ACCLAIM FOR THE QUEEN OF SUSPENSE
MARY HIGGINS CLARK

DADDY'S LITTLE GIRL

"Clark certainly has a few tricks left in her bag."

—*Boston Globe*

"Hard to resist."

—*Toronto Sun*

"Her best in years . . . a tightly woven, emotionally potent tale of suspense and revenge. . . . With its textured plot, well-sketched secondary characters, strong pacing and appealing heroine, this is Clark at her most winning."

—*Publishers Weekly*

"Few stories of obsession will grab readers quite like this one."

—*Ottowa Citizen*

"A fast and fascinating read."

—*Knoxville News-Sentinel* (TN)

"*Daddy's Little Girl* is the best book Clark has written in two years. Her work seems somehow more solid, the plotting more deft. The . . . ending is so unexpected and harrowing I just had to sit back and allow the story to run through my mind until I absorbed the depth of all I'd just read."

—*Tulsa World* (OK)

Mary Higgins Clark

Daddy's Little Girl

POCKET BOOKS
New York   London   Toronto   Sydney

POCKET BOOKS, a division of Simon & Schuster, Inc.
1230 Avenue of the Americas, New York, NY 10020

Copyright © 2002 by Mary Higgins Clark

Originally published in hardcover in 2002 by Simon & Schuster, Inc.

ISBN: 1-4165-0374-9

This Pocket Books trade paperback edition August 2004

10 9 8 7 6 5 4 3

POCKET and colophon are registered trademarks of
Simon & Schuster, Inc.

Printed in the U.S.A.

For information regarding special discounts for bulk purchases,
please contact Simon & Schuster Special Sales at 1-800-456-6798
or business@simonandschuster.com.

Acknowledgments

THIS STORY, written in the first person, has been a different kind of journey for me. That is why I am so truly grateful for the guidance, encouragement, and support of my longtime editor, Michael Korda, and his associate, senior editor Chuck Adams. *Mille grazie,* dear friends.

Always thanks to Eugene Winick and Sam Pinkus, my literary agents, for all their constant care, assistance, and friendship.

Lisl Cade, my dear publicist, remains as always my right hand. My gratitude to her always.

Continuing thanks to Associate Director of Copyediting Gypsy da Silva, with whom I have worked for so many years. A kiss to the memory of copyeditor Carol Catt who shall be sorely missed.

Kudos to Sgt. Steven Marron and Detective Richard Murphy, Ret. NYPD, New York County District Attorney's Office, for their advice and assistance in matters of investigation and detection.

Blessings to my assistants and friends, Agnes Newton and Nadine Petry, and my reader-in-progress, my sister-in-law, Irene Clark.

Judith Kelman, author and pal, once again came through instantly when I called on her. Love you, Judith.

My gratitude to Fr. Emil Tomaskovic and Fr. Bob Warren, Franciscan Friars of the Atonement at Graymoor, Garrison, New York, for their valuable help with the setting of scenes in this book, and for the wonderful work they and their brother Friars do for those who need help most.

My love and gratitude to my husband, John Conheeney, our children, and grandchildren only grows and multiplies. They are what I am all about.

Greetings to all my friends who have been waiting for me to finish this book so that we can "get together soon."

I'm ready!

In loving memory of my father,

Luke Joseph Higgins

Daddy's Little Girl

Part One

1

WHEN ELLIE AWOKE that morning, it was with the sense that something terrible had happened.

Instinctively she reached for Bones, the soft and cuddly stuffed dog who had shared her pillow ever since she could remember. When she'd had her seventh birthday last month, Andrea, her fifteen-year-old sister, had teased her that it was time to toss Bones in the attic.

Then Ellie remembered what was wrong: Andrea hadn't come home last night. After dinner, she had gone to her best friend Joan's house to study for a math test. She had promised to be home by nine o'clock. At quarter of nine, Mommy went to Joan's house to walk Andrea home, but they said Andrea had left at eight o'clock.

Mommy had come back home worried and almost crying, just as Daddy got in from work. Daddy was a lieutenant in the New York State Police. Right away he and Mommy had started calling all of Andrea's friends, but no one had seen her. Then Daddy said he was going to drive around to the bowling alley and to the ice cream parlor, just in case Andrea had gone there.

"If she lied about doing homework until nine o'clock, she won't set foot out of this house for six months," he'd said angrily, and then he'd turned to Mommy: "If I said it once, I've said it a thousand times—I don't want her to go out after dark alone."

Despite his raised voice, Ellie could tell that Daddy was more worried than angry.

"For heaven's sake, Ted, she went out at seven o'clock. She got to Joan's. She was planning to be home by nine, and I even walked over there to meet her."

"Then *where is* she?"

They made Ellie go to bed, and, eventually, she fell asleep waking only now. Maybe Andrea was home by now, she thought hopefully. She slipped out of bed, rushed across the room, and darted down the hall to Andrea's room. Be there, she begged. *Please* be there. She opened the door. Andrea's bed had not been slept in.

Her bare feet silent on the steps, Ellie hurried downstairs. Their neighbor, Mrs. Hilmer, was sitting with Mommy in the kitchen. Mommy was wearing the same clothes she had on last night, and she looked as if she'd been crying for a long time.

Ellie ran to her. "Mommy."

Mommy hugged her and began to sob. Ellie felt Mommy's hand clutching her shoulder, so hard that she was almost hurting her.

"Mommy, where's Andrea?"

"We ... don't ... know. Daddy and the police are looking for her."

"Ellie, why don't you get dressed, and I'll fix you some breakfast?" Mrs. Hilmer asked.

No one was saying that she should hurry up because the school bus would be coming pretty soon. Without asking, Ellie knew she wouldn't be going to school today.

She dutifully washed her face and hands and brushed her teeth and hair, and then put on play clothes—a turtleneck shirt and her favorite blue slacks—and went downstairs again.

Just as she sat at the table where Mrs. Hilmer had put out juice and cornflakes, Daddy came through the kitchen door. "No sign of her," he said. "We've looked everywhere. There was a guy collecting for some phony charity ringing doorbells in town yesterday. He was in the diner last night and left around eight o'clock. He would have passed Joan's house on the way to the highway around the time Andrea left. They're looking for him."

Ellie could tell that Daddy was almost crying. He also hadn't seemed to notice her, but she didn't mind. Sometimes when Daddy came home he was upset because something sad had happened while he was at work, and for a while he'd be very quiet. He had that same look on his face now.

Andrea was hiding—Ellie was sure of it. She had probably left Joan's house early on purpose because she was meeting Rob Westerfield in the hideout, then maybe it got late and she was afraid to come home. Daddy had said that if she ever lied again about where she'd been, he'd make her quit the school band. He'd said that when he found out she had gone for a ride with Rob Westerfield in his car when she was supposed to be at the library.

Andrea loved being in the band; last year she'd been the only freshman chosen for the flute section. But if she'd left Joan's house early and gone to the hideout to meet Rob, and Daddy found out, that would mean she'd have to give it up. Mommy always said that Andrea could twist Daddy around her little finger, but she didn't say that last month when one of the state troopers told Daddy he'd stopped Rob Westerfield to give him a ticket for speeding and that Andrea was with him at the time.

Daddy hadn't said anything about it until after dinner. Then he asked Andrea how long she'd been at the library.

She didn't answer him.

Then he said, "I see you're smart enough to realize that the trooper who gave Westerfield the ticket would tell me you were with him. Andrea, that guy is not only rich and spoiled, he's a bad apple through and through. When he kills himself speeding, you're not going to be in the car. You are *absolutely forbidden* to have anything to do with him."

The hideout was in the garage behind the great big house that old Mrs. Westerfield, Rob's grandmother, lived in all summer. It was always unlocked, and sometimes Andrea and her friends sneaked in there and smoked cigarettes. Andrea had taken Ellie there a couple of times when she was babysitting her.

Her friends had been really mad at Andrea for bringing her along, but she had said, "Ellie is a good kid. She's not a snitch." Hearing that had made Ellie feel great, but Andrea hadn't let Ellie have even one puff of the cigarette.

Ellie was sure that last night Andrea had left Joan's house early because she was planning to meet Rob Westerfield. Ellie had heard her when she talked to him on the phone yesterday, and when she was finished, she was practically crying. "I told Rob I was going to the mixer with Paulie," she said, "and now he's really mad at me."

Ellie thought about the conversation as she finished the cornflakes and juice. Daddy was standing at the stove. He was holding a cup of coffee. Mommy was crying again but making almost no sound.

Then, for the first time, Daddy seemed to notice her: "Ellie, I think you'd be better off in school. At lunchtime I'll take you over."

"Is it all right if I go outside now?"

"Yes. But stay around the house."

Ellie ran for her jacket and was quickly out the door. It was the fifteenth of November, and the leaves were damp and felt sloshy underfoot. The sky was heavy with clouds, and she could tell it was going to rain again. Ellie wished they were back in Irvington where they used to live. It was lonesome here. Mrs. Hilmer's house was the only other one on this road.

Daddy had liked living in Irvington, but they'd moved here, five towns away, because Mommy wanted a bigger house and more property. They found they could afford that if they moved farther up in Westchester, to a town that hadn't yet become a suburb of New York City.

When Daddy said he missed Irvington, where he'd grown up and where they'd lived until two years ago, Mommy would tell him how great the new house was. Then he'd say that in Irvington we had a million-dollar view of the Hudson River and the Tappan Zee Bridge, and he didn't have to drive five miles for a newspaper or a loaf of bread.

There were woods all around their property. The big Westerfield house was directly behind theirs, but on the other side of the woods. Glancing back at the kitchen window to make sure no one had seen her, Ellie began to dart through the trees.

Five minutes later she reached the clearing and ran across the field to where the Westerfield property began. Feeling more and more alone, she raced up the long driveway and darted around the mansion, a small figure lost in the lengthening shadows of the approaching storm.

There was a side door to the garage, and that was the one that was unlocked. Even so, it was hard for Ellie to turn the handle. Finally she succeeded and stepped into the gloom of the interior. The garage was big enough to hold four cars, but the only one Mrs. Westerfield left after the summer was the van. Andrea and her friends had brought some old blankets to sit on when they went there. They always sat in the same spot, at the back of the garage behind the van, so that if anyone happened to look in the window, they wouldn't be able to see them. Ellie knew that was where Andrea would be hiding if she was here.

She didn't know why she felt suddenly afraid, but she did. Now, instead of running, she had to practically drag her feet to make them move toward the back of the garage. But then she saw it—the edge of the blanket peeking out from behind the van. Andrea *was* here! She and her friends would never have left the blankets out; when they left, they always folded them and hid them in the cabinet with the cleaning supplies.

"Andrea . . ." Now she ran, calling softly so that Andrea wouldn't be scared. She was probably asleep, Ellie decided.

Yes, she was. Even though the garage was filled with shadows, Ellie could see Andrea's long hair trailing out from under the blankets.

"Andrea, it's me." Ellie sank to her knees beside Andrea and pulled back the blanket covering her face.

Andrea had a mask on, a terrible monster mask that looked all sticky and gummy. Ellie reached down to pull it off, and her fingers went into a broken space in Andrea's forehead. As she jerked back, she became aware of the pool of Andrea's blood, soaking through her slacks.

Then, from somewhere in the big room, she was sure she heard someone breathing—harsh, heavy, sucking-in breaths that broke off in a kind of giggle.

Terrified, she tried to get up, but her knees slid in the blood and she fell forward across Andrea's chest. Her lips grazed something smooth and cold—Andrea's gold locket. Then she managed to scramble to her feet, and she turned and began to run.

She did not know she was shrieking until she was almost home, and Ted and Genine Cavanaugh ran into the backyard to see their younger daughter burst out of the woods, her arms outstretched, her little form covered in her sister's blood.

2

WITH THE EXCEPTION of when his team practiced or had a game during the baseball season, sixteen-year-old Paulie Stroebel worked in Hillwood's service station after school and all day Saturday. The alternative was to help out during those same hours at his parents' delicatessen a block away on Main Street, something he'd been doing from the time he was seven years old.

Slow academically, but good with things mechanical, he loved to repair cars, and his parents had been understanding of his desire to work for someone else. With unruly blond hair, blue eyes, round cheeks, and a stocky five-foot-eight frame, Paulie was considered a quiet, hardworking employee by his boss at the service station and something of a dopey nerd by his fellow students at Delano High. His one achievement in school was to be on the football team.

On Friday, when word of Andrea Cavanaugh's murder reached the school, guidance counselors were sent to all the classes to break the news to the students. Paul was in the middle of a study period when Miss Watkins came into his classroom, whispered to the teacher, and rapped on the desk for attention.

"I have very sad news for all of you," she began. "We have just learned . . ." In halting sentences she informed them that sophomore Andrea Cavanaugh had been killed, the victim of foul play. The reaction was a chorus of shocked gasps and tearful protests.

Then a shouted "No!" silenced the others. Quiet, placid Paulie Stroebel, his face twisted in grief, had sprung to his feet. As his classmates stared at him, his shoulders began to shake. Fierce sobs racked his body, and he ran from the room. As the door closed behind him, he said something in a voice too muffled for most of them to hear. However, the student seated nearest the door later swore that his words were "I can't believe she's dead!"

Emma Watkins, the guidance counselor, already stunned by the tragedy, felt as though a knife had gone through her. She was fond of Paulie and understood the isolation of the earnestly plodding student who tried so hard to please.

She herself was positive that the anguished words he shouted were "I didn't think she was dead."

That afternoon, for the first time in the six months he'd been working at the service station, Paulie did not show up, nor did he call his boss to explain his absence. When his parents got home that evening, they found him lying on top of the bed, staring at the ceiling, pictures of Andrea scattered beside him.

Both Hans and Anja Wagner Stroebel had been born in Germany, and they immigrated to the United States with their parents when they were children. They had met and married in their late thirties and used their combined savings to open the delicatessen. By nature undemonstrative, they were fiercely protective of their only son.

Everyone who came into the store was talking about the murder, asking each other who could possibly have committed such a terrible crime. The Cavanaughs were regular customers at the deli, and the Stroebels joined in the shocked discussion that Andrea might have been planning to meet someone in the garage on the Westerfield estate.

They agreed that she was pretty, but a bit headstrong. She was supposed to be doing homework with Joan Lashley until nine o'clock, but had left unexpectedly early. Had she planned to meet someone, or had she been waylaid on the way home?

Anja Stroebel acted instinctively when she saw the pictures on her son's bed. She swooped them up and put them in her pocketbook. At her husband's questioning glance, she shook her head, indicating that he was to ask no questions. Then she sat down next to Paulie, and put her arms around him.

"Andrea was such a pretty girl," she said soothingly, her voice heavy with the accent that became stronger when she was upset. "I remember how she congratulated you when you made that great catch and saved the game last spring. Like her other friends, you are very, very sad."

At first it seemed to Paulie that his mother was talking to him from a distant place. Like her other friends. What did she mean?

"The police will be looking for anyone who has been a particular friend to Andrea, Paulie," she said slowly but firmly.

"I invited her to a mixer," he said, the words coming haltingly. "She said she would go with me."

Anja was sure her son had never asked a girl for a date before. Last year he had refused to go to his sophomore dance.

"Then you liked her, Paulie?"

Paulie Stroebel began to cry. "Mama, I loved her so much."

"You *liked* her, Paul," Anja said insistently. "Try to remember that."

On Saturday, composed and quietly apologetic for not showing up on Friday afternoon, Paulie Stroebel reported for work at the gas station.

Early Saturday afternoon, Hans Stroebel personally delivered a Virginia ham and salads to the Cavanaugh home and asked their neighbor Mrs. Hilmer, who answered the door, to convey his deepest sympathy to the family.

3

"IT'S A SHAME Ted and Genine are both only children," Ellie heard Mrs. Hilmer say a couple of times on Saturday. "It makes it easier when there's a lot of family around at a time like this."

Ellie didn't care about having more family. She just wanted Andrea back, and she wanted Mommy to stop crying and she wanted Daddy to talk to her. He'd hardly said a word to her since she came running home and he grabbed her up in his arms and she managed to tell him where Andrea was and that she'd been hurt.

Later, after he'd gone to the hideout and had seen Andrea, and all the police came, he'd said, "Ellie, you knew last night she might have gone to the garage. Why didn't you *tell* us then?"

"You didn't ask me, and you made me go to bed."

"Yes, I did," he admitted. But then later she heard him say to one of the cops, "If only I had known Andrea was there. She might still have been alive at nine o'clock. I might have found her in time."

Somebody from the police talked to Ellie and asked her questions about the hideout and about who else went there. In her head Ellie could hear Andrea saying, "Ellie is a good kid. She's not a snitch."

Thinking about Andrea, and knowing that she'd never come home again, made Ellie begin to cry so hard that the police stopped questioning her.

Then on Saturday afternoon a man who said he was Detective Marcus Longo came to the house. He took Ellie into the dining room and closed the door. She thought he had a nice face. He told her that he had a little boy exactly her age and that they looked a lot alike. "He has the same blue eyes," he said. "And his hair is just the color of yours. I tell him it reminds me of sand when the sun is shining on it."

Then he told her that four of Andrea's friends had admitted they went to the hideout with her, but none of them had been there that night. He named the girls, then asked, "Ellie, do you know any other girls who might have met your sister there?"

It wasn't like snitching on them if they had already told on themselves. "No," she whispered. "That was all of them."

"Is there anyone else Andrea might have met at the hideout?"

She hesitated. She couldn't tell him about Rob Westerfield. That would really be telling on Andrea.

Detective Longo said, "Ellie, someone hurt Andrea so much that she isn't alive anymore. Don't protect that person. Andrea would want you to tell us anything you know."

Ellie looked down at her hands. In this big old farmhouse, this room was her favorite. It used to have ugly wallpaper, but now the walls were painted a soft yellow, and there was a new chandelier over the table and the bulbs looked like candles. Mommy had found the chandelier at a yard sale and said it was a treasure. It had taken her a long time to clean it, but now anyone who visited admired it.

They always ate dinner in the dining room, even though Daddy thought it was silly to go to all the fuss. Mommy had a book that showed how to set the table for a formal dinner. It was Andrea's job to set the table that way every Sunday, even when it was just them. Ellie would help her, and they would have fun putting out the good silver and china.

"Lord Malcolm Bigbottom is the guest of honor today," Andrea would say. Then reading from the book of etiquette, she'd place him at the seat to the right of where Mommy would sit. "Oh, no, Gabrielle, the water glass must be placed slightly to the right of the dinner knife."

Ellie's real name was Gabrielle, but no one called her that, except Andrea when she was joking. She wondered if it would be her job to set the table that way on Sunday from now on. She hoped not. Without Andrea it wouldn't be a game.

It felt funny to be thinking like that. On one hand, she knew that Andrea was dead and would be buried Tuesday morning in the cemetery in Tarrytown with Grandma and Grandpa Cavanaugh. On the other hand, she still expected Andrea to come into the house any minute, pull her close, and tell her a secret.

A secret. Sometimes Andrea met Rob Westerfield in the hideout. But Ellie had crossed her heart and promised not to tell.

"Ellie, whoever hurt Andrea may hurt somebody else if he isn't stopped," Detective Longo said. His voice was quiet and friendly.

"Do you think it's my fault that Andrea is dead? Daddy thinks so."

"No, he doesn't think that, Ellie," Detective Longo said. "But anything you can tell us about secrets you and Andrea shared may help us now."

Rob Westerfield, Ellie thought. Maybe it wouldn't really be breaking a promise to tell Detective Longo about him. If Rob had been the one who hurt Andrea, everybody should know it. She looked down at her hands. "Sometimes she would meet Rob Westerfield at the hideout," she whispered.

Detective Longo leaned forward. "Do you know if she was going to meet him there the other night?" he asked. Ellie could tell that he was excited to hear about Rob.

"I think she was. Paulie Stroebel had asked her to go to the Thanksgiving mixer with him, and she said yes. She didn't really *want* to go with him, but Paulie had told her he knew she was sneaking off to meet Rob Westerfield, and she was afraid he would tell Daddy if she didn't go with him. But then Rob was mad at her, and she wanted to explain to him that that was why she agreed to go out with Paulie, to keep him from telling Daddy. So maybe that's why she left Joan's house early."

"How did Paulie know that Andrea was seeing Rob Wester-field?"

"Andrea said that she thought he sometimes followed her to the hideout. Paulie wanted her to be *his* girlfriend."

4

THE WASHING MACHINE had been used.

"What was so important it couldn't wait until I got back, Mrs. Westerfield?" Rosita asked, her tone a touch defensive, as though fearful she had left a task undone. She had gone out of town to visit her ailing aunt on Thursday. It was now Saturday morning, and she had just arrived back. "You shouldn't bother yourself with wash when you have your hands full decorating all those houses."

Linda Westerfield did not know why a sudden alarm bell went off in her head. For some reason she did not respond directly to Rosita's remarks.

"Oh, every once in a while, if I'm checking on the decorative painting and touch it up myself, it's just as easy to run the paint cloths through the machine as to leave them around," she said.

"Well, judging from the amount of detergent you used, you must have had a whole heap of them. And Mrs. Westerfield, I heard about the Cavanaugh girl on the news yesterday. I can't stop thinking about her. Who would believe that kind of thing could happen in this little town? It breaks your heart."

"Yes, it does." It had to be Rob who used the machine, Linda thought. Vince, her husband, would certainly not have used a washing machine at any time. Probably didn't even know how.

Rosita's dark eyes glistened, and she dabbed her hand over them. "That poor mother."

Rob? What would be so important for him to wash?

It was an old trick of his. When he was eleven, he'd tried to wash the smell of cigarette smoke from his play clothes.

"Andrea Cavanaugh was the prettiest thing. And her father a lieutenant in the state troopers! Somehow you'd think a man like that would be able to protect his child."

"Yes, you would." Linda was sitting at the counter in the kitchen, going over the sketches she had made for window treatments for a client's new home.

"To think that anybody would smash that girl's head in. Had to be a monster. I hope they string him up when they find him."

Rosita was talking to herself now and didn't seem to expect a response. Linda slipped the sketches into the portfolio. "Mr. Westerfield and I are meeting some friends at the inn for dinner, Rosita," she said as she slid off the stool.

"Will Rob be home?"

A good question, Linda thought. "He went out for a run and should be back any minute. Check with him then." She thought she detected a quiver in her voice. Rob had been agitated and moody all day yesterday. When the news about Andrea Cavanaugh's death flashed through the town, she had expected him to be upset. Instead, he'd been dismissive. "I hardly knew her, Mom," he said.

Was it simply that Rob, like many nineteen-year-olds, could not confront the death of a young person? Was it that somehow he felt as though his own mortality was threatened?

Linda went up the stairs slowly, suddenly weighted down with a sense of impending disaster. They had moved from the townhouse on Manhattan's East Seventieth Street to this pre-Revolutionary house six years ago, when Rob went away to boarding school. By then they both knew that the town where they'd traditionally summered at Vince's mother's home was where they wanted to live permanently. Vince had said that there were great opportunities to make money here, and he had begun investing in real estate.

The house, with its sense of timelessness, was a continuing source of quiet pleasure to her, but today Linda did not pause to feel the polished wood of the banister under her hand or stop to enjoy the view of the valley from the window at the top of the stairs.

She walked directly to Rob's room. The door was closed. He had been gone an hour and would be back from jogging any minute. Nervously she opened the door and stepped inside. The bed was unmade, but the rest of the room was oddly tidy. Rob was meticulous about his clothing, sometimes even pressing slacks fresh from the cleaners to sharpen the crease, but he was downright careless about discarded garments. She would have expected to see the clothes he had worn Thursday and yesterday thrown on the floor, waiting for Rosita's return.

She walked quickly across the room and looked into the hamper in his bathroom. That, too, was empty.

Sometime between Thursday morning, when Rosita left, and early this morning, Rob had washed and dried the clothes he'd been wearing Thursday and yesterday. *Why?*

Linda would have liked to go through his closet but knew she risked having him find her there. She wasn't prepared for a confrontation. She left his room, remembering to close the door, and went down the hall and around the corner to the master suite she and Vince had added when they expanded the house.

Suddenly aware that she might be feeling the onslaught of a migraine, she dropped the portfolio onto the sofa in the sitting room, went into the bathroom, and reached in the medicine chest. As she swallowed two prescription pills, she looked into the mirror and was shocked to see how pale and anxious she looked.

She was wearing her jogging suit because she had planned to go for a run after she'd worked on the sketches. Her short chestnut hair was held back by a band, and she hadn't bothered with makeup. To her own hypercritical gaze, she looked older than her forty-four years, with tiny wrinkles forming around her eyes and the corners of her mouth.

The bathroom window looked out over the front yard and the driveway. As she glanced out, she saw an unfamiliar car driving up. A moment later the doorbell rang. She expected Rosita to use the intercom to let her know who it was, but instead Rosita came upstairs and handed her a card.

"He wants to talk to Rob, Mrs. Westerfield. I told him Rob was out jogging, and he said he'd wait."

Linda was nearly eight inches taller than Rosita, who was only a shade over five feet, but she almost had to grab the small woman to support herself after she read the name on the card: Detective Marcus Longo.

5

WHEREVER ELLIE WENT, she felt in the way. After the nice detective left, she tried to find Mommy, but Mrs. Hilmer said that the doctor had given her something to help her rest. Daddy spent almost all the time in his little den with the door closed. He said he wanted to be left alone.

Grandma Reid, who lived in Florida, came up late Saturday afternoon, but all she did was cry.

Mrs. Hilmer and some of Mommy's friends from her bridge club sat in the kitchen. Ellie heard one of them, Mrs. Storey, say, "I feel so useless, but I also feel as though seeing us around may make Genine and Ted realize they're not alone."

Ellie went outside and got on the swing. She pumped her legs until the swing went higher and higher. She wanted it to go over the top. She wanted to fall from the top and hit the ground and hurt herself. Then maybe she'd stop hurting inside.

It had stopped raining, but there still was no sun and it was cold. After a while, Ellie knew that it was no use; the swing wouldn't go over the top. She went back into the house, entering the small vestibule off the kitchen. She heard Joan's mother's voice. She was with the other ladies now, and Ellie could tell that she was crying. "I was surprised that Andrea left so early. It was dark out, and it crossed my mind to drive her home. If only . . ."

Then Ellie heard Mrs. Lewis say, "If only Ellie had told them that Andrea used to go to that garage that the kids called 'the hide-out.' Ted might have gotten there in time."

"If only Ellie . . ."

Ellie went up the back stairs, careful to walk very quietly so they wouldn't hear her. Grandma's suitcase was on her bed. That was funny. Wasn't Grandma going to sleep in Andrea's room? It was empty now.

Or maybe they'd let *her* sleep in Andrea's room. Then, if she woke up tonight, she could pretend that Andrea would be coming back any minute.

The door to Andrea's room was closed. She opened it as quietly as she always did on Saturday mornings when she'd peek in to see if Andrea was still sleeping.

Daddy was standing at Andrea's desk. He was holding a framed picture in his hands. Ellie knew it was the baby picture of Andrea, the one in the silver frame that had "Daddy's Little Girl" engraved across the top.

As she watched, he lifted the top of the music box. That was another present he had bought for Andrea right after she was born. Daddy joked that Andrea never wanted to go to sleep when she was a baby, and so he'd wind up the music box and dance around the room with her and play the song from it, singing the words softly, until she dozed off.

Ellie had asked if he did that with her, too, but Mommy said no, because she was always a good sleeper. From the day she was born, she'd been no trouble at all.

Some of the song's words ran through Ellie's head as the music drifted through the room. ". . . You're daddy's little girl to have and to hold. . . . You're the spirit of Christmas, my star on the tree. . . . And you're daddy's little girl."

As she watched, Daddy sat on the edge of Andrea's bed and began to sob.

Ellie backed out of the room, closing the door as quietly as she had opened it.

Part Two

Twenty-three Years Later

6

MY SISTER, ANDREA, was murdered nearly twenty-three years ago, yet it always seems as though it was just yesterday.

Rob Westerfield was arrested two days after the funeral and charged with first degree murder. Almost solely from the information I provided them, the police were able to obtain a search warrant of the Westerfield home and Rob's car. They found the clothes he had worn the night he took her life, and though he had thoroughly bleached them, the police lab was able to identify bloodstains. The tire jack that had been the murder weapon was found in the trunk of his car. He had washed that, too, but a tiny strand of Andrea's hair still clung to it.

Rob's defense was that he had gone to the movies the night Andrea was murdered. The cinema parking lot was full, and he left his car at the service station next door. He said that the pumps were closed, but he found Paulie Stroebel working in the enclosed garage. He said he looked in on Paulie and told him he was leaving the car there and would pick it up after the movies.

He claimed that while he was watching the movie, Paulie Stroebel must have driven to the hideout in his car, killed Andrea, then left the car back at the service station. Rob said he'd left the car at the station at least half a dozen times to get dents fixed, and that on any of those occasions Paulie could have had an extra key made.

He tried to explain away the blood on his clothes and in the ridges of his sneakers by claiming that Andrea had begged him to meet her at the hideout. He said that she had been pestering him with phone calls and phoned him at dinnertime the night she died. She told him that she was going to a mixer with Paulie Stroebel and didn't want him to be mad at her.

"I didn't care who she went out with," Rob explained when he testified at the trial. "She was just a kid in town who had a crush on me. She followed me everywhere. I'd be hanging out in town, and she'd walk by. I'd go bowling, and suddenly she's playing in the next lane. I caught her and her friends hanging out in my grandmother's garage, having a cigarette. I wanted to be nice, so I told her it was all right. She was always begging me to take her for a ride in my car. She was always calling me."

He had an explanation for why he went to the garage-hideout that night. "I got out of the movie," he testified, "and started to drive home. Then I got worried about her. Even though I told her that I wasn't going to meet her, she said she'd wait there for me anyway. I thought I'd better drop by and make sure she went home before her dad got angry. The light in the garage had burned out. I kind of fumbled along and walked around behind the van. That's where Andrea and her friends used to sit on blankets and smoke cigarettes.

"I felt the blanket under my foot. I could just about make out that someone was lying there, and I figured Andrea must have been waiting for me and fallen asleep. Then I knelt down, and I could feel the blood on her face. I ran."

He was asked why he ran. "Because I was scared somebody might think I did it."

"What did you think happened to her?"

"I didn't know. I was scared. But when I found out that the tire jack in my trunk had blood on it, I knew it had to be Paulie who killed her."

He was very slick, and his testimony was well rehearsed. A

good-looking young guy, he made a strong impression. But I was
Rob Westerfield's nemesis. I remember being on the stand and answering the questions the prosecutor asked.

"Ellie, did Andrea call Rob Westerfield before she went to do
homework with Joan?"

"Yes."

"Did he ever make phone calls to her?"

"Sometimes he did, but then if Daddy or Mommy answered, he
always hung up. He wanted Andrea to call him because he had his
own phone in his room."

"Was there a special reason Andrea called him the night she
died?"

"Yes."

"Did you hear the conversation?"

"Just a little of it. I went into her room. She was almost crying.
She was telling Rob that she couldn't help it that she was going with
Paulie to the mixer, that she had to do it. She didn't want Paulie to
tell Daddy that she sometimes met Rob in the hideout."

"Then what happened?"

"She told Rob she was going to Joan's to do homework, and he
told her to meet him at the hideout."

"Did you hear him tell her that?"

"No, but I heard her say, 'I'll try, Rob,' and when she hung up,
she said, 'Rob wants me to leave Joanie's early and meet him in the
hideout. He's mad at me. He said I'm not supposed to go out with
anyone else.'"

"Andrea told you that?"

"Yes."

"Then what happened?"

And then on the stand I gave away Andrea's last secret and
broke the sacred promise I had made to her—the "cross-my-heart-
and-hope-to-die" promise that I would never tell anyone about the
locket Rob had given her. It was gold and heart-shaped, and had
little blue stones. Andrea had shown her that Rob had had their ini-

tials engraved on the back. I was crying by then because I missed my sister so much, and it hurt to talk about her. And so, without being asked, I added, "She put on her locket before she left, so I was pretty sure she would meet him."

"A locket?"

"Rob gave her a locket. Andrea wore it under her blouse so no one could see it. But I could feel it when I found her in the garage."

I remember sitting on the witness stand. I remember trying not to look at Rob Westerfield. He kept staring at me; I could feel the hatred coming from him.

And I swear I could read the thoughts of my mother and father who were sitting behind the prosecutor: Ellie, you should have told us; you should have told us.

My testimony was pounced on by the defense attorneys. They brought out that Andrea often wore a locket that my father had given her, that it was on top of her dresser after her body was found, that I was making up stories or that I was repeating the stories Andrea had made up about Rob.

"Andrea was wearing the locket when I found her," I insisted. "I could feel it." I burst out, "That's why I know it was Rob Westerfield who was in the hideout when I found Andrea. He came back for the locket."

Rob's attorneys became furious, and that remark was ordered stricken from the record. The judge turned to the jurors and told them not to consider it in any way

Did anyone believe what I told them about the locket Rob gave Andrea? I don't know. The case went to the jury, and they were out for nearly a week. We learned that a few jurors leaned at first toward a manslaughter verdict, but the rest insisted on a murder conviction. They believed that Rob had carried that tire jack into the garage because he intended to kill Andrea.

I reread the transcript of the trial the first few times Westerfield came up for parole, and I wrote vehement letters protesting his release. But since he has served nearly twenty-two years, I knew that this time the parole may well be granted, and that is why I have come back to Oldham-on-the-Hudson.

I AM THIRTY YEARS OLD, live in Atlanta, and work as an investigative reporter with the *Atlanta News*. The editor in chief, Pete Lawlor, considers it a personal affront if anyone on the staff takes even a yearly vacation, so I expected him to hit the ceiling when I told him I needed a few days off immediately and might need more later.

"You getting married?"

I told him that was the last thing on my mind.

"Then what's up?"

I had not told anyone at the newspaper anything about my personal life, but Pete Lawlor is one of those people who seemed to know everything about everybody. Thirty-one years old, balding, and always fighting to get off those ten extra pounds, he was probably the smartest man I've ever met. Six months after I'd started at the *News* and covered the story of a murdered teenager, he said in an offhand manner, "That must have been a tough one for you to write. I know about your sister."

He didn't expect a response, nor did I give him one, but I felt his empathy. It did help. It had been an emotionally wrenching assignment.

"Andrea's killer is coming up for parole. I'm afraid he may get it this time, and I want to see if there's anything I can do to stop it."

Pete leaned back in his chair. He always wore an open-necked shirt and a sweater. Sometimes I've wondered if he even *owns* a jacket. "How long has he served?"

"Almost twenty-two years."

"How many times has he come up for parole?"

"Twice."

"Any problems while he was in prison?"

I felt like a schoolgirl being grilled. "None that I know of."

"Then he'll probably get out."

"I expect he will."

"So why bother?"

"Because I must."

Pete Lawlor doesn't believe in wasting either time or words. He didn't ask any more questions. He just nodded. "Okay. When's the hearing?"

"The hearing is next week. I get to speak to someone on the staff of the parole board on Monday."

He turned back to the paperwork on his desk, effectively dismissing me. "Go ahead," he said. But, as I turned away, he added, "Ellie, you're not as tough as you think you are."

"Yes, I am." I didn't bother to thank him for the time off.

That was yesterday. The next day, Saturday, I flew from Atlanta to the Westchester County Airport and rented a car.

I could have stayed at a motel in Ossining, near Sing Sing, the prison where Andrea's killer has been incarcerated. Instead I drove fifteen miles further to my old hometown, Oldham-on-the-Hudson, and managed to find the quaint Parkinson Inn that I vaguely remembered as a place where we sometimes went for lunch or dinner.

The Inn was obviously flourishing. On this chilly Saturday afternoon in October, the tables in the dining room were filled with casually dressed people, mostly twosomes and family groups. I felt a moment of acute nostalgia. This is the way I remembered my early life, the four of us having lunch here on Saturday, and then sometimes Dad would drop Andrea and me at the movies. She'd be meeting her friends, but she didn't mind that I tagged along.

"Ellie is a good kid, she's not a snitch," she'd say. If the movie got out early enough, we'd all rush to the garage-hideout where Andrea and Joan and Margy and Dottie would share a quick cigarette before going home.

Andrea had an answer ready if Daddy said he smelled smoke

on her clothing. "Can't help it. We had pizza after the movie and a lot of other people were smoking." Then she'd wink at me.

The Inn had only eight guest rooms, but one was still available, a spartan space containing a bed with an iron headboard, a two-drawer bureau, a night table, and a chair. It faced east, the direction where the house we lived in was located. The sun that afternoon was uncertain, slipping in and out of clouds, one moment blinding, the next completely concealed.

I stood at the window, staring out, and it seemed to me I was seven years old again and watching my father holding the music box.

7

I REMEMBER THAT afternoon as the defining day of my life. Saint Ignatius of Loyola said, "Give us the child until he is seven years old, and I will show you the man."

I assume that he meant the woman as well. I stood there, quiet as a mouse, watching the father I worshiped, sobbing and hugging my dead sister's picture against his chest, while the fragile sounds from that music box drifted around him.

I look back and wonder if it ever occurred to me to run to him, throw my arms around him, absorb his grief and let his mingle with mine. But the fact is, even then I understood that his grief was unique and that no matter what I did, I could never really ease his pain.

Lieutenant Edward Cavanaugh, decorated officer of the New York State Police, hero of a dozen life-threatening situations, had not been able to prevent the murder of his beautiful, headstrong, fifteen-year-old daughter, and his agony could not be shared with a fellow mourner, however close by blood.

Over the years I came to understand that when grief is not shared, blame is passed around like a hot potato instead, thrust from one to the other, eventually sticking to the hands of the one least able to throw it away.

In this case, that person was me.

Detective Longo lost no time following up on my violation of

Andrea's trust. I had given him two leads, two possible suspects: Rob Westerfield, who used his stunning, sultry, rich playboy persona to turn Andrea's head, and Paul Stroebel, the shy and backward teenager with the crush on the gorgeous band member who had enthusiastically cheered his game-winning performances on the football field.

Root, root, root for the home team—no one was better at that than Andrea!

As Andrea's autopsy results were being studied, and preparations made for her interment in Gate of Heaven Cemetery, next to the paternal grandparents I only dimly remembered, Detective Longo was interrogating both Rob Westerfield and Paul Stroebel. Both protested that they had not seen Andrea on Thursday evening, nor had either made plans to meet her.

Paul was working in the gas station, and although it closed at seven, he claimed he had stayed longer in the shop to complete some minor repairs on several cars. Rob Westerfield swore that he had gone to the local cinema, and even produced a ticket stub as proof.

I remember standing at Andrea's grave, a single long-stemmed rose in my hand, and after the prayers had been offered, being told to place it on Andrea's casket. I remember, too, that I felt dead inside, as dead and still as Andrea had been when I knelt over her in the hideout.

I wanted to tell her how sorry I was that I had told her secret about her meetings with Rob, and with equal passion I wanted to tell her that I was sorry I hadn't told about them the minute we knew she had left Joan's but not reached home. But of course I said nothing. I dropped the flower, but it slid off the casket, and before I could retrieve it, my grandmother stepped past me to place her flower on the casket and her foot crushed my rose into the muddy earth.

A moment later we filed out of the cemetery, and in that crowd of solemn faces I caught angry stares directed at me. The Westerfields stayed away, but the Stroebels were there, standing on either side of Paulie, their shoulders touching his. I remember the feeling of blame surrounding me, overwhelming me, choking me. It was a feeling I have never lost.

I had tried to tell them that when I was kneeling at Andrea's body, I heard someone breathing, but they were skeptical because I was so hysterical and frightened. My own breathing when I ran from the woods was as labored and rattling as it became during my bouts of croup. But over the years I have been awakened many times by the same nightmare: I am kneeling over Andrea's body, slipping in her blood and listening to the harsh, animal-like breathing and high-pitched giggle of a predator.

I know with the instinct of fear that has saved humankind from extinction that Rob Westerfield has a beast lurking inside him, and if he is freed, he will strike again.

8

WHEN I FELT tears stinging the back of my eyes, I turned away from the window, reached for my backpack, and tossed it on the bed. I almost smiled as I unpacked, realizing that I had a nerve to even mentally criticize Pete Lawlor's casual wardrobe. I was wearing jeans and a turtleneck sweater. In the bag, besides a nightshirt and underwear, I was carrying only a long wool skirt and two other sweaters. My favorite shoes are clogs, which is just as well because I'm five feet nine. My hair has kept its sandy shade. I wear it long and either twist it up or clip it at the back of my neck.

Pretty, feminine Andrea resembled Mother. I have my father's strong features, which work better on a man than on a woman. No one would ever call me the star on the Christmas tree.

Tantalizing aromas were drifting up from the dining room, and I realized I was hungry. I'd caught an early flight from Atlanta and, of course, had to be at the airport well ahead of departure time. The food service—excuse me, *beverage* service—had consisted of a cup of bad coffee.

It was one-thirty when I went down to the dining room, and the lunch crowd was thinning out. It was easy to get a table, a small booth near the blazing fire. I didn't realize how chilled I felt until the warmth penetrated my hands and feet.

"May I get you a beverage?" asked the waitress, a smiling gray-haired woman with the name tag "Liz."

Why not? I thought, and ordered a glass of red wine.

When she came back, I told her I'd decided on the onion soup, and she said that it was always a favorite.

"Have you been here long, Liz?" I asked.

"Twenty-five years. Hard for me to believe."

She might have waited on us years ago. "Still fix peanut butter and jelly sandwiches?" I asked.

"Oh, sure. Did you used to have them?"

"Yes, I did." I was immediately sorry I'd mentioned it. The last thing in the world I wanted was for old-timers to realize I was the "sister of the girl who was murdered twenty-three years ago."

But Liz was obviously used to having passersby mention having dined at the Inn years ago, and without further comment she left the table.

I sipped the wine and gradually began to remember specific occasions when we'd been here as a family, back when we *were* a family. Birthdays, usually, and stopping for dinner after we'd gone for drives. The last time we came here, was, I think, during my grandmother's visit after she'd lived in Florida for nearly a year. I remember that my father picked her up at the airport and met us here. We had a cake for her. The pink lettering on the white frosting read, "Welcome home, Grandma."

She began to cry. Happy tears. The last happy tears ever shed in our family. And that thought wrenched me back to the tears shed the day of Andrea's funeral and the terrible public confrontation between my mother and father.

9

AFTER THE FUNERAL, we went back to the house. The women in the neighborhood had put together a spread, and a lot of people were there: our old neighbors from Irvington, my mother's new friends from our parish, her Wednesday bridge club members, and her fellow volunteers from the hospital. Many of my father's long-time friends and fellow officers were there as well, some of them in uniform and on duty, able to pause only long enough to offer brotherly solace.

The five girls who were Andrea's particular pals, their eyes swollen with tears, were clustered in a corner. Joan, whose house Andrea had been visiting, was especially distressed and was being comforted by the other four.

I felt apart from all of them. My mother, looking very sad in a black suit, was sitting on the couch in the living room, friends on either side, holding her hand or pressing a cup of tea on her. "It will warm you up, Genine. Your hands are so cold." She was composed even though her eyes kept welling with tears, and several times I heard her say, "I can't believe she's gone."

She and my father had clung together at the graveside, but now they sat in different rooms, she in the living room, he on the enclosed back porch that had been turned into a sort of den for him. My grandmother was in the kitchen with some of her old friends from Irvington, sadly reliving happier times in their lives.

I wandered among them, and even though there is no question that people spoke to me and told me what a brave little girl I was, I felt acutely alone. I wanted Andrea. I wanted to go up to my sister's room and find her there and curl up on the bed with her while she chatted endlessly on the phone with her friends or with Rob Westerfield.

Before she called him, she would say, "Can I trust you, Ellie?"

Of course she could. He almost never called her at home because she was forbidden to have anything to do with him, and there was always the worry that even if she answered the phone on her extension, my mother or father might pick up downstairs and hear his voice.

My mother or father? Or was it just my father? Would my mother have been upset? After all, Rob was a Westerfield, and both Mrs. Westerfields, senior and junior, occasionally attended meetings of the Women's Club, to which my mother belonged.

We got back to the house at noon. At two o'clock, people started to say things like "After all you've been through, you folks need a rest."

I knew that meant that, having paid their respects to the afflicted, having sincerely grieved, they were ready to go home. Any reluctance in leaving was caused by the fact they were also eager to be in our house the moment any developments in tracking down Andrea's killer were reported.

By then everyone had heard about Paulie Stroebel's outburst in school and knew that Andrea had been in Rob Westerfield's car when it was stopped for speeding on the thruway last month.

Paulie Stroebel. Who would ever have guessed that a quiet, introverted kid like that would have a crush on a girl like Andrea, or that she would have agreed to go to the Thanksgiving dance with him?

Rob Westerfield. He had finished a year at college, and he certainly was no dope—anyone could see that. But the rumor was he'd been asked to leave. Apparently he'd just wasted his whole freshman year. He was nineteen when he noticed my sister. What business did he have fooling around with Andrea, a sophomore in high school?

"Wasn't there some story about his having been involved in what happened to his grandmother at her house?"

It was precisely as I overheard that particular remark that the doorbell rang and Mrs. Storey from the bridge club, who was already in the vestibule, went to answer it. Standing on the porch was Mrs. Dorothy Westerfield, Rob's grandmother and the owner of the estate with the garage where Andrea had died.

She was a handsome, impressive woman, broad-shouldered and full-bosomed. She stood very straight, which made her seem taller than she was. Her iron-gray hair had a natural wave, and she wore it brushed back from her face. At seventy-three, her eyebrows were still dark and drew attention to the intelligent expression in her light brown eyes. A heavy jaw line kept her from ever having been considered pretty, but on the other hand, it added to her overall impression of commanding strength.

She was hatless and wearing a beautifully cut dark gray winter coat. She stepped into the vestibule, and her eyes swept the interior as she looked for my mother, who by then was pulling her hands away from her friends and struggling to stand up.

Mrs. Westerfield went directly to her. "I was in California and could not get back until now, but I had to tell you, Genine, how heartbroken I am for you and your family. Many years ago I lost a teenage son in a skiing accident, so I do understand what you are going through."

As my mother nodded gratefully, my father's voice rang through the room. "But it wasn't an accident, Mrs. Westerfield," he said. "My daughter was *murdered*. She was bludgeoned to death, and your grandson may have been the one who killed her. In fact, knowing his reputation, you must be aware that he is the prime suspect. So please get out of here. You're damn lucky that you're still alive yourself. You still don't believe he was involved in that burglary when you were shot and left for dead, do you?"

"Ted, how can you *say* that?" my mother pleaded. "Mrs. Westerfield, I apologize. My husband . . ."

Except for the three of them, the crowded house might have been empty. Everyone was frozen in place, as in the statues game I used to play as a child.

My father might have been a figure from the Old Testament. He had taken off his tie, and his shirt was open at the collar. His face was as white as the shirt, and his blue eyes were almost black. He had a full head of naturally dark brown hair, but at that moment it seemed even thicker, as if anger had sent bolts of electricity through it.

"Don't you *dare* apologize for me, Genine," he shouted. "There isn't a cop in this house who doesn't know that Rob Westerfield is rotten through and through. My daughter—*our* daughter—is *dead*. Now you—" he walked over to Mrs. Westerfield—"you get out of my house, and take your crocodile tears with you."

Mrs. Westerfield had turned as pale as my father. She did not answer him, but gave my mother's hand a squeeze and walked unhurriedly to the door.

When she spoke, my mother did not raise her voice, but her tone was a whiplash. "You *want* Rob Westerfield to be the one who took Andrea's life, don't you, Ted? You know Andrea was crazy about him, and you couldn't stand that. You want to know something? You were *jealous!* If you had been reasonable and let her go out with him, or any other boy for that matter, she wouldn't have had to make secret dates . . ."

Then my mother imitated my father's way of speaking: "Andrea, you may only go to a school function with a high school boy. You will *not* drive in his car. I will pick you up, and I will deliver you."

The skin over my father's cheekbones reddened, whether from

embarrassment or fury I am still not sure. "If she had obeyed me, she would still be alive today," he said evenly, his voice quiet, but bitter. "If you had not been kissing the hand of anyone named Westerfield—"

"It's a damn good thing you're not investigating this case," my mother said, interrupting him. "What about that Stroebel kid? What about that handyman, Will Nebels? What about that salesman? Have they found *him* yet?"

"What about the tooth fairy?" Now my father's tone was contemptuous. He turned and went back into the den where his friends were gathered. He closed the door behind him. Finally there was complete silence.

10

MY GRANDMOTHER HAD planned to stay with us that night, but sensing that it would be better if my father and mother were alone, she packed her bag and departed with a friend from Irvington. She would stay there overnight and be driven to the airport the next morning.

Her hope for some sort of reconciliation between my mother and father after the bitter exchange of words was not to be.

My mother slept in Andrea's room that night and every night for the next ten months, until after the trial, when not even all the Westerfield money and a high-powered defense team could save Rob Westerfield from being found guilty of murder in Andrea's death.

Then the house was sold. My father moved back to Irvington, and my mother and I began a nomadic life, starting in Florida near my grandmother. My mother, who had worked briefly as a secretary before marriage, got a job with a national hotel chain. Always very attractive, she was also smart and diligent, and worked her way up rapidly to being a kind of troubleshooter, which entailed moving every eighteen months or so to a different hotel in a different city.

Unfortunately, she applied that same diligence to concealing from everyone—except me—the fact that she became an alcoholic, drinking steadily each day from the moment she arrived home from work. For years she managed to retain enough control to do her job, with only occasional bouts of "flu" when she needed several days to sober up.

The drinking sometimes made her silent and morose. At other times she became loquacious, and it was during those sessions that I realized how passionately in love she was with my father.

"Ellie, I was crazy about him from the time I first laid eyes on him. Did I ever tell you how we met?"

Over and over again, Mother.

"I was nineteen and had been working six months at my first secretarial job. I bought a car, an orange crate on wheels with a gas tank. I decided to see how fast I could go in it on the thruway. Then all of a sudden I heard a siren and in the rearview mirror saw a dome light flashing behind me, and then a voice on a bullhorn told me to pull over. Your father gave me a ticket and a lecture that had me in tears. But when he showed up for my court date, he announced he was going to give me driving lessons."

Other times she would lament, "He was terrific in so many ways. He's a college graduate; he's got looks and brains. But he was only comfortable with his old friends and didn't like change. That's why he didn't want to move to Oldham. The problem wasn't where we lived. It was that he was too strict with Andrea. Even if we'd stayed in Irvington, she'd still have been making secret dates."

Those recollections almost always ended with "If only we'd known where to look when she didn't come home." Meaning, if only I had told them about the hideout.

The third grade in Florida. The fourth and fifth in Louisiana. The sixth in Colorado. The seventh in California. The eighth in New Mexico.

My father's check for my support arrived without fail on the first of the month, but I saw him only occasionally those first few years and then not at all. Andrea, his golden child, was gone. There was nothing left between him and my mother except bitter regret and frozen love, and whatever he felt for me was not enough to make him desire my presence. Being under the same roof with me seemed to open whatever scar tissue he had managed to grow over his wounds. If only I had told about the hideout.

As I grew up, my adoration of my father was replaced with resentment. What about asking yourself: If only I had questioned Ellie instead of ordering her to bed? What about that, Daddy?

Fortunately, by the time I began college we had been in California long enough to establish residency, and I went to UCLA as a journalism major. My mother died of liver failure six months after I received my master's degree, and, wanting yet another fresh start, I applied for and got the job in Atlanta.

Rob Westerfield did more than murder my sister that November night twenty-two years ago. As I sat in the Inn and watched Liz place the steaming onion soup in front of me, I began to wonder what our lives would have been if Andrea were still alive.

My mother and father would still be together, would still be living here. My mother had great plans for improving the house, and my father undoubtedly would have settled in. Driving through the town, I observed that the rural village I remembered had grown considerably. It now had the look of an upscale Westchester town, which was exactly what my mother had foreseen. My father would no longer have had to drive five miles for a quart of milk.

Whether or not we had remained here, there was no question that if Andrea had lived, my mother would still be alive. She'd have had no need to find comfort and forgetfulness in alcohol.

My father might even have taken note of my hero worship, and in time, perhaps when Andrea went off to college, he might have given me some of the attention I craved from him.

I sipped my soup.

It was exactly as I remembered it.

11

LIZ WAS BACK at the table, a basket of crusty bread in her hands. She lingered for a moment. "From what you mentioned about the peanut butter and jelly sandwiches, I guess you used to come here."

I had piqued her curiosity.

"A long time ago," I said, trying to sound casual. "We moved away when I was a child. I live in Atlanta now."

"I was there once. It's a nice city." She drifted away.

Atlanta, the Gateway to the South. It proved to be a good move for me. When so many of my journalism classmates were only interested in breaking into television, I for some reason always knew that the printed word held the greatest attraction for me. And at last I began to develop a sense of permanence.

Fresh-out-of-college employees are not paid much at newspapers, but my mother had a modest life insurance policy that gave me the freedom to furnish a small three-room apartment. I shopped carefully in secondhand furniture stores and at closeout sales. When the apartment was furnished, I was almost dismayed to realize that I had unconsciously recreated the overall effect of the living room of our home in Oldham: Blues and reds in the carpet. A blue upholstered couch and club chair. Even an ottoman, although it was a tight fit.

It brought back so many memories: My father dozing in the club chair, his long legs stretched on the ottoman; Andrea uncere-

moniously pushing them over and plopping down; his eyes opening, his smile of welcome to his saucy, pretty, golden child . . .

I always tiptoed around when he was napping, not wanting to
disturb his sleep. When Andrea and I were clearing the table after
dinner, I would listen intently as he began to unwind over a second
cup of coffee and tell my mother what had happened that day on
the job. I was in awe of him. My father, I bragged to myself, saved
people's lives.

Three years after the divorce, he remarried. By then I had paid
my second and final visit to him in Irvington. I did not want to go to
his wedding, nor did I care when he wrote to tell me I had a baby
brother. His second marriage had produced the son I was supposed
to be. Edward James Cavanaugh, Jr., is about seventeen now.

My last contact with my father was to write and inform him
that my mother had died and I would like to have her ashes shipped
to Gate of Heaven Cemetery and interred in Andrea's grave. If that
did not meet with his approval, I would have her buried with her
own parents in their plot in the cemetery.

He wrote back, expressing sympathy for me, and told me he
had made the arrangements I requested. He also invited me to
come and visit in Irvington.

I sent the ashes and declined the invitation.

THE ONION SOUP had warmed me up, and the memories had
made me restless. I decided to go upstairs to my room, get my
jacket, and drive around town. It was only two-thirty, and I was already beginning to wonder why I hadn't waited until tomorrow to
come here. I had an appointment with someone named Martin
Brand at the parole office at ten o'clock on Monday morning. I
would make an impassioned effort to convince him that Rob Westerfield should not be released, but as Pete Lawlor told me, it was
probably a useless gesture.

The message light on the phone in my room was blinking. I had an urgent message to call Pete Lawlor. He picked up on the first ring. "You seem to have a gift for being in the right place at the right time, Ellie," he said. "It's just coming over the wire services. The Westerfields are holding a press conference in fifteen minutes. CNN is covering it. Will Nebels, the handyman who was questioned in your sister's murder, has just made a statement claiming he saw Paul Stroebel in Rob Westerfield's car the night Andrea was killed. He claims he saw him go into the garage with something in his hand, then run out ten minutes later, get back in the car, and drive away."

"Why didn't Nebels tell that story years ago?" I snapped.

"He claims he was afraid someone would try to blame him for your sister's death."

"How was it that he saw all this happen?"

"He was in the grandmother's house. He'd done some repairs there and knew the code for the alarm. He also knew that the grandmother had a habit of leaving loose cash in drawers around the house. He was broke and needed money. He was in the master bedroom, which has windows overlooking the garage, and when the car door opened, he got a good look at Stroebel's face."

"He's lying," I said flatly.

"Watch the press conference," Pete told me, "then cover the story. You're an investigative reporter." He paused. "Unless it's too close to home for you."

"It's not," I said. "I'll talk to you later."

12

THE NEWS CONFERENCE was held in the White Plains office of William Hamilton, Esq., the criminal attorney retained by the Westerfield family to prove Robson Parke Westerfield's innocence.

Hamilton opened the proceedings by introducing himself. He was standing between two men. One I recognized from his pictures as Rob's father, Vincent Westerfield. He was a distinguished figure in his mid-sixties, with silver hair and patrician features. On Hamilton's other side, a visibly nervous, somewhat bleary-eyed fellow, who could have been anywhere between sixty and seventy, was compulsively opening and closing his interlocked fingers.

He was introduced as Will Nebels. Hamilton gave a brief summary of his background. "Will Nebels has worked in Oldham for years as a handyman. He often worked for Mrs. Dorothy Westerfield at her country home, the one at which Andrea Cavanaugh's body was found in the garage. Along with many other people, Mr. Nebels was questioned as to his whereabouts that Thursday evening when Andrea lost her life. Mr. Nebels claimed at the time that he had dinner at the counter in the local diner and went directly home. He had been seen at the diner, and there was no reason to doubt his story.

"However, when best-selling true-crime writer Jake Bern, who is writing a book about Andrea Cavanaugh's death and Rob Westerfield's claim of innocence, spoke to Mr. Nebels, new facts came to light."

Hamilton turned to Will Nebels. "Will, may I ask you to tell the media exactly what you told Mr. Bern."

Nebels shifted nervously. He looked uncomfortable dressed as he was in a shirt and tie and suit that I was sure they'd put on him just for the occasion. It's an old defense trick, one I've seen hundreds of times in court. Dress up the defendant, cut his hair, make sure he's clean-shaven, give him a shirt and tie, even if he's never buttoned a collar in his life. The same was often true for defense witnesses.

"I feel bad," Nebels began, his voice hoarse. I noticed how thin and pale he was and wondered if he were ill. I only vaguely remembered him. He had done some odd jobs for us, but I remembered him as being pretty beefy.

"It's something I've been living with, and when the writer fellow started talking to me about the case, I knew I had to get it off my chest."

He then gave the same story that had come over the wires. He had seen Paul Stroebel drive up to the garage-hideout in Rob Westerfield's car and go into the garage carrying a heavy object. The insinuation, of course, was that the object was the tire jack that had been used to bludgeon Andrea to death, the one that had been found in the trunk of Rob Westerfield's car.

Then it was Vincent Westerfield's turn to speak. "For twenty-two years my son has been locked in a prison cell amidst hardened criminals. He has always protested his innocence in this terrible crime. He went to the movies that night. He parked at the service station next door to the cinema where the family cars are routinely serviced and where the key to his car could easily have been duplicated. It had been in the station at least three times in the previous months to have minor dents removed.

"Paul Stroebel was working there that night. The pumps had closed at seven o'clock, but he was servicing a car in the interior service area. Rob spoke to Paul, told him he was leaving his car in the service lot while he was at the film. We know Paul has always denied this account of events, but now we have proof he was lying. While my son was watching that movie, Stroebel took his car, went to what they called the hideout, and killed that girl."

He drew himself up, and his voice became deeper and louder. "My son is coming up for parole. From what we are led to understand, he will be released from prison. That isn't good enough. With this newly discovered evidence we will seek a new trial, and we believe that this time Rob will be acquitted. We can only hope that Paul Stroebel, the real killer, will be put on trial and placed behind bars for the rest of his life."

I was watching the news conference on a television in the little sitting room on the main floor of the Inn. I was so enraged I wanted to throw something at the screen. For Rob Westerfield it was a win-win situation. If he was found guilty again, they couldn't put him back in prison. He'd already served his sentence. If he was acquitted, the state would never put Paulie Stroebel on trial on the word of an unreliable witness like Will Nebels. Nonetheless, in the eyes of the world, he would be the murderer.

I guess other people had heard about the conference because as soon as I turned it on, they began drifting in. The desk clerk was the first to make a comment. "Paulie Stroebel. Come on, that poor guy wouldn't hurt a fly."

"Well, a lot of people think he did a lot more than hurt a fly," said one of the waitresses I'd noticed in the dining room. "I wasn't here when it happened, but I've heard a lot of talk. You'd be surprised how many people think Rob Westerfield is innocent."

The members of the media at the conference were hurling questions at Will Nebels. "Do you realize you could go to prison for breaking, entering, and perjury?" I heard a reporter ask.

"Let me answer that," Hamilton said. "The statute of limitations has passed. Mr. Nebels is in no danger of incarceration. He has come forward to right a wrong. He had no idea that Andrea

Cavanaugh was in the garage that night, nor at the time did he know what had happened to her. Unfortunately, he panicked when he realized that his testimony would put him at the scene of a murder, so he kept quiet."

"Were you promised any money in exchange for this testimony, Mr. Nebels?" another reporter asked.

Exactly my question, I thought.

Again Hamilton took over. "Absolutely not."

Will Mr. Nebels get to play himself in the movie? I wondered.

"Has Mr. Nebels made a statement to the district attorney?"

"Not yet. We wanted the fair-minded public to be aware of his statement before there is any spin put on it by the prosecutor. The point is this—it is a terrible thing to say, but if Andrea Cavanaugh had been sexually molested, Rob Westerfield would have been out of prison long ago on DNA evidence. As it stands, it was his very concern that entrapped him. Andrea had begged him to meet her at the hideout. Over the phone she told him that she had agreed to a date with Paul Stroebel only because she thought he was the last person who would provoke jealousy in a young man like Rob Westerfield.

"The fact is that Andrea Cavanaugh was chasing Rob Westerfield. She called him frequently. He didn't care whom she dated. She was a flirt, boy crazy, a 'popular' girl."

I cringed at the insinuation.

"Rob's only mistake was to panic when he found Andrea Cavanaugh's body. He went home, never realizing that he was transporting the murder weapon in his car and that Andrea's blood was already staining the trunk of that car. That night he put his slacks and shirt and jacket in the washing machine because he was frightened."

Not too frightened to bleach the color out of them in his effort to get rid of bloodstains, I thought.

The cameras switched to the CNN anchor. "Observing this interview with us from his home in Oldham-on-the-Hudson is retired detective Marcus Longo. Mr. Longo, what do you think of Mr. Nebel's statement?"

"It is a total fabrication. Robson Westerfield was found guilty of murder because he *is* guilty of murder. I can understand the anguish of his family, but to try to shift the blame to an innocent, special-needs person is beneath contempt."

Bravo, I thought. The memory of Detective Longo years ago sitting with me in the dining room, telling me that it was all right to give up Andrea's secrets, vividly replayed itself in my mind. Longo was about sixty now, a long-faced man with heavy, dark brows and a roman nose. His remaining hair was a salt-and-pepper fringe around his head. But he had an innate dignity that heightened the effect of his obvious scorn for the charade we had just witnessed.

He still lived in Oldham. I decided that at some point I would call him.

The news conference was over, and people began to drift out of the room. The desk clerk, a studious-looking young man who looked as if he was fresh out of college, came over to me. "Is everything okay with your room, Miss Cavanaugh?"

The waitress was passing the sofa where I was sitting. She turned and looked at me sharply, and I knew she wanted to ask if I was any relation to the young girl who was murdered in the Westerfield case.

It was the first indication that I would have to give up the personal anonymity I craved if I stayed in Oldham.

So be it, I thought. This is something I have to do.

13

MRS. HILMER STILL lived in the same house down the street from ours. There were four other houses now separating it from the home we had lived in for those few years. It was obvious that the people who now owned ours had fulfilled Mother's dream for it. It had been expanded on both sides and in the back. It had always been a good-sized farmhouse, but now it was a truly lovely dwelling, substantial yet graceful, with gleaming white clapboard and dark green shutters.

I slowed the car as I drove past, and then, because on this quiet Sunday morning I didn't think anyone would notice, I stopped.

The trees had grown of course. It had been a warm autumn in the Northeast this year, and even though it was now downright chilly, there was still an abundance of gold and crimson leaves shimmering on the branches.

The living room of our house had obviously been expanded. What about the dining room? I wondered. For an instant I was standing there, holding in my arms the box of silver—or was it silverplate—as Andrea carefully arranged the place settings. *"Today Lord Malcolm Bigbottom will be our guest."*

Mrs. Hilmer had been watching for me. The minute I got out of the car, the front door opened. A moment later I felt her fierce hug. She had always been a small woman, cozily plump with a motherly face and vivacious brown eyes. Now her medium-brown hair was completely silver, and there were lines around her eyes and mouth. But basically she was as I remembered her. For years she sent Mother a Christmas card with a long note, and Mother, who never sent cards, would write back, putting a good face on our newest move and saying how well I was doing in school.

I had written to let her know when Mother died and received a warm and comforting note. I did not send her word when I moved to Atlanta, so I imagine any holiday cards or notes she might have sent were returned. The post office doesn't forward mail for too long these days.

"Ellie, you're so tall," she said now with something between a smile and a laugh. "You were such a little bit of a thing."

"It happened somewhere between my junior and senior years in high school," I told her.

There was coffee perking on the stove and blueberry muffins fresh from the oven. At my insistence we stayed in the kitchen and sat at the banquette. For a few minutes she told me about her family. I had hardly known her son and daughter. Both had been married when we moved to Oldham. "Eight grandchildren," she said proudly. "Unfortunately, none of them live around here, but I still get to see a lot of them." I knew she'd been widowed for many years. "The kids tell me this place is too big for me, but it's home and I love it. When I can't get around anymore, I'll sell it, I guess, but not now."

Briefly I told her a little about my job, and then we began to talk about the reason I was back in Oldham. "Ellie, since the day Rob was led out of the courtroom in handcuffs and shackles, the Westerfields have been insisting that he's innocent and have been fighting to get him released. They've got a lot of people convinced of it, too." Her expression became troubled. "Ellie, having said that, I've got to admit something. I'm beginning to wonder myself if Rob Westerfield wasn't convicted partly because of his reputation as a troublemaker. Everybody thought of him as a bad kid and was only too ready to believe the worst about him."

She had seen the press conference. "There's one thing I believe in that speech Will Nebels made," she said flatly, "and that's that he'd go into old Mrs. Westerfield's house to look for money to steal. Was he there that night? It is possible. On one hand, I wonder what they're giving him to tell that story, and on the other, I think how Paulie went to pieces in class when they announced that Andrea was dead. I watched that teacher testify in court. You never saw a more reluctant witness. You could tell how protective she was of Paulie, but she had to admit that she thought when he ran out of the classroom that he had said, 'I didn't think she was dead.' "

"How is Paulie Stroebel now?" I asked.

"Actually, he's been doing very well. For ten or twelve years after the trial he was terribly reticent. He knew that some people believed he had killed Andrea, and that just about destroyed him. He started working in the deli with his mother and father, and from what I understand stayed very much to himself. But since his father died and he's had to take on more and more responsibility, he's really kind of blossomed. I hope this story of Will Nebels's doesn't unravel him now."

"If Rob Westerfield gets a new trial and is acquitted, it will be as though Paulie has been found guilty," I said.

"Would they arrest him, put him on trial?"

"I'm not a lawyer, but I doubt it. Will Nebels's new testimony might be enough to get Rob Westerfield a new trial and an acquittal, but he'd never be considered credible enough to convict Paulie Stroebel. But the damage will be done, and Paulie will be another Westerfield victim."

"Maybe, maybe not. That's what makes it so hard." Mrs. Hilmer hesitated, then went on. "Ellie, that fellow who's writing a book about the case came to see me. Somebody had told him I was close to your family."

I sensed a warning in her words. "What's he like?"

"Polite. Asked a lot of questions. I was careful of every word that passed my lips. But I'm telling you right now that Bern has a point of view, and he's going to make the facts fit it. He asked if the reason your father was so strict with Andrea was that she would sneak off to meet a lot of different boys."

"That's not true."

"He's going to make it seem as if it was true."

"Yes, she had a crush on Rob Westerfield, but at the end she was afraid of him, too." It was something I hadn't expected to say, but when I did, I realized it was true. "And I was afraid for her," I whispered. "He was so angry at her because of Paulie."

"Ellie, I was in your house. I was there when you testified in court. You never said that you or Andrea were afraid of Rob Westerfield."

Was she implying that I might be creating a dishonest memory to justify my childhood testimony? But then she added, "Ellie, be careful. That writer suggested to me that you were an emotionally unstable child. It's something he's going to imply in his book."

So that's the tack he's going to take, I thought: Andrea was a tramp, I was emotionally unstable, and Paulie Stroebel is a killer. If I hadn't been sure of it before, I knew now that I had my job cut out for me.

"Rob Westerfield may get out of prison, Mrs. Hilmer," I said, and then I added firmly, "but by the time I finish investigating and writing about every dirty detail of his rotten life, no one will want to walk down the block with him, day or night. And if he gets a second trial, no jury will acquit him."

14

ON MONDAY MORNING at ten o'clock I had my meeting in Albany with Martin Brand, who was on the staff of the parole board. He was a tired-looking man of about sixty, with pouches under his eyes and a thick head of gray hair that was overdue for attention from his barber. He had opened the top button of his shirt and pulled the knot of his tie down a few inches. His florid complexion suggested a problem with high blood pressure.

There was no doubt that he had heard many versions of my protest a thousand times over the years.

"Ms. Cavanaugh, Westerfield has been turned down for parole twice. This time it's my guess the decision will be to let him out."

"He's a recidivist."

"You can't be sure of that."

"You can't be sure that he's not."

"He was offered parole two years ago if he'd admit to killing your sister, accept responsibility for the crime, and express remorse. He didn't take the offer."

"Oh, come on, Mr. Brand. He had too much to lose by being truthful. He knew you couldn't hold him much longer."

He shrugged. "I forgot that you're an investigative reporter."

"I'm also the sister of the fifteen-year-old girl who didn't get a chance to have a sweet-sixteen party."

The world-weary expression left his eyes for a moment. "Ms.

Cavanaugh, I have little doubt that Rob Westerfield is guilty, but I think you have to resign yourself to the fact that he's served his time and that, after a couple of incidents during the first years, he's behaved himself."

I would love to have known what those couple of incidents were, but I was sure Martin Brand was not going to share them with me.

"Something else," he went on. "Even if he is guilty, it was a crime of passion directed at your sister, and the odds of him repeating this kind of crime are almost nil. We have the statistics. Incidents of recidivism decline after age thirty and almost vanish after age forty."

"And there are people who are born without a conscience and once they are uncaged become walking time bombs."

I pushed the chair back and got up. Brand stood up, too. "Ms. Cavanaugh, here's a piece of unwelcome advice. I get the feeling you've lived with the memory of your sister's brutal murder all your life. But you can't bring her back, and you can't keep Rob Westerfield in prison any longer. And if he goes for a new trial and is acquitted, that's the way it is. You're a young woman. Go home to Atlanta and try to put this tragedy behind you."

"That's good advice, Mr. Brand, and I'll probably take it someday," I said. "But not now."

15

THREE YEARS AGO, after I'd written a series of articles about Jason Lambert, a serial killer in Atlanta, I received a call from Maggie Reynolds, a New York book editor I'd met on a crime panel. She offered me a contract to convert the articles into a book.

Lambert was a Ted Bundy–type killer. He'd hang around campuses, passing himself off as a student, and then trick young women into getting into his car. Like Bundy's victims, those girls simply disappeared. Fortunately, he hadn't had time to dispose of his last victim when he was captured. He's in prison in Georgia now with 149 years left to serve on his sentence and no chance of parole.

The book did surprisingly well, even clinging for a few weeks to the bottom of *The New York Times* best-seller list. I called Maggie after I left Brand's office. After describing the case and the investigative track I intended to pursue, she readily agreed to give me a contract for a book about Andrea's murder, a book that I promised her would conclusively prove Rob Westerfield's guilt.

"There's a lot of hype about the one Jake Bern is writing," Maggie told me. "I'd like to go toe-to-toe on it with a book from you. Bern broke his contract with us after we spent a fortune on publicity on his last book, trying to build him up."

I figured the project would take about three months of intensive research and writing, and then if Rob Westerfield succeeded in getting a new trial, several months beyond that. The inn would be too confining and too expensive to stay in over the long haul, so I asked Mrs. Hilmer if she knew of any rental apartments in the area. She waved my suggestion away, insisting that I stay in the guest apartment over her garage.

"I put it in a few years ago in case I ever felt I needed someone around all the time," she explained. "Ellie, it's comfortable, it's quiet, and I'll be a good neighbor, not a nuisance who runs in and out."

"You were always a good neighbor." It was a great solution, and perhaps the only drawback was that it meant driving past our old house on a regular basis. I assumed that eventually repetition would dull the instant flash of pain that hit me now as I passed that acre of property.

"God's Little Acre." Mother had laughingly called it that. She was thrilled to have so much property and was determined to cultivate a garden that would be one of the highlights on the Oldham Garden Club spring tour.

I checked out of the Inn, moved into Mrs. Hilmer's guest apartment, and on Wednesday flew back to Atlanta, arriving in the office at quarter of six in the evening. I knew there was no chance that Pete would have gone home. He was married to the job.

He looked up, saw me, grinned briefly, and said, "Let's talk over a plate of spaghetti."

"What about those ten pounds you're trying to lose?"

"I've decided not to think about them for the next couple of hours."

Pete has an intensity about him that sends electric jolts into the people around him. He went with the *News,* a privately owned daily, right out of graduate school, and within two years he was managing editor. By the time he was twenty-eight he was wearing two hats, editor in chief and publisher, and the "dying Daily," as it had been labeled, suddenly had a new lease on life.

Hiring an investigative crime reporter was one of his ideas to rev up circulation, and getting the job six years ago was a stroke of luck for me. I had just been taken on as a cub reporter. When the guy Pete wanted for the position backed out at the last minute, I was told to fill in, but only until a permanent replacement was found. Then one day, without comment, Pete stopped looking for that replacement. I had the job.

Napoli's is truly the kind of neighborhood restaurant you find all over Italy. Pete ordered a bottle of Chianti and grabbed a chunk of the warm bread that had been deposited on our table. My thoughts went back to the semester I had spent in Rome during my college years. It was one of the few genuinely happy periods of my adult life.

My mother was trying to get on the wagon and was doing reasonably well. She visited me there during my spring break, and we had a wonderful time together. We explored Rome and spent a week in Florence and the hill towns of Tuscany. We capped that off with a visit to Venice. Mother was such a pretty woman, and on that trip, when she was smiling, she looked like her old self. By unspoken agreement the names of Andrea and my father never crossed our lips.

I'm glad I have that memory of her.

The wine came, was approved by Pete, and uncorked. I took a sip of it and plunged into what I had to say. "I've been doing a lot of homework. The whitewash job on Westerfield has every possibility of succeeding. Jake Bern is a good writer. He's already done an article on the case that will be coming out next month in *Vanity Fair.*"

Pete reached for another piece of warm bread. "What can you do about it?"

"I am writing a book that will come out in the spring, the same week Bern's is published." I told him about my call to Maggie Reynolds. Pete had met her at the book party she threw for me in

Atlanta. "Maggie is doing it, and she'll put me on the fast track for publication. But in the meantime I've got to counteract Bern's articles and the Westerfield family's press releases."

Pete waited. That was another thing about him—he didn't rush to reassure. And he didn't fill in dead spots in the conversation.

"Pete, I'm fully aware that a series of articles about a crime committed twenty-two years ago in Westchester County, New York, might not be of great interest to a readership in Georgia, and anyhow, I don't think it's the right place to publish them. The Westerfield family is identified with New York."

"Agreed. So what do you propose to do?"

"Take a leave of absence if you can give it to me. Or if that isn't feasible, quit, write the book, and take my chances after it's finished."

The waiter came to the table. We both ordered cannelloni and a green salad. Pete hemmed and hawed for a minute, but then decided on Gorgonzola dressing.

"Ellie, I'll hold your job open for you as long as it's in my power to do it."

"What does that mean?"

"I may not be around much longer myself. I've had a couple of interesting offers that I'm considering."

I was shocked. "But the *News* is your baby."

"We're getting too big for the competition. There's real talk of our being bought out for big bucks. The family is interested. This generation doesn't give a damn about the paper; it's only about the revenue."

"Where are you thinking of going?"

"The *L. A. Times* is probably going to make an offer. The other possibility is Houston."

"Which would you prefer?"

"Until there's an offer on the plate, I'm not wasting my time making choices that may not exist."

Pete didn't wait for me to comment before he went on.

"Ellie, I've been doing a little research of my own on your case. The Westerfields are getting good at criminal defense strategy. They have an impressive team of lawyers just waiting to get a chance to earn a fortune. They have that Nebels guy, and, weasel that he is, some people are going to believe his story. Do what you have to, but please, if Westerfield goes to trial and gets acquitted, swear to yourself that you'll walk away from it."

He looked directly at me. "Ellie, I can tell that you're thinking, 'Not a chance.' I wish I could make you understand that no matter what books you and Bern write, some people are going to go to their graves believing that Westerfield got a bum deal, while others will still be convinced that he's guilty."

Pete meant his advice kindly, but that night as I packed the things I needed for an extended stay in Oldham, I realized that even he had the feeling that, guilty or innocent, Rob Westerfield had served his time, that people would think whatever they wanted about the merits of the case, and that it was time for me to drop it.

Nothing wrong with righteous wrath, I thought. Except when it hangs around too long.

I drove back to Oldham, and the following week Rob Westerfield's parole hearing was held. As expected, the parole was granted, and it was announced that he would be released on October 31.

Halloween, I thought. How appropriate. The night that demons walk the earth.

16

PAULIE STROEBEL WAS behind the counter when I opened the door of the delicatessen, setting off the jingling of the bell attached to it.

My vague memory of him was centered at the old service station where he'd worked years ago. He would pump gas into the tank of our car and then spray and polish the windshield until it gleamed. I remember my mother saying, "What a nice boy Paulie is," a sentiment that was never again uttered after he came under suspicion in Andrea's death.

I believe my memory of his physical appearance was partially—or perhaps even solely—based on the pictures of him I saw in the newspapers my mother had kept, newspapers that reported every detail of Andrea's murder and the trial. There is nothing that piques the reading public's interest more than having the handsome son of a wealthy and socially prominent family as the defendant in the murder of a lovely young teenager.

Of course, there were pictures accompanying the text: Andrea's body being carried out of the garage-hideout; her casket being carried out of the church; my mother, her hands clasped, her face contorted with grief; my father, his expression agonized; myself, small and lost; Paulie Stroebel, bewildered and nervous; Rob Westerfield, arrogant, handsome, and sneering; Will Nebels, with an inappropriate ingratiating smile.

Photographers hell-bent on capturing raw human emotion had a field day.

Mother had never told me that she had this collection of newspapers or the transcript of the trial. After her death I was shocked to learn that the bulky suitcase which accompanied us in all our moves was actually a Pandora's box of misery. I suspect now that when drink sent Mother into depressed reverie, she may have opened that suitcase and relived her private crucifixion.

I knew Paulie and Mrs. Stroebel must have heard that I was in town. When he looked up and saw me, he was startled, but then his expression became guarded. I inhaled the wonderful mingled aroma of ham and beef and condiments that seems to be indigenous to fine German delicatessens, and we stood there and took each other's measure.

Paulie's stolid body was more appropriate on a mature man than it had been on the teenager in the newspaper photographs. His pudgy cheeks had thinned out, and the expression in his eyes no longer had the bewildered look of twenty-three years ago. It was a few minutes before six o'clock, closing time, and as I had hoped, there were no last-minute customers waiting to be served.

"Paulie, I'm Ellie Cavanaugh." I walked over to him and extended my hand across the counter. He took it, his grasp firm, even uncomfortably strong.

"I heard you were back. Will Nebels is lying. I wasn't in the garage that night." His voice was a hurt protest.

"I know you weren't."

"It's not fair for him to say that."

The door that separated the kitchen from the front of the store opened, and Mrs. Stroebel came out. I had the immediate impression that she was always alert for even a hint that something wasn't going smoothly with her son.

She had aged, of course, and was no longer the apple-cheeked woman I remembered. Her body was thinner now. Her hair was gray, with only a hint of the daffodil shade I recalled, and she walked with a slight limp. When she saw me, she said, "Ellie?" and when I nodded, her concerned expression lightened into a welcoming smile. She hurried around the counter to embrace me.

After I testified in court, Mrs. Stroebel had come up to me, taken both my hands in hers, and, close to tears, thanked me. The defense attorney had tried to get me to say that Andrea was afraid of Paulie, and I guess on the stand I got pretty definite. "I *didn't* say Andrea was afraid of Paulie 'cause she *wasn't*. She was afraid Paulie would tell Daddy that she sometimes met Rob in the hideout."

"It is so good to see you, Ellie. You're a young lady now, and I'm an old lady," Mrs. Stroebel told me as her lips brushed my cheek. The accent of her native land flowed like honey through her words.

"No, you're not," I protested. The warmth of her welcome, like the warmth of Mrs. Hilmer's greeting, was a dart of light flashing through the unshakable sadness that accompanies my every waking moment. It is a sense of coming home to people who care about me. Here in their presence, even after all this time, I am not a stranger and I am not alone.

"Put the 'Closed' sign on the door, Paulie," Mrs. Stroebel said briskly. "Ellie, you will come home and have dinner with us, won't you?"

"I'd love to."

I followed them in my car. They lived about a mile away in one of the older sections of town. The houses were all late-nineteenth-century and relatively small. But they looked cozy and well kept, and I could imagine generations of families sitting on those front porches in the summertime.

The Stroebels' dog, a yellow Lab, greeted our arrival enthusiastically, and Paulie immediately got his leash and took him for a walk.

Their home was just what I'd expected—inviting, immaculate, and comfortable. I vetoed Mrs. Stroebel's suggestion that I sit in one of the overstuffed chairs in the living room and watch the news on television while she prepared dinner in the kitchen. Instead, I followed her there and sat on a stool at the counter, watching her work, offering to help, but confident she'd decline.

"A simple meal," she warned. "I made a beef stew yesterday. I always serve it the second day. Better that way. Much tastier."

Her hands worked swiftly, preparing the last-minute vegetables to add to the stew, rolling dough for biscuits, breaking greens for a salad. I sat quietly, suspecting she wanted to get the dinner on track and then would talk.

I was right.

It was about fifteen minutes later when, with a nod of satisfaction, she said, "Good. Now before Paulie gets back, you must tell me. Can the Westerfields do this? After twenty-two years, can they try again to make my son a killer?"

"They can try, but they won't succeed."

Mrs. Stroebel's shoulders slumped. "Ellie, Paulie has come such a long way. You know when he was a boy, it was so hard for him. He's not a student. There is a kind of knowledge that is not for him. His father and I always worried so much. Paulie is such a sweet, good person. In school he was so lonely except when he played football. It was the only time he felt he was liked."

It was obviously hard for her to continue. "Paulie was on the second team, so he didn't play much. But then one day they put him in the game, and the other team scored and then—I don't understand all about these games; if his father were alive, he could tell you—Paulie at the last minute got the ball and made a touchdown that won the game.

"Your sister was in the band, the prettiest one of all, as I remember. She was the one who grabbed a megaphone and rushed out onto the field. Paulie told me about it over and over—the cheer Andrea led for him."

Mrs. Stroebel paused, cocked her head as though listening, and then, in a low but exuberant voice, sang: *"We'll cheer for Paulie Stroebel, the best of them all. He's merry, he's jolly, we love him by golly, we'll cheer for Paulie Stroebel, the best of them all."*

Her eyes glistened as she said, "Ellie, that was the most wonderful moment of Paulie's life. You can't know what it was for him after Andrea died and the Westerfields tried to blame him. I believe he would have died to save her. Our doctor was worried that he might do something to himself. When you are a little different, a little slower, it is very easy to become depressed.

"He's been doing so well in the last few years. More and more he makes the decisions in the store. You know what I mean. Like last year he decided we should put in some tables and hire a girl to serve. Just a simple breakfast, then sandwiches in the afternoon. It's been very popular."

"I noticed the tables."

"Paulie will never have it easy. He will always have to work harder than anyone else. He will be okay unless—"

"Unless people actively start to point at him again and wonder if he's the one who should have been in prison for twenty-two years," I said, interrupting.

She nodded. "Yes. That's what I mean."

We heard the front door open. Paulie's footsteps and the Lab's short bark announced their arrival.

Paulie came into the kitchen. "It's not fair of that man to say I hurt Andrea," he said, then abruptly went upstairs.

"It is beginning to consume him again," Mrs. Stroebel said flatly.

17

THE DAY AFTER I saw the Stroebels I tried to reach Marcus Longo, the detective who had investigated Andrea's murder. The answering machine picked up, and I left a message explaining who I was and gave my cell phone number. For a few days I heard nothing.

I was terribly disappointed. After seeing how strongly Longo had expressed himself on television about Rob Westerfield's guilt, I'd thought he'd leap to the phone to get back to me. I'd just about given up on him when, on October 30, my cell phone rang. When I answered, a quiet voice asked, "Ellie, is your hair still the color of sand with sunbeams running through it?"

"Hello, Mr. Longo."

"I just got back from Colorado, which is why you haven't heard from me," he said. "Our first grandchild arrived Tuesday. My wife is still out there. Can you have dinner with me tonight?"

"I'd love to." I told him I was staying in Mrs. Hilmer's guest apartment.

"I know where Mrs. Hilmer lives."

There was the slightest pause as we both thought that of course he did—it's just down the road from our old house.

"I'll pick you up at seven, Ellie."

I was watching for his car and hurried downstairs when it pulled off the road and onto the long driveway. The driveway forks, and the garage with the guest apartment is at the end on the right side. At one time it had been a stable, and it is actually a distance from the house. I didn't want him to take the wrong turn.

There are some people in this world with whom we feel immediately comfortable. That was the way it was with Marcus Longo as soon as I slid into the passenger seat.

"I've thought a lot about you over the years," he said as he made a U-turn. "Have you been to Cold Spring since you've been back?"

"I drove through it one afternoon, but I didn't get out of the car. I remember being there when I was a kid. My mother was always browsing around antique shops."

"Well, it still has those, but now it also has some good restaurants."

Oldham is the northernmost town bordering the Hudson River in Westchester County. Cold Spring on the Hudson is just over the line in Putnam County, directly across the Hudson from West Point. It is a particularly beautiful town with a Main Street that has the look and feel of the nineteenth century.

I did have strong memories of being there with my mother. In fact, over the years she would sometimes talk about Cold Spring.

"Remember how on Saturday afternoons we would drive down Main Street and stop in all those little antique shops? I was training you girls to have an eye for lovely things. Was that so bad?"

The reminiscences usually began over her second or third scotch. By the time I was ten, I was watering the bottle of Dewar's in the hope of slowing her down. It never really seemed to help.

Longo had made a reservation at Cathryn's, an intimate Tuscan-style grill in a courtyard off Main Street. There, at a corner table, we took each other's measure. Oddly, in person he looked older than he did on television. There were furrows around his eyes and mouth, and even though his body was broad, he did not seem physically strong. I wondered if he had been ill.

"I don't know why I thought you'd be about five feet three," he said. "You were small for your age when you were young."

"I grew quite a bit in high school."

"You look like your father, you know. Have you seen him?"

The question surprised me. "No. And I don't intend to." I didn't want to ask, but I was too curious not to. "Do you see him, Mr. Longo?"

"Please call me Marcus. I haven't seen him in years, but his son, your half-brother, is a terrific all-around athlete. Gets lots of press in the local papers. Your father retired from the state troopers eight years ago when he was fifty-nine. There were some very nice write-ups in the local papers about him. He had an impressive career with the state troopers."

"I assume Andrea's death was mentioned?"

"Yes, and there were quite a few pictures, both recent and from the files. That's how I can see how much you resemble him now."

I didn't answer, and Longo raised his eyebrows. "Obviously that's a compliment. Anyhow, as my mother used to say, 'You grew up nice.'" Abruptly he changed the subject. "Ellie, I read your book and liked it a lot. In it you captured the gut-wrenching pain of the victims' families better than anything I've ever read. I understand where that's coming from."

"I guess you do."

"Why are you here, Ellie?"

"I came because I had to protest against Rob Westerfield getting out on parole."

"Even though you must have known you were wasting your frequent flier miles," he said quietly.

"I knew it was useless."

"Do you feel it necessary to be a voice crying out in the wilderness?"

"My message is not to prepare the way for the Lord. Mine is 'Beware. You're uncaging a killer.'"

"It's still a voice in the wilderness. The doors will open tomorrow morning for Rob Westerfield, and he will walk out of prison. Listen to me carefully now, Ellie. There isn't the faintest doubt that he'll get a new trial. Nebels's testimony will probably be enough to cause reasonable doubt in the jurors' minds, and Westerfield will be acquitted. His record will be expunged, and the Westerfields will live happily ever after."

"That can't happen."

"Ellie, you've got to understand something: The Westerfields need to *make* it happen. Robson Parke Westerfield is the last of the line of what used to be a fine and respected name. Don't be fooled by his father's public image. Behind that philanthropic facade, Vincent Westerfield, Rob's father, is a greedy robber baron, but he craves respectability for his son. And *old* Mrs. Westerfield demands it."

"What does that mean?"

"It means that at age ninety-two she is still as sharp as a tack and in control of the family fortune. If Rob's name isn't cleared, she's leaving everything to charity."

"Surely Vincent Westerfield has plenty of money in his own right."

"Of course. But nothing compared to his mother's wealth. Mrs. Dorothy Westerfield is a class act, and she no longer has blind faith in her grandson's innocence. Didn't your father throw her out of your house the day of the funeral?"

"Yes, he did. My mother never got over being mortified about that."

"Apparently neither did Mrs. Dorothy Westerfield. Your father publicly confronted her with the fact that the guy who robbed and shot her claimed to be in collusion with Rob."

"Yes, I remember him shouting that."

"And apparently Mrs. Westerfield has remembered it, too. Naturally she has wanted to believe that Rob was wrongly convicted, but I gather the seeds of doubt have always been there and have only grown stronger over the years. Now that she obviously is running out of time, she's put it to the father. If Rob is innocent, see that he's vindicated and the stain removed from the family name. Otherwise, her money, the Westerfield fortune, will go to charity."

"I'm surprised she has that much discretion over it."

"Maybe her husband, Vincent's father, saw something in his son that caused him to set it up that way. Fortunately for him, he didn't live to see his grandson convicted of murder."

"So the father has to prove Rob's innocence, and suddenly there's an eyewitness who saw Paulie Stroebel go into the hideout. Is old Mrs. Westerfield buying that story?"

"Ellie, what she wants is a new jury to review the case and render the verdict she wants."

"And Vincent Westerfield is going to make sure what that verdict is."

"Let me tell you about Vincent Westerfield. For years he's been hell-bent on destroying the character of the Hudson Valley by getting residential areas zoned for business. He'd put a shopping mall in the middle of the Hudson River if he could figure out how to do it. Do you think he cares what happens to Paulie Stroebel?"

The menus came. I decided on one of the specials, rack of lamb. Marcus ordered salmon.

Over our salads I told him my plans. "When I saw that interview on television with Will Nebels, I originally decided to try to get some investigative articles published. What I've gotten so far is a contract to write a book to refute the one Jake Bern is writing."

"They not only have Bern writing a book but they have a publicity machine geared up and ready to blitz the media. What you saw on television was only the beginning," Longo warned. "I wouldn't be surprised if they suddenly released a picture of Rob in an Eagle Scout uniform."

"I remember my father saying he was rotten through and through. What was the story about the break-in at his grandmother's home?"

Marcus had a cop's memory for crimes. "The grandmother was staying at her house in Oldham. In the middle of the night she heard some kind of noise and woke up. There was a live-in maid, but she was in a separate wing. When Mrs. Westerfield opened the bedroom door, she was shot at point-blank range. She never saw her assailant, but he was arrested a couple of days later. He claimed Rob had put him up to it, said he promised him ten thousand dollars if he finished her off.

"Needless to say, there was no proof. It was the word of a twenty-one-year-old high school dropout with a long juvenile record against a Westerfield."

"What would Rob's motive have been?"

"Money. His grandmother was leaving one hundred thousand dollars directly to him. She thought that sixteen wasn't too young to begin to handle and invest money intelligently. She didn't know that Rob had a drug problem."

"She believed he wasn't involved in the shooting?"

"Yes. Nevertheless, she changed her will. That bequest disappeared."

"So she may have had her doubts about him even then?"

Longo nodded. "And that doubt, combined with the doubt about your sister's murder, has come to a head. In essence she's telling her son and grandson to put up or shut up."

"What about Rob Westerfield's mother?"

"Another very nice lady. She spends almost all her time in Florida. She has an interior design business in Palm Beach. Under her maiden name, I might add. She's very successful. You can look her up on the Internet."

"I've opened a Website," I said.

Longo's eyebrows raised.

"It's the fastest way to spread information. Every day starting with tomorrow and every single day after that I'm going to write about Andrea's murder and Rob Westerfield's guilt on my Website. I'm going to follow up every nasty rumor about him and try to verify each one. I'm going to interview his teachers and classmates from his two prep schools and from his freshman year in Willow

College. You don't get thrown out of schools without a reason. It's a long shot, but I'm going to see if I can trace the locket he gave Andrea."

"How well do you remember it?"

"Now, it's blurry, of course. But at the trial I described it specifically. I have the trial transcript, so I know exactly what I said then—that it was gold, heart-shaped, and had three blue stones in the center, and that the letters R and A were engraved on the back."

"I was in court when you described it. I remember thinking that it sounded expensive, but in reality it was probably one of those twenty-five-dollar pieces of junk that you buy from a cart in a shopping mall. They initial them for a couple of bucks."

"But you didn't believe that I actually touched it when I found Andrea's body in the hideout or that I heard someone breathing near me or that the locket disappeared before the police came?"

"Ellie, you went from hysteria to shock. You testified that when you knelt down, you slid and fell over Andrea's body. I don't think that in the dark, and with what must have been going on in your head, that you could have identified feeling the locket. You said yourself that she always wore it under her blouse or sweater."

"She was wearing it that night. I'm certain of it. Why wasn't it on her when the police came?"

"A reasonable explanation is that he took it after he killed her. His defense was predicated on his claim that she was just a kid with a crush on him and that he had absolutely no interest in her."

"Let's leave it at that for now," I said. "I want to talk about something else. Tell me about your brand-new grandchild. He's the only baby ever born, I assume."

"Of course he is." Marcus Longo seemed as glad as I to change the subject. Dinner was served, and he told me about his family. "Mark's your age. He's a lawyer. He married a girl from Colorado and got a job with a firm out there. Loves it. I retired a couple of years ago and had heart surgery last winter. We spend most of the cold months in Florida now and are talking about selling out here and buying a little place around Denver so that we can see the kids without crowding in on them."

"Mother and I spent a year or so in Denver."

"You've been in Atlanta for a while, Ellie. Do you consider that home?"

"It's a great city. I have a lot of good friends. I've enjoyed my job, but if the paper I work for is sold as rumored, I don't know that I'll stay there. Maybe someday I'll get that nice feeling of putting down roots and being settled. I don't have it yet. I always feel there is unfinished business. As a kid did you ever go to the movies when you had homework due the next day?"

"Sure."

"You really couldn't enjoy the movie, could you?"

"It's a long time ago, but I guess not."

"I have homework to finish before I can enjoy the movie," I told him.

I HADN'T TURNED a light on before I left, and when we got back to Mrs. Hilmer's place, the garage apartment looked dark and lonely. Marcus Longo ignored my protests and insisted on walking me upstairs. He stood there while I fished for my key, and then when I inserted it in the lock and stepped inside, he said firmly, "Double-lock the door."

"Any special reason?" I asked.

"Ellie, to quote you, 'Beware, you're uncaging a killer.' "

"That's right."

"Then listen to your own voice. I'm not telling you not to go after Westerfield, but I *am* telling you to be careful."

I was home just in time to catch the ten o'clock news. The big story was that Rob Westerfield was being released from prison in the morning and that there would be an interview with the press from the family home in Oldham at noon.

I wouldn't miss it for the world, I thought.

18

SLEEP DID NOT come easily that night. I would doze and then wake up, knowing that each tick of the clock was bringing Rob Westerfield closer to the moment when he would be released from prison.

I could not take my mind off him or off the event that had kept him behind bars for twenty-two years. In fact, the closer he came to freedom, the more alive Andrea and Mother were to me. If only . . . if only . . . if only . . .

Give it up, part of me screamed. Walk away from it. Put it in the past. I know what I'm doing to my life, and it's not something I want to happen. Somewhere around two o'clock I got up and made a cup of cocoa. I sat by the window as I drank it. The woods that separated our house from old Mrs. Westerfield's estate extend past the Hilmer property and are still there, her privacy buffer. I could slip through them as Andrea did that night, and on the other side make my way to the garage-hideout.

Now there is a tall fence defining the several acres around the Westerfield house. I'm sure there is now a security system that would signal an interloper, or a fifteen-year-old kid. At ninety-two, people don't usually require much sleep. I wondered if Mrs. Westerfield was awake right now, glad to see her flesh and blood released from prison but cringing at the publicity that would accompany it. Her need to clear the family name was as powerful as mine was to see that Paulie Stroebel was not destroyed and that Andrea's name was not dragged in the dirt.

She was an innocent, young kid whose head was turned; then her crush on Rob Westerfield became fear, which was why she went to the hideout that night. She was afraid *not* to meet him when he ordered her to show up.

Sitting in the predawn hours, my subconscious feeling that she was afraid of him, and that I was afraid of him for her, crystallized in my mind. I could vividly see Andrea as she had been that night, clasping the locket around her neck, choking back tears. She didn't want to meet him, but she was caught between a rock and a hard place. And so I added another "if only" to the list. If only she had gone to my parents and confessed to them that she had been meeting Rob.

In that moment we reversed roles, and I became her big sister. I went back to bed and slept fitfully until seven o'clock. I was in front of the television when the media covered Rob Westerfield's exit from Sing Sing prison in a limousine that met him at the gate. The on-the-spot reporter of the channel I watched emphasized that Rob Westerfield had always sworn he was innocent of the crime.

At noon I was back in front of the set for the unveiling of Rob Westerfield to the world.

The interview took place in the library of the family home in Oldham. The sofa on which he sat was placed in front of a wall of leatherbound books, inferring, I assume, his scholarly mind.

Rob was wearing a tan cashmere jacket, an open-necked sport shirt, dark trousers, and loafers. He was always handsome but had become much more so in his maturity. He had his father's patrician features and had learned to conceal the condescending sneer that appeared in all of his early pictures. There was the faintest touch of gray in the roots of his dark hair. His hands were clasped in front of him, and he was leaning slightly forward in a relaxed but attentive pose.

"Good setting," I said aloud. "The only thing missing is a dog at his feet." At the sight of him I could feel the bile rising in my throat.

His interviewer was Corinne Sommers, host of *The Real Story,* the popular syndicated Friday night program. She did a brief intro: "Just released after twenty-two years in prison . . . always protested his innocence . . . will now fight to have his name cleared . . ."

Get on with it, I thought.

"Rob Westerfield, it's an obvious question, but how does it feel to be a free man?"

His smile was warm. His dark eyes under well-shaped eyebrows seemed almost amused. "Unbelievable, wonderful. I'm too big to cry, but that's what I feel like doing. I just go around the house, and it's so wonderful to be able to do normal things, like going into the kitchen and getting a second cup of coffee."

"Then you'll be staying here for a while?"

"Absolutely. My father has furnished a wonderful apartment for me near this house, and I want to work with our lawyers to get a speedy retrial." Now he looked earnestly into the camera. "Corinne, I could have gotten parole two years ago if I'd been willing to say I killed Andrea Cavanaugh and that I regretted that terrible deed."

"Weren't you tempted to do that?"

"Not for a minute," he said promptly. "I have always maintained my innocence, and now, thanks to Will Nebels coming forward, I may at last have a chance to prove it."

You couldn't admit it, you had too much to lose, I thought. Your grandmother would have disowned you.

"You went to the movies the night Andrea Cavanaugh was murdered."

"Yes, I did. And I stayed until the movie was over at nine thirty. My car was parked at the service station for over two hours. It's only a twelve-minute drive to my grandmother's place from the center of town. Paulie Stroebel had access to the car, and he had been following Andrea around. Even her sister admitted that on the stand."

"The ticket taker at the theater remembers you buying the ticket."

"That's right. And I had the stub to prove it."

"But no one saw you leave the theater at the end of the film?"

"No one *remembers* seeing me," he corrected. "There's a difference."

For just an instant I saw a flash of temper under the amiable smile, and I sat up.

The rest of the interview, however, might have been with a newly returned hostage. "Besides clearing your name, what are you looking forward to doing?"

"Going to New York. Dining in the restaurants that probably didn't exist twenty-two years ago. Traveling, eventually. Getting a job." Now a warm smile from him. "Meeting a special someone. Getting married. Having kids."

Getting married. Having kids. All the things Andrea would never do.

"What are you having for dinner tonight, and who is going to be with you?"

"Just the four of us—my mother, my father, and my grandmother. We just want to be reunited as a family. I asked for a pretty basic dinner: shrimp cocktail, prime rib, baked potato, broccoli, a salad."

How about apple pie? I wondered.

"And apple pie," he concluded.

"And champagne, I imagine."

"Definitely."

"It seems as though you have pretty definite plans for the future, Rob Westerfield. We wish you luck and hope that in a second trial you can prove your innocence."

This is a journalist? I snapped the remote button and went to the table in the dining area where I had my laptop ready and waiting. I got online to my Website and began to write.

"Robson Westerfield, the convicted murderer of fifteen-year-old Andrea Cavanaugh, has just been released from prison and is looking forward to roast beef and apple pie. The sanctification of this killer has just begun, and it will be made at the expense of his young victim and of Paulie Stroebel, a quiet, hardworking man who has had to overcome many difficulties.

"He shouldn't have to overcome this one."

Not bad for a beginning, I thought.

19

EVERY DAY Sing Sing Correctional Facility discharges prisoners who have completed serving their sentences or have been paroled. When they leave, they are given jeans, work boots, a jacket, and $40, and unless they are picked up by a family member or friend, they are driven to the bus station or issued a train ticket.

The train station is the equivalent distance of four blocks from the prison. The discharged prisoner walks to the station and takes a train going either north or south.

The train going south terminates in Manhattan. The one going north travels up New York as far as Buffalo.

I reasoned that anyone getting out of Sing Sing at this time would almost certainly have known about Rob Westerfield.

That was why early the next morning I dressed warmly, parked at the station, and walked toward the prison. There is constant activity at the gates. I had checked some statistics and knew there were about twenty-three hundred inmates housed there. Jeans, work boots, and a jacket are not particularly distinctive apparel. How would I be able to tell the difference between someone who might be an employee getting off duty and a newly released inmate? The answer is I couldn't.

Anticipating the problem, I had made a cardboard sign. I stood beside the gate and held it. It read: "Investigative journalist seeking information about just-released prisoner Robson Westerfield. Substantial payment."

Then it occurred to me that someone driving out of the prison in a car or taxi, or someone who did not want to be seen talking to me, might come forward if he could reach me by phone. At the last minute I added the number of my cell phone—917-555-1261—in large, easy-to-read numbers.

It was a cold, windy morning. The first of November. All Saints Day. Since Mother died I've attended Mass only on days such as Christmas and Easter, when even fallen-away Catholics like me hear the bells of a nearby church and reluctantly make our way to it.

I'm like a robot when I get there. I dutifully kneel and stand with the others, never sharing in the prayers. I like to sing, and I can feel throbbing in my throat when the congregation joins the choir. At Christmas it's joyous music: "Hark the Herald Angels Sing" or "Away in a Manger." At Easter the song is triumphant: "Jesus Christ Is Risen Today." But my lips always stay closed. Let others sing in exultation.

I used to be angry; now I am only weary. *One way or another you've taken them all, O Lord. Are you finally satisfied?* I know when I watch television and learn of whole families wiped out in bombings, or see them starving in refugee camps, I should be able to realize how much more I have, how much better off I am. I do grasp that intellectually, but it doesn't help. *Let's make a deal, God. We'll leave each other alone.*

I stood for two hours holding the sign. Most people passing in or out of the gates stared at it, curiosity in their eyes. A few of them spoke to me. A bulky man in his late forties, the earmuffs of his cap pulled down for warmth, snapped, "Lady, haven't you got anything better to do with your time than investigate that creep?" He would only tell me that he worked in the prison, but he refused to give his name.

I did notice, however, that some people, including those who looked like employees, studied the sign as though memorizing my phone number.

At ten o'clock, chilled to the bone, I gave up and walked back to the parking lot at the train station. I was just at the driver's door of my car when a man came up to me. He appeared to be about thirty, rawboned, with mean eyes and narrow lips. "Why are you picking on Westerfield?" he asked. "What's he ever done to you?"

He was wearing jeans, a jacket, and work boots. Had he just been released and followed me? I wondered. "Are you a friend of his?" I asked.

"What do you care?"

We have an instinctive reaction to step back when people get too close to us, when they are literally "in our faces." My back was against the side of the car, and this guy was crowding me. From the corner of my eye I was relieved to see a van pulling into the parking area. The thought rushed through my head that at least if I needed help there was someone around.

"I want to get in my car, and you're in my way," I said.

"Rob Westerfield was a model prisoner. We all looked up to him. He set a great example for the rest of us. Now, how much are you going to pay me for that information?"

"Let him pay you." I turned and shouldered the guy away from me, pushed the remote to release the lock, and yanked the door open.

He did not try to stop me, but before I could close the door again, he said, "Let me give you a little free advice. Burn your sign."

20

WHEN I GOT BACK to the Hilmer apartment, I began to peruse the old newspapers Mother had kept. They were a godsend in my research on the life of Rob Westerfield. In several of them I found a mention of the two prep schools he had attended. The first one, Arbinger Preparatory School, in Massachusetts, is one of the toniest in the country. Interestingly, he stayed there only a year and a half before switching to Carrington in Rhode Island.

I didn't know anything about Carrington and looked it up on the Internet. The Website of Carrington Academy made it sound like a country estate where learning, sports, and friendship intertwined to create a sort of paradise. But behind the glowing description of all that it had to offer, the nitty-gritty became obvious: It was a school for "students who haven't realized their academic or social potential," for "students who may have difficulty adjusting to disciplined study."

In other words, it was a place for kids with a behavior problem.

Before I placed an inquiry on my Website, looking for information about Rob Westerfield's school days, from fellow students or former Carrington employees, I decided to see both places for myself. I phoned the schools and explained that I was a journalist writing a book on Robson Westerfield who had been a student there. In both cases I reached the president's office. At Arbinger I was immediately referred to Craig Parshall in the media relations office.

Mr. Parshall told me it was school policy that students, former or present, were never discussed with the press.

I took a stab. "Isn't it a fact that you gave an interview to Jake Bern concerning Robson Westerfield?"

There was a long pause, and I knew I was right.

"There was an interview granted," Parshall said, his voice stiff and condescending. Then he added, "If the family of a present student or a former student grants permission for an interview, we would within reason honor that request. You must understand, Ms. Cavanaugh, that our pupils come from distinguished families, including the sons of presidents and royalty. There are times when it is appropriate to allow carefully monitored media access."

"And of course that publicity enhances the name and reputation of the school," I said. "On the other hand, if every day on a Website the fact that the convicted murderer of a fifteen-year-old girl had been rubbing shoulders with some of those distinguished students, they and their families might not be too happy. And other families might think twice about sending their sons and heirs to you. Isn't that right, Mr. Parshall?"

I didn't give him a chance to answer. "In fact, it might serve the school much better to be cooperative. Don't you agree?"

When, after a long moment of silence, Parshall responded, he clearly was not a happy man. "Miss Cavanaugh, I will grant your request for an interview. I will, however, warn you that the only information released to you will be the dates Robson Westerfield was a student here and the fact that he requested and received a transfer."

"Oh, I don't expect you to admit that you booted him out," I said scornfully. "But I'm sure you managed to find a little more than that to tell Mr. Bern."

We agreed that I would be in his office at eleven the next morning.

Arbinger is about forty miles north of Boston. I found the town on the map and figured out the best route to take and how much time I'd need.

Then I called Carrington Academy, and this time was passed through to Jane Bostrom, director of admissions. She acknowledged that Jake Bern had been granted an interview at the request of the Westerfield family, and added that without the family's permission she could not grant me an interview.

"Ms. Bostrom, Carrington is a kind of prep school of last resort," I pointed out firmly. "I want to be fair to its reputation, but the reason for its existence is to accept and try to straighten out problem kids. Right?"

I liked the fact that she leveled with me. "There are a lot of reasons why kids have problems, Ms. Cavanaugh. The majority of those reasons have to do with the family. They're kids of divorce, kids with high-powered parents who don't have time for them, kids who are loners or the butt of jokes by their peers. It doesn't mean they're not capable academically or socially. It just means that they're overwhelmed and need help."

"Help that sometimes, no matter how hard you try, you simply can't give?"

"I can give you a list of our graduates who went on to become very successful."

"I can name one who succeeded at the very first murder he committed—or at least the very first he is known to have committed." Then I added, "I don't want to do a hatchet job on Carrington. I want to find out what I can about what Rob Westerfield was up to in his teenage years before he murdered my sister. If you gave a lot of information to Jake Bern, and he can extrapolate the good stuff and leave out the rest, I want the same kind of access."

Since I'd be at Arbinger tomorrow, which was Friday, I made an appointment with Ms. Bostrom at Carrington for Monday morning. I debated about spending some time before the meetings tomorrow and Monday in the neighborhood of the schools. From what I could tell, they both were located in small towns. That had to mean there were places where the kids would congregate, such as a pizza parlor or fast-food joint. Sitting around the local off-campus hangout had worked for me when I did an earlier follow-up article on a kid who tried to kill his parents.

I hadn't run into Mrs. Hilmer in a couple of days, but in the late afternoon she phoned. "Ellie, this is a suggestion more than an invitation. I had one of my urges to cook today and ended up with a roast chicken in the oven. If you don't have plans, would you like to come over for dinner? But please don't say yes if you'd rather just be quiet."

I hadn't bothered to go to the grocery that morning and knew that my at-home choices were an American cheese sandwich or an American cheese sandwich. And I also remembered that Mrs. Hilmer was a good cook.

"What time?" I asked.

"Oh, about seven."

"I'll not only be there, I'll be early."

"Wonderful."

As I hung up I realized that Mrs. Hilmer must think of me as something of a loner. She's partially right, of course. But despite my interior core of isolation, or maybe even because of it, I am a reasonably outgoing person. I enjoy being with people, and after a busy day at the newspaper, I often get together with friends. When I worked late, I'd end up having pasta or a hamburger with whoever was around. There were always two or three of us there who weren't rushing home to the spouse or significant other after wrapping up a story or finishing a column.

I was one of the regulars in that group, and so was Pete. As I washed my face, brushed my hair, and twisted it back up, I wondered when he'd let me know which job he'd taken. I was sure that even if the paper *wasn't* sold immediately, he wouldn't stay at it much longer. The fact that the family was trying to sell it would be enough to make him move on. Where would he end up? Houston?

L.A.? Whichever, chances were that our paths wouldn't cross much after the move.

It was a suddenly disquieting thought.

The cozy apartment consisted of a large living room with a galley kitchen at one end and a medium-sized bedroom. The bath was off the short hallway between them. I had set up my computer and printer on the table in the dining area near the kitchen. I'm not a neat worker, and as I was about to put on my coat, I looked around as if with Mrs. Hilmer's eyes.

The newspapers I'd been going through were scattered on the floor in an arc around the chair I'd been sitting in. The decorative fruit bowl and brass candlesticks that had been primly centered on the colonial table were shoved together on the buffet. My appointment book lay open on one side of the computer, and my pen was tossed on top of it. The bulky bound copy of the thick trial transcript, complete with vivid yellow markers, was next to the printer.

Suppose for some reason Mrs. Hilmer walked back with me and saw this mess, I thought. How would she react? I was pretty sure I knew the answer to that question, since there was absolutely nothing out of place in her home.

I bent down, scooped up the papers, and straightened them into something of an orderly pile. Then, on further consideration, I dug out the big duffel bag in which I always carried them and dropped them into it.

The trial transcript followed. I reasoned that the notebook, my pen, and the laptop and printer weren't too asthetically offensive. I moved the fruit bowl and candlesticks back to their decorative positions on the table. I had started to put the duffel bag in the closet when it dawned on me that if the apartment were to catch on fire, I would lose all this material. I dismissed that notion as improbable but nonetheless decided to take the bag with me. I don't know why I did that, but I did. Call it a hunch, one of those *feelings* you just get, as my grandmother used to say.

It was still cold outside, but at least the wind had died down.

Even so, the walk from the apartment to the house seemed pretty long. Mrs. Hilmer had told me that after her husband died she had an attached garage added to the house because she didn't want to have to walk back and forth from the old one. Now the old garage beneath the apartment was empty except for gardening supplies and lawn furniture.

Walking to the house in the dark silence, I could well understand why she hadn't wanted to make the trip at night alone.

"Don't think I'm moving in here as well as in the apartment," I told Mrs. Hilmer when she opened the door and spotted the duffel bag. "It's just become my constant companion."

Over a glass of sherry I explained what was in it, then a thought occurred to me. Mrs. Hilmer had lived in Oldham for nearly fifty years. She was active in the parish and in the town activities— meaning she knew everyone. There were local people mentioned in those newspaper stories whose names meant nothing to me, but they would surely be familiar to her.

"I wonder if you'd consider going through these papers with me," I asked her. "There are people quoted whom I'd love to talk to, assuming they're still around. For example, some friends of Andrea's from school, neighbors at that time of Will Nebels, some of the guys Rob Westerfield hung around with. I'm sure most of Andrea's classmates are married, and probably a lot of them have moved away. I wonder if it would upset you to read through these old articles and maybe make a list of the people who talked to reporters who are still around here. I'm hoping, of course, that they may have known something that didn't come out at the time."

"I can tell you about one of them off the top of my head," Mrs. Hilmer said. "Joan Lashley. Her parents retired, but she married Leo St. Martin. She lives in Garrison."

Joan Lashley was the girl with whom Andrea had been doing homework that last night! Garrison was near Cold Spring, only a fifteen-minute drive from here. It was obvious that Mrs. Hilmer was going to be a treasure trove of information about people I might want to see.

While we were having coffee, I opened the duffel bag and put some of the newspapers on the table. I saw the look of pain that came over Mrs. Hilmer's face when she picked up the first one. The headline read, "Fifteen-Year-Old Bludgeoned to Death." Andrea's picture filled the front page. She was wearing her band uniform: a red jacket with brass buttons and a matching short skirt. Her hair was falling around her shoulders, and she was smiling. She looked happy and vibrant and young.

That picture had been taken at the first game of the season in late September. A few weeks later Rob Westerfield first met her when she was bowling with friends at the sports center in town. It was the next week that she went for the drive in his car and he was stopped by the state trooper for speeding.

"Mrs. Hilmer, I warn you," I said. "It's not easy going through this material, so if you think it would be too much for you—"

She interrupted me. "No, Ellie, I want to do it."

"Okay." I took out the rest of the newspapers. The trial transcript was still in the duffel bag. I took it out. "This makes pretty unpleasant reading."

"Leave it with me," she said firmly.

MRS. HILMER INSISTED on lending me a small flashlight for my return to the apartment, and I must say I was glad to have it. The night had continued to clear, and now a sliver of the moon was visible. I guess I was getting fanciful, but I could only think of those Halloween images of black cats sitting on crescent moons, grinning as though they were reveling in some secret knowledge.

I'd left on only a small night-light in the stairwell—again my conscious effort to be considerate of my hostess, this time by not running up her electricity bill. As I walked up the stairs, I suddenly was not sure if it was the best idea to be so frugal. The staircase was dark and shadowed, and it creaked under my steps. I suddenly became acutely aware that Andrea was murdered in a garage very similar to this one. They both originally had been barns. The old hayloft here is now the apartment, but the feeling of the structures is similar.

By the time I was at the head of the stairs, the key was in my hand and with a quick turn of the lock I was inside and had bolted the door. I immediately stopped worrying about running up bills and began to turn on every light I could find: the lamps on either side of the couch, the chandelier over the dining room table, the hallway light, the bedroom lights. At last I was able to draw a sigh of relief and begin to shake off the sense of alarm that had seized me.

The table looked strangely neat, with only the laptop and printer, my pen and appointment book at one end, and the fruit bowl and candlesticks in the center. Then I realized that something had changed. I had left my pen to the right of the appointment book, next to the computer. It was now on the left side of the book, away from the computer. A chill shot through me. Someone had been here and must have moved it. But why? To go through the appointment book and check on my activities—that would have to be the only reason. What else had been examined?

I turned on the computer and rushed to check the file where I kept my notes on Rob Westerfield. Just that afternoon I had jotted in a quick description of the man who stopped me in the parking lot at the railroad station. It was still there, but now a sentence had been added. I had described him as average height, gaunt, with mean eyes and mouth. The new sentence was "Considered dangerous, so approach with extreme caution."

My knees felt weak. It was bad enough that someone had come in while I was with Mrs. Hilmer, but that he would flaunt his presence was frightening. I was absolutely certain that I had locked the apartment door when I left, but the lock was basic and inexpensive, and wouldn't be much of a challenge for a professional burglar. Was anything missing? I ran into the bedroom and could see that the closet door, which I had left closed, was now slightly ajar. My clothes and shoes inside, however, seemed to be exactly as I'd left them. In the top drawer of the dresser I had a leather case of jewelry. Earrings, a gold chain, and a simple long strand of pearls are pretty much all I bother with, but the case also held my mother's engagement ring and wedding band, and the diamond earrings my father had given her for their fifteenth wedding anniversary, the year before Andrea died.

The jewelry was all there, so it was clear that whoever came in was not a common thief. He had been after information, and I realized how blessed I was that I had not left the trial transcript and all the old newspapers there. I had not the slightest doubt that they would have been destroyed. I could replace the trial transcript, but it would take a lot of time and those newspapers were irreplaceable. It was not just the accounts of the trial that the articles contained, but all the interviews and background that would be lost if they were to disappear.

I decided not to call Mrs. Hilmer immediately. I was sure she would be awake all night if she knew that an intruder had been in the apartment. I resolved that in the morning I would take the newspapers and the transcript and have copies made of them. It would be a tiresome job but well worth it. I simply couldn't afford to take a chance on losing them.

I checked the door again. It was bolted, but I wedged a heavy chair against it. Then I locked all the windows except the one in the bedroom that I wanted open for fresh air. I love a cold bedroom and didn't want to be deprived of that pleasure by the unknown visitor. Besides, the apartment is on the second floor, and there's no way anyone could get in through a window without a ladder. I was very sure that if anyone wanted to harm me, he'd find an easier way than dragging a ladder that I might hear. Still, when I finally did fall asleep, I kept waking with a start, always listening intently. But the sounds I heard were simply the wind blowing the few remaining leaves from the trees behind the garage.

It was only at dawn when I woke for the fourth or fifth time that I realized what I should have picked up on immediately: Whoever had gone through my appointment book knew that I had a meeting that morning at Arbinger and another one at Carrington Academy on Monday.

I planned to leave for Arbinger at seven o'clock. I knew Mrs. Hilmer was an early bird, so at ten of seven I called her and asked if I could stop by for a moment. Over a cup of her excellent coffee I told her about the intruder and that I would take the transcript and newspapers and get copies made of them.

"No, you won't," she said. "I have nothing else to do. I'm a volunteer at the library and use the machines there all the time. I'll use the copier in the office. That way no one has to know what's going on. Except Rudy Schell, of course. He's been there forever, and I'd trust him not to say a word."

She hesitated for a moment, then said, "Ellie, I want you to move in with me. I don't want you alone in the apartment. Whoever was in last night might come back, and, anyhow, I think we should call the police."

"No to moving in with you," I said. "If anything, I should leave the apartment." She began to shake her head, and I said, "But I won't. I'm too comfortable being near you. And I've thought about notifying the police and decided it's a bad idea. There's no sign of breaking and entering. My jewelry is still there. If I tell a cop that the only disturbance was that someone moved a pen and added a couple of words to a computer file, what do you think he'll believe?" I didn't wait for her to answer. "The Westerfields are already putting out the scenario that I was an overly imaginative and troubled child, and that my testimony at the trial was unreliable. Can you imagine what they'd make of a story like this? I'd sound like one of those people who send threatening letters to themselves just to get attention."

I gulped the last of the coffee. "There is something you can do,

though, if you will. Call Joan Lashley and ask her if I can come and
see her tomorrow."

It was comforting to hear Mrs. Hilmer say, "Drive carefully,"
and feel her quick kiss on my cheek.

ON MY WAY around Boston I got caught in some of the commuter
traffic, so it was almost eleven o'clock when I drove through the
carefully guarded gates of Arbinger Preparatory School. It was
even more impressive in real life than the photographs on its Website suggested. The handsome pink brick buildings looked mellow
and tranquil under the November sky. The long driveway through
the campus was lined with mature trees that in season must form a
lush canopy of leaves. It was easy to imagine why most of the kids
who graduate from a place such as this received with their diplo-
mas a sense of entitlement, a feeling of having been made special, of
being a cut above the rest.

As I steered the car into the area designated for visitors, I recalled the list of high schools I had attended. Freshman year in
Louisville. Second half of sophomore year in Los Angeles. No, I
was there until the middle of my junior year. Where was I next?
Oh, yes, Portland, Oregon. And finally back to Los Angeles, which
for my senior year and the four years of college offered some sort of
stability. Mother continued to move around in the hotel chain until
I was a senior in college. That was when the damage to her liver became accelerated, and she shared my tiny apartment until her
death.

*I always wanted you girls to know how to do things nicely, Ellie.
That way if you met someone with a very good background, you'd be
able to hold your own.*

Oh, Mother, I thought as I was admitted to the main building
and directed to Craig Parshall's office. The walls along the corridor
were lined with portraits of grave-faced figures, and from what I

could discern from quick glances, most of them were former school presidents.

Craig Parshall was less impressive in appearance than his cultured voice suggested. He was a man in his late fifties who still wore his school ring. His thinning hair was too perfectly combed—in a vain attempt to conceal the empty space on the dome of his head—and he could not conceal the fact that he was downright nervous.

His office was large and very handsome, with paneled walls, formal draperies, a Persian carpet just threadbare enough to guarantee its antiquity, comfortable leather chairs, and a mahogany desk, behind which he promptly retreated after greeting me.

"As I told you on the phone, Ms. Cavanaugh—" he began.

"Mr. Parshall, why don't we not waste each other's time?" I suggested, interrupting him. "I am totally aware of the constraints on you, and I appreciate them. Just answer a few questions, and I'll be on my way."

"I will give you the dates that Robson Westerfield attended—"

"I'm aware of the dates he was a student here. That came out at his trial for the murder of my sister."

Parshall winced.

"Mr. Parshall, the Westerfield family has a goal in life and that is to whitewash Robson Westerfield's reputation, have a new trial, and get him acquitted. Success will have the *de facto* effect of having the world believe that another young man—one, I might add, who has neither the money nor the intellectual capacity to walk through these doors—is guilty of my sister's death. My goal is to see that that does not happen."

"You must understand—" Parshall began.

"I understand that you can't be quoted on the record. But you can open some doors for me. By that I mean that I want the list of students who were in class with Rob Westerfield. I want to know if any of them was known to be a particular friend of his—or, better yet, if there was someone who simply couldn't stand him. Who was his roommate? And off the record—and I do mean off the record—why was he kicked out?"

We looked at each other in silence for a long minute, and neither one of us blinked.

"On my Website I could easily refer to Robson Westerfield's exclusive prep school and not name it," I said, "or I could put it this way: Arbinger Preparatory School, alma mater to His Royal Highness Prince Gregory of Belgium, His Serene Highness Prince—"

He interrupted me. "Off the record?"

"Absolutely."

"No naming of the school or of me?"

"Absolutely."

He sighed, and I almost felt sorry for him. "Have you ever heard the quote 'Put not your trust in princes?' Ms. Cavanaugh?"

"As a matter of fact, I'm quite familiar with it—not only the biblical reference, but the way it's been paraphrased to me: 'Put not your trust in investigative reporters.'"

"Is that a warning, Ms. Cavanaugh?"

"If the investigative reporter has a sense of integrity, the answer is no."

"Understanding that, I'm going to put my trust in you, in the sense that I can rely on your discretion. Off the record?"

"Absolutely."

"The only reason Robson Westerfield was accepted here is that his father offered to rebuild the science building. And without a hint of publicity, I might add. Rob was presented to us as a troubled student who was never at home among his grade-school peers."

"He went to Baldwin in Manhattan for eight years," I said. "Were there problems there?"

"None reported to us, except perhaps a peculiarly absent—or listless—endorsement from his teachers and guidance counselor."

"And the science lab here needed rebuilding?"

Parshall looked pained. "Westerfield was from a fine family. His intelligence is in the very superior category."

"All right," I said. "Now let's get down to the nitty-gritty. What was it like having that guy on these hallowed grounds?"

"I had just begun teaching here, so I'm a firsthand witness. It was about as bad as it gets," Parshall said frankly. "I assume you know the definition of a sociopath?" He waved his hands in an impatient sort of gesture. "Sorry. As my wife reminds me, my classroom warm-ups can be quite annoying. I am talking of the sociopath as someone who is born without a conscience, who has a disregard for and is in conflict with the social code as you and I understand it. Robson Westerfield was a poster boy for that kind of personality."

"Then you had problems with him from the beginning?"

"Like so many of his ilk, he is blessed with looks and intelligence. He also is the last of a distinguished family line. His grandfather and father were students here. We hoped that we would be able to bring out whatever good qualities there were in him."

"People don't think much of his father, Vincent Westerfield. What kind of record did he have here?"

"I looked him up. Academically, only fair. Nothing like the grandfather, from what I gather. Pearson Westerfield was a United States senator."

"Why did Rob Westerfield leave in the middle of his sophomore year?"

"There was a serious incident stemming from his losing a starting spot on the football team. He attacked another student. The family was persuaded not to sue, and the Westerfields paid all the bills. Maybe more—to that I can't swear."

It dawned on me that Craig Parshall was being unusually frank. I told him so.

"I do not like to be threatened, Ms. Cavanaugh."

"Threatened?"

"This morning, shortly before you arrived, I received a telephone call from a Mr. Hamilton, an attorney who represents the Westerfield family. I was warned that I should give you no negative information about Robson Westerfield."

They work pretty fast, I thought. "May I ask what kind of information you gave Jake Bern about Westerfield?"

"His sports activities, such as they were. Robson was a powerful young man; even as a thirteen-year-old he was nearly six feet tall. He played on the squash team, the tennis team, and the football team. He was also in the theater group. I told Bern that he was a genuinely talented actor. That was the kind of information Bern was seeking. He managed to elicit some quotes from me that will sound very favorable in print."

I could just imagine how Bern would write the chapter on Rob at Arbinger. He'd come out looking like an all-around preppie in the three-generation family prep school. "How will his leaving Arbinger be explained?"

"He took the second semester of his sophomore year abroad, then decided to switch."

"I realize we're going back nearly thirty years, but could you give me a list of his former classmates?"

"You didn't get it from me, of course."

"That's understood."

WHEN I LEFT ARBINGER an hour later, I had a list of the freshmen and sophomores who had been classmates of Rob Westerfield. Comparing them with the active alumni list, Parshall identified ten who were in the Massachusetts-to-Manhattan area. One of them was Christopher Cassidy, the football player Rob Westerfield had severely beaten. He now had his own investment firm and lived in Boston.

"Chris was a scholarship student," Parshall explained. "And because he is grateful for having had the opportunity to attend this school, he is one of our most generous donors. In his case, I don't mind making a phone call. Chris has always been blunt about his feelings about Westerfield. But, again, if I hook you up with him, it has to be confidential."

"Absolutely."

Parshall walked with me to the door. It was break time between classes, and the soft pealing of a bell was followed by a steady stream of small groups of students emerging from various rooms. The current generation of Arbinger scholars, I thought as I studied their young faces. Many of them were destined for future leadership roles, but I couldn't help but wonder if there was also another Robson Westerfield–type sociopath incubating within these privileged walls.

I drove out of the school grounds and along the town's main street, which begins at the school. From the map I could see that it runs in a direct line from Arbinger Prep on the south end of town to Jenna Calish Academy for girls on the north end. New Cotswold is one of those charming New England villages that is built around the schools in its vicinity. It has a large bookstore, a cinema, a library, a number of clothing stores, and several small restaurants. I had given up the thought of hanging around with the chance of learning something from students. Craig Parshall had given me the kind of information that I wanted, and I knew that I'd be better off pursuing Rob Westerfield's classmates than spending more time around Arbinger.

But it was nearly noon, and I realized that I had the beginnings of a headache, partly due to the fact that I was getting hungry and partly because I hadn't slept much the previous evening.

About three blocks from the school I passed a restaurant called The Library. The quaint hand-painted sign caught my eye, and I suspected that it might be the kind of place where the soup was homemade. I decided to give it a try and pulled into a parking space nearby.

Because it was before noon, I was the first lunch customer, and the hostess, a cheery, bustling lady in her late forties, was happy not only to give me my choice of the dozen or so smaller tables, but to fill me in on the history of the establishment. "It's been in our family for fifty years," she assured me. "My mother, Antoinette Duval, opened it. She was always a marvelous cook, and my father, to indulge her, staked her to it. She was so successful, he ended up quitting his job and handling the business end here. They're retired now, and my sisters and I have taken it over. But Mother still comes in a couple of days a week to make some of her specials. She's in the kitchen now, and if you like onion soup, she just made it."

I ordered it, and it was every bit as good as I'd hoped. The hostess came over to check my reaction, and my reassurance that the soup was heavenly caused her to beam with delight. Then, since only a few other diners had arrived, she stood at the table and asked me if I were staying locally or just passing through. I decided to be totally honest. "I'm a journalist, and I'm doing a story on Rob Westerfield who was just released from Sing Sing. Do you know who he is?"

Her expression changed instantly from friendly to stern and tight-lipped. She turned abruptly and walked away from me. Oh, boy, I thought. It's a good thing I've almost finished the soup. She looks as though she's ready to throw me out.

A moment later she was back, this time with a plump white-haired woman in tow. The older woman was wearing a chef's apron and drying her hands on a corner of it as she came to the table. "Mom," the hostess said, "this lady is doing a story on Rob Westerfield. Maybe you'd like to tell her something."

"Rob Westerfield." Mrs. Duval practically spat out the name. "He's a bad one. Why did they let him out of prison?"

She didn't need encouragement to tell her story. "He came in here with his mother and father during one of the parents' weekends. How old was he? Fifteen, maybe. He was arguing with his father. Whatever happened, he jumped up to leave. The waitress was walking behind him, and he knocked into the tray. The food went all over him. I tell you, Miss, I never saw anything like it. He grabbed that girl's arm and twisted it until she screamed. He's an *animal*."

"Did you call the police?"

"I was about to, but his mother begged me to wait. Then the father opened his wallet and handed the waitress five hundred dollars. She was just a kid. She wanted to take it. She said she wouldn't press charges. Then the father told me to add the price of the food that was lost to his check."

"What did Rob Westerfield do?"

"He stalked out and left his parents to deal with the mess. The mother was terribly embarrassed. After the father paid the waitress, he told me that it was all her fault and that his son had reacted that way because he had been scalded. He told me I should train waitresses before I let them carry trays."

"What did you do?"

"I told him that we would no longer continue to serve him and that they should leave my restaurant."

"You can't imagine what Mama is like when she's angry," her daughter said. "She picked up the plates that had just been put in front of them and carried them back to the kitchen."

"But I was very sorry for Mrs. Westerfield," Mrs. Duval said. "She was so upset. In fact, she wrote me a very nice letter of apology. I still have it in my files."

When I left The Library half an hour later, I had permission to tell that story on my Website and a promise that I would receive a copy of the letter Mrs. Westerfield had written to Mrs. Duval. Plus, I was on my way to visit Margaret Fisher, the young waitress whose arm Rob had twisted. She was now a psychologist living two towns away, and, yes, she would be very happy to talk to me. She remembered Rob Westerfield very well indeed.

"I WAS SAVING MONEY for college," Dr. Fisher told me. "The five hundred dollars his father gave me seemed like a fortune at the time. Looking back, I'm sorry I didn't sign a complaint against him. The guy is violent, and if I know anything about the human mind, I suspect that twenty-two years in prison didn't change him a bit."

She was an attractive woman in her early forties, with prematurely gray hair and a young face. She told me that she had appointments only until noon on Friday and was just about to leave her office when I phoned. "I saw the interview with him the other night on television," she said. "Butter wouldn't melt in his mouth. It sickened me, so I can understand how *you* feel."

I told her what I was doing with the Website and how I had gone to stand outside Sing Sing with the sign requesting information about Rob's conduct in prison.

"I'd be very surprised if there weren't more incidents there that you may find out about," she said. "But what about the years between the time he was in school here and when he was arrested for your sister's death? How old was he when he went to prison?"

"Twenty."

"With his history, I seriously doubt there weren't other situations that were hushed up or never reported. Ellie, has it occurred to you that you're setting yourself up as a constant menace to him? You tell me that his grandmother is very alert. Suppose she learns about your Website and visits it, or has someone in her employ visit it for her every day. If she reads enough negative facts about him, what's to keep her from deciding to change her will even before Westerfield has a second trial?"

"Wouldn't that be absolutely wonderful!" I said. "I'd love to think that I was responsible for having the family money go to charity."

"I would be *very* careful if I were you," Dr. Fisher said quietly.

I THOUGHT ABOUT her advice as I drove back to Oldham. There had been a break-in at my apartment and then what amounted to a threat lodged in my computer file. I turned over in my mind the question of whether I should have notified the police. But for the reason I had given Mrs. Hilmer, I knew I was right not to notify them; I wasn't going to put myself at risk of being considered some kind of nut case. On the other hand, I had no right to put Mrs. Hilmer in any kind of jeopardy. I decided I'd have to find another place to live.

Dr. Fisher had given me permission to use her name when I wrote about what had happened in the restaurant. That was something else I'd do on the Website—invite people to share any problems they'd had with Rob Westerfield in the years before he went to prison.

IT WAS LATE AFTERNOON when I pulled into the driveway and parked in front of the apartment. I'd stopped at the supermarket in Oldham and picked up some much needed supplies. My plan was to make a simple dinner: a shell steak, baked potato, and salad. Then I'd watch television and get to bed reasonably early. I needed to begin to write the book I had contracted to do about Westerfield, and while the material I used on the Website could be repeated in the book, it would have to be presented differently.

Her house was dark, so I wasn't sure if Mrs. Hilmer was home. I reasoned that her car might be in the garage and that she might not have turned any lights on yet, so I phoned her when I got into the apartment. She answered on the first ring, and I could tell that her voice was troubled.

"Ellie, this may sound crazy, but I think someone followed me today when I went to the library."

"Why do you think that?"

"You know how quiet this street is. But I was hardly out of the driveway when I could see a car in the rearview mirror. It stayed a distance behind me, but it didn't turn off until after I'd turned into the parking area next to the library. Then I think the same car followed me home."

"Did it keep going when you turned off?"

"Yes."

"Can you describe it?"

"It was midsize, dark, either black or dark blue. It was far enough behind me that I couldn't see the driver, but I have the impression that it was a man. Ellie, do you think that whoever was in the apartment last night is hanging around here?"

"I don't know."

"I'm going to call the police, and that means I'll have to tell them about last night."

"Yes, of course." I hated myself for the nervousness I heard in Mrs. Hilmer's voice. Until now, she obviously had always felt secure in her home. I only prayed that by being a lightning rod for trouble I had not destroyed that sense of security for her.

A squad car pulled up at the house ten minutes later, and after debating for a few minutes, I decided to walk over to talk to the police. The officer who looked to be a longtime veteran of the force obviously did not think much of Mrs. Hilmer's suspicions. "Whoever was in that car didn't try to stop you or contact you in any way?" he was asking her when I arrived.

"No." She introduced us. "Ellie, I've known Officer White for many years."

He was a craggy-faced man who looked as though he'd spent a lot of time outdoors. "And what's this about an intruder, Ms. Cavanaugh?"

His skepticism was apparent when I told him about the pen and the entry in the file. "You mean your jewelry wasn't touched and the only evidence you have of someone having been in the apartment is that you think your pen had been moved from one side of your notebook to the other and there are a couple of words in a file in the computer that you don't remember writing."

"That I *didn't* write," I corrected him.

He was polite enough not to contradict me directly, but then he said, "Mrs. Hilmer, we'll keep an eye on the house for the next few days, but my guess is that you were a little nervous after hearing Ms. Cavanaugh's story this morning and that's why you picked up on that car. Chances are it was nothing."

My "story," I thought. Thanks for nothing. But then he said he'd like to examine the lock in the door of the apartment. Promising Mrs. Hilmer that I'd call her, I walked back to the apartment with him. He did take a look at the lock and came to the same conclusion I had reached: It had not been forced in any way.

He lingered for a moment, obviously trying to make up his mind about something, and then he said, "We heard about you being at Sing Sing yesterday, Ms. Cavanaugh."

I waited. We were standing in the hall outside the apartment. He had not asked to see the computer file, which showed just how much credence he had put in my "story." I was not about to invite him in to shrug it off any further.

"Ms. Cavanaugh, I was here when your sister was murdered, and I do understand the pain your family experienced. But if Rob Westerfield did commit the crime, he has served his sentence, and I have to tell you there are plenty of people in this town who had no use for him as a wild kid, but who think he got a bum rap."

"Is that your opinion, Officer?"

"Frankly, it is. I've always thought that Paulie Stroebel was guilty. There was a lot that didn't come out at the trial."

"Such as . . ."

"He'd bragged to a number of kids in school that your sister was going to the Thanksgiving mixer with him. If she told any of them, I mean some of her close friends, that she was going only because Rob Westerfield wouldn't get jealous of a guy like Paulie and it got back to him, he might have gone crazy. Rob Westerfield's car was parked at the service station. You said yourself on the witness stand that Paulie told Andrea he'd followed her to the hideout. And then there was that guidance counselor who swore on the stand that when Paulie heard about Andrea's body being found, she heard him say, 'I didn't think she was dead.' "

"And there was a student nearer to him who swore that he said, 'I can't believe she's dead.' A big difference, Officer."

"It's obvious we're not going to see eye to eye on this, but let me give you a warning." He must have sensed that I stiffened, because he said, "Hear me out. You're in way over your head, carrying signs around Sing Sing. The guys getting out of there are hardened criminals. You're standing there, a young, very attractive woman with a sign giving your phone number and begging them to call you. Half of those bums are going to end up back in there within a couple of years. What do you think goes through their heads when they see a woman like you just begging for trouble?"

I looked at him closely. There was sincere concern on his face. And he certainly had a point. "Officer White, it's you and people like you I'm trying to convince," I said. "I understand now that my sister was terrified of Rob Westerfield, and after what I've just learned about him today, I can understand why. If I'm in any danger, I'll take my chances with the people who saw that sign—unless, of course, they're in any way connected to Rob Westerfield and his family."

That was when it occurred to me to describe the man who had spoken to me in the parking lot of the railroad station. I asked him to see if he could learn whether a prisoner of that description had been released yesterday.

"What would you do with that information?" he asked me.

"All right. Let's forget it, officer," I said.

Mrs. Hilmer must have been watching for Officer White to leave. My cell phone rang just as the taillights of his squad car disappeared onto the road.

"Ellie," she said, "I made a copy of the newspapers and the trial transcript. Do you need the originals this evening for any reason? I'm meeting some friends for a movie and dinner and won't be back until ten o'clock."

I hated the thought that I was afraid to have both the originals and the copies under one roof, but I was.

"I'll be right over," I said.

"No, I'll call you when I'm leaving. I'll drive past the apartment, and you can run down and get the duffel bag."

She came a few minutes later. It was only four-thirty, but already the sky was dark. Even so, I could see the tension in her face when she opened the window to speak to me.

"Did anything else happen?" I asked.

"Just a minute ago I got a phone call. I don't know who it was. The caller ID was blocked."

"Tell me about it."

"I know it's crazy, but somebody said I should be careful keeping a psycho around me. He said that you'd been institutionalized for setting fire in a classroom."

"That's absolutely untrue. My God, I've never spent a day in a hospital since I was born, never mind an institution."

I knew from the relief on her face that Mrs. Hilmer believed me. But that meant, of course, that she had not instantly disbelieved the caller. After all, the first time I visited her, she had suggested that Rob Westerfield might be innocent and that I was obsessed with Andrea's death.

"But, Ellie, why would anyone say such a terrible thing about you?" she protested. "And what can you do to stop him from saying it to someone else?"

"Someone's trying to discredit me, of course, and the answer is that I can't stop it." I opened the back door of the car and retrieved the duffel bag. I tried to choose my words carefully. "Mrs. Hilmer, I think it's better if I move back to the Inn tomorrow morning. Officer White thinks that I'm going to attract some pretty strange people as a result of standing outside Sing Sing with a sign, and I can't have them finding their way here. I'm safer in an Inn, and certainly you'll have your peace back."

She was not dishonest enough to contradict me. There was relief in her voice when she said, "I think you *would* be safer, Ellie."

She paused, then added in all honesty, "I guess I would feel safer, too." After that she was gone.

I walked back up to the apartment, the duffel bag in my hand, feeling almost bereft. In biblical days the lepers were made to wear bells around their necks and to shout, "Unclean, unclean," if anyone happened to wander near them. At that moment I swear I felt like a leper.

I dropped the bag and went into the bedroom to change. I replaced my jacket with a loose sweater, kicked off my shoes, and stuffed my feet into ancient fleece-lined slippers. Then I went into the living room, poured myself a glass of wine, and settled in the big club chair with my feet on the hassock.

The sweater and slippers were my comfort clothes. For a fleeting moment I thought about my old comforter, Bones, the floppy stuffed animal who had shared my pillow when I was a child. He was in a box on the top shelf of a closet in my apartment in Atlanta. He shared the box with other mementos my mother had kept of the past, including her wedding album, pictures of the four of us, baby clothes, and, most wrenching of all, Andrea's band uniform. For a moment I felt a childish resentment that Bones wasn't with me now.

Then, as I sipped the wine, I thought of how often when Pete and I went out after work we'd linger over a glass of wine before ordering dinner.

Two memories: my mother drinking to seek peace, and Pete and I relaxing and joking about what had sometimes been a wildly busy or frustrating day.

I hadn't heard from him in the ten days since we'd had dinner in Atlanta. Out of sight, out of mind, I decided. Looking for another job. "Pursuing other interests," as the business jargon goes when an executive is told to clean out his desk.

Or when he decides to cut his ties. All of them.

21

AN HOUR LATER there was a subtle change in the weather. The faint rattle of a loose pane in the window over the sink was the first hint of a shift in the wind. I got up and pushed up the thermostat, then went back to the computer. Realizing that I was in acute danger of feeling sorry for myself, I had begun to work on what would become the opening chapter of the book.

After some false starts, I knew that I should begin with my final memory of Andrea, and, as I wrote, my memory seemed to sharpen. I could see her room with the white organdy bedspread and frilly curtains. I remembered in sharp detail the old-fashioned dresser Mother had so carefully antiqued. I could visualize the pictures of Andrea and her friends stuck in the frame of the mirror over that dresser.

I could see Andrea in tears as she talked on the phone to Rob Westerfield, and then I saw her putting on the locket. As I wrote, I realized that there was something about the locket that still eluded me. I knew that I couldn't positively identify it now if I saw it, but at the time, I gave a clear description of it to the police—a description that years ago had been dismissed as childish fantasy.

But I knew she had been wearing it when I found her, and I was certain I had heard Rob Westerfield in the garage-hideout. Mother told me later that it had taken her and my father ten or fifteen minutes to calm me down so that I was coherent enough to tell them where I had found Andrea's body. Plenty of time for Rob to get away. And he had taken the locket with him.

On the witness stand he claimed that he'd been out jogging at that time and had been nowhere near the garage. Nevertheless, he had washed and bleached the sweats he'd worn that morning, along with the bloodied clothes from the night before.

Once again I was struck by the terrible risk he had taken in coming back to the garage. Why did he retrieve the locket? Was he afraid that it would be enough to confirm that Andrea was not just a kid with an annoying crush on him? Even as I thought of that morning, and the harsh breathing and the nervous giggling sound he had made as he hid on the other side of the van, my hands turned clammy on the keyboard.

Suppose I had *not* slipped through the woods alone but had brought my father with me? Rob would have been caught in the garage. Did sheer panic bring him back? Was it possible that he needed to confirm to himself that what he had done wasn't just a nightmare? Or, worst of all, had he gone back to make certain Andrea was not alive?

At seven o'clock I turned on the oven and put in the lone potato to bake; then I went back to work. Shortly afterward the phone rang; it was Pete Lawlor.

"Hi, Ellie."

There was something in his voice that immediately warned me to brace myself.

"What's the matter, Pete?"

"You don't waste time on chitchat, do you?"

"We never do. That's our agreement."

"I guess it is. Ellie, the paper is being sold. It's definite now. The announcement will be made on Monday. The staff will be cut to the bone."

"What about you?"

"They offered me a job. I turned them down."

"You said you were going to do that."

"I asked about you, but off the record they told me they don't plan to keep up the investigative reporter series."

I'd been expecting that bit of news, but I realized how suddenly rootless it made me feel. "Have you decided where you're going, Pete?"

"I'm not sure yet, but I may be seeing some people in New York before I decide. Maybe when that happens, I'll rent a car and drive up to see you, or you can meet me in the city."

"I'd like that. I was kind of expecting that I'd get a postcard from Houston or L.A."

"I never send postcards. Ellie, I've been watching your Website."

"There isn't much on it yet. It's sort of like a sign, the kind you put on a shop you've rented. You know what I mean: 'Watch for the grand opening.' But I am digging up a lot of nasty stuff on Westerfield. If Jake Bern tries to portray him as an all-American kid, his book will have to be published as fiction."

"Ellie, it is not in my nature to—"

I cut him off. "Ah, come on, Pete. You're not going to warn me to be careful, are you? I've already been warned by my neighbor—a psychologist—and by a cop. And that's just today."

"Then let me join the chorus."

"Let's change the subject. Have you lost any of those ten pounds yet?"

"I did better than that. I decided I look good just the way I am. Okay, I'll call you when I know I'm coming in. Or you can always call me, you know. Long-distance rates are pretty cheap at night."

He disconnected before I could even say good-bye.

I pressed the "end" button on my cell phone and laid the phone down next to the computer. As I made a salad, the ramifications of losing my job began to sink in. The advance on signing the contract to write my book would keep me going for a while, but what would I do when that was finished and I had given my best shot to torpedoing Rob Westerfield's reinvention of himself?

Go back to Atlanta? But my friends at the paper would be scattered. Another thing to ponder: It isn't that easy to get a newspaper job these days. Too many newspapers have been swallowed up or have folded. And when the book is finished and I've put all this behind me, where did I want to live? It was a question that I kept pondering all through dinner, even as I tried to concentrate on the news magazine I'd picked up at the supermarket.

The cell phone rang again as I was clearing the table. "You the lady who was standing outside the prison with a sign yesterday?" a husky male voice asked.

"Yes, I am." Mentally I was crossing my fingers. The caller ID registered "unavailable."

"I might have something to tell you about Westerfield. How much you gonna pay?"

"I guess it depends on the information."

"You pay first, then you hear."

"How much?"

"Five thousand dollars."

"I haven't got that much money."

"Then forget it. But what I can tell you would put Westerfield back in Sing Sing for the rest of his life."

Was he bluffing? I wasn't sure, but I couldn't take a chance on losing the caller. I thought of my advance. "I have some money coming in the next week or two. Just give me some hint of what you know."

"How's this? When he was whacked out on cocaine last year, Westerfield told me he killed a guy when he was eighteen. Is the name of that guy worth five thousand dollars? Think about it. I'll call back next week."

I heard a click in my ear.

Margaret Fisher had told me only that afternoon that in her professional opinion Rob Westerfield had been guilty of other crimes before he murdered Andrea. I thought of incidents I had heard earlier that day, like the ones at school and at the restaurant. But if he had really murdered someone . . .

Suddenly it was a whole new ball game. If the guy who had just called me was on the level and could give the name of a murder victim I could verify, it would be easy enough to find out the facts of the case. Of course, it might be that this was a hoax, just a way for a crook to make a fast $5,000. I had to decide if that was a risk I was willing to take.

I was standing at the computer, looking down at the open file. As I read my description of Andrea in those last few moments that I was with her, I knew that to help put Rob Westerfield back in prison was worth every cent I would ever earn in my life.

There was a glass of water at the side of the computer. I picked it up and lifted it in a kind of salute, a toast to Andrea and to the prospect of sending Westerfield back to prison.

I tidied up the kitchen and turned on the TV to watch the local news. The sports editor was showing clips of a basketball game. The winning basket had been made by Teddy Cavanaugh, and as I stared, I saw the face of the half-brother I'd never met.

He was close to being a mirror image of me. He was younger, of course, boyish, but our eyes and noses and lips and cheekbones were the same. He was looking straight into the camera, and I felt as if we were staring at each other.

Then before I could change the station, in a final touch of irony, the cheerleaders began to chant his name.

22

MRS. HILMER HAD TOLD ME that Joan Lashley St. Martin lived on the road not far beyond Graymoor, the monastery and retreat house of the Franciscan Friars of the Atonement. When I passed the lovely Graymoor property, I had a vague memory of driving up the winding driveway to attend Mass in the main chapel with my parents and Andrea.

Mother had sometimes reminisced about the last time we were there; it had been shortly before Andrea died. Andrea had been feeling silly that day and kept whispering jokes in my ear; during the sermon, I even laughed out loud. My mother had firmly separated us and after Mass told my father that we should go straight home and forget about having the brunch we'd been looking forward to at the Bear Mountain Inn.

"Even Andrea couldn't charm your father that day," Mother recalled. "Of course when everything happened a few weeks later, I was sorry we didn't have that last happy time together having brunch."

The day before . . . the last happy time . . . I wondered if I'd ever be free of that kind of remark. It certainly won't be today, I thought, as I slowed down to check Joan's address again.

She lived in a three-story frame house in a lovely wooded area. The white clapboard shingles glistened in the sunshine and were complemented by the hunter green shutters framing the windows.

I parked in the semicircular driveway, went up the porch steps, and rang the bell.

Joan answered the door. She had always seemed tall to me, but I realized instantly that she hadn't grown an inch in these twenty-two years. Her long brown hair was now collar length, and her thin frame had filled out. I remembered her as being very attractive. I would say the definition still fit, at least until she smiled—she is one of those people whose smile is so vivid and warm that it makes the whole face seem beautiful. As we looked at each other, Joan's green eyes became moist for a moment, then she grasped my hands.

"Little Ellie," she said. "Dear God, I thought you'd be shorter than I am. You were such a tiny kid."

I laughed. "I know. It's the reaction I'm getting from everyone who used to know me."

She put her arm through mine. "Come in, I have a pot of coffee going, and I stuck a couple of bake-and-serve muffins in the oven. No guarantees that they're any good. Sometimes they're fine; other times they taste like lead balloons."

We walked through the living room that ran from the front to the back of the house. It was the kind of room I loved—deep couches, club chairs, a wall of books, a fireplace, wide windows that looked out at the surrounding hills.

We share similar taste, I thought. Then I realized that the similarity also extended to clothing. We were both dressed casually in sweaters and jeans. I had been expecting to see a tall fashionable woman with long hair. In addition to expecting me to be small, I'm sure she also thought I'd be dressed in something frilly. Mother's taste in dress-up clothes for Andrea and me had been very feminine.

"Leo is out with the boys," she said. "Between the three of them, life is one long basketball game."

The table in the breakfast room was already set for the two of us. The percolator was plugged in on the sideboard. The picture window offered a stunning view of the palisades and the Hudson River.

"I would never get tired of looking out this window," I said as I sat down.

"I never do. So many of the old crowd went down to the city, but, you know something? A lot of them are coming back. The commute into Manhattan is only an hour, and they think it's worth it." Joan was pouring the coffee as she spoke, then abruptly set the percolator back on the sideboard. "Oh, my Lord, it's time to rescue the bake-and-serves." She disappeared into the kitchen.

She may not look as I visualized her, I thought, but one thing hadn't changed! Joan was always fun to be with. She was Andrea's best friend and therefore was in and out of our house all the time. Of course, I had my own friends, but if I didn't have one of them around, Andrea and Joan would let me join them, often to listen to records with them in Andrea's room. Sometimes when they were doing their homework together, they'd let me do mine with them, just as long as I wasn't a pest.

Joan returned triumphantly carrying a plate of corn muffins. "Congratulations are in order, Ellie," she said. "I caught them just before the bottoms started to burn."

I helped myself to one. Joan sat down, cut a muffin open, spread butter on it lightly, tasted it, and said, "My God, it's edible!"

We laughed together and began to talk. She wanted to know about me, what I had been doing, and I briefly sketched in the years between age seven and the present. She had heard of Mother's death. "Your father put a notice in the local papers," she said. "A very sweet one. Didn't you know that?"

"He didn't send it to me."

"I have it somewhere. If you'd like to see it, I can dig it out. It might take a while, though. My filing is about on a par with my baking."

I wanted to say no, don't bother, but I was curious to see what my father had written. "If you come across it, I would like to see it," I said, trying to sound offhand. "But please don't go to any trouble."

I was sure Joan wanted to ask me if I had been in touch with my father, but she must have sensed that I did not want to talk about him.

Instead she said, "Your mother was so lovely. And of course your father was very handsome. I remember that I was intimidated by him, but I think I also had a crush on him. I was so sorry when I heard they separated after the trial. The four of you always seemed so happy, and you did so many things together. I always wished my family would go to Sunday brunches at the Bear Mountain Inn the way you did."

"Only an hour ago I'd been thinking of the brunch that we didn't go to there," I said, and then told Joan about Andrea making me laugh in church.

Joan smiled. "She did that to me sometimes in school assemblies. Andrea could keep a straight face, and I'd get in trouble for laughing when the principal was speaking."

As she sipped her coffee, she reflected. "My parents are good people, but, to be perfectly frank, they're not much fun. We never went out to a restaurant, because my father said the food was cheaper and tasted better at home. Fortunately, he's loosened up a bit now that they've retired to Florida."

She laughed. "But when they go out, the rule is they have to be in the restaurant by five o'clock to get the early bird prices, and if they have a cocktail, they fix it at home and sip it in the van in the parking lot of the restaurant before dinner. Don't you love it?"

Then she added, "I mean, it would be different if he couldn't afford to do otherwise, but he can. Dad is just plain cheap. My mother says he still has his First Communion money."

She poured us a second cup of coffee. "Ellie, like everybody else around here, I saw the Rob Westerfield interview on television. My cousin is a judge. He says there's so much pressure for that second trial that he's surprised they're not already into jury selection. You have no idea how manipulative the father is, and, of course, Dorothy Westerfield, the grandmother, has made *huge* donations to hospitals and libraries and schools around here. She wants the second trial for Rob, and the powers that be want her to have it."

"You'll be called as a witness, of course, Joan," I said.

"I know it. I was the last person to see Andrea alive." She hesitated, then added, "Except for her murderer, of course."

We were both silent for a moment. Then I said, "Joan, I need to know everything that you remember about that last night. I've read the trial transcript over and over, and it strikes me that your testimony was very brief."

She put her elbows on the table and folded her hands together, resting her chin on them. "It *was* brief, because neither the prosecutor nor the defense attorney asked me questions that, looking back, I think they should have asked."

"What kind of questions?"

"About Will Nebels, for one," she said. "You remember how he was a handyman and worked for just about everyone in town at some point. He helped build your porch, didn't he?"

"Yes."

"He fixed our garage door when my mother backed the car into it. As my father used to say, when Will wasn't three sheets to the wind, he was a good carpenter. But, of course, you could never count on him showing up."

"I kind of remember that."

"Something you wouldn't remember was that Andrea and I used to talk about the fact that he was a bit *too* friendly."

"Too friendly?"

Joan shrugged. "Today, knowing what I know, I would say that he was one step away from being a child molester. I mean, we all knew him because he'd been in our houses. But any number of times when we bumped into him in the street, he'd give us each a big hug—although never if an adult was around, of course."

I was incredulous. "Joan, I'm sure even at that age I would have been aware if Andrea had complained about him to my father. I certainly knew when he ordered Andrea to stay away from Westerfield."

"Ellie, twenty-two years ago we kids simply weren't aware that he was potentially more than a nuisance. At that time we told each other how yucky it was when Nebels would give us a hug and call us 'his girls.' 'How do you like the new porch I built with your daddy, Andrea?' he'd say with an overly friendly smile, or 'Didn't I fix your garage good, Joanie?' he'd whine.

"Now understand, he didn't molest us, but in retrospect, he was just a boozy sleaze who had a hell of a nerve, and there was no question in my mind that the one he really had his eye on was Andrea. I remember I joked to your mother and father that Andrea was going to invite Will Nebels to the Christmas dance. They never picked up that there was anything behind the joking."

"My father missed that!"

"Andrea could do a great imitation of Will sneaking beer out of his toolbox and getting bombed while he was working. There was no reason for your father to look behind the joking for a potential problem."

"Joan, I don't understand why you're telling me this now. Are you saying that you think that this story Will Nebels is telling now is anything but an outright lie that the Westerfields are paying him to tell?"

"Ellie, ever since I heard Will Nebels with Rob Westerfield during that interview, I'm wondering if there's *any* truth to what he said. Was he really in old Mrs. Westerfield's house that night? Did he actually see Andrea go into the garage? Well after the fact, I wondered if I'd seen someone coming down the road when Andrea left our house that night. But I was so vague about it when I talked to the police and the attorneys then that it was pretty much dismissed as teenage hysteria."

"What I told them was dismissed as childish imagination."

"I do know for certain that Will Nebels had lost his driver's license at that time and was always wandering around town. I also know he had a thing for Andrea. Suppose she was hoping to meet Rob Westerfield in the garage hideout and got there early. Suppose Will had followed her there and made a pass at her. Suppose there was a struggle, and she fell backward? That was a cement floor. There was an injury on the back of her head that they blamed on the fact that she'd fallen after she was hit with the tire jack. But isn't it possible she fell *before* she was hit with the tire jack?"

"The blow on the back of her head would only have stunned her," I said. "I know that from the records."

"Hear me out. Let's assume for one single minute that, lowlife that he is, Rob Westerfield's story is true. He parked his car at the service station, went into the movie, and after it was over, drove to the hideout, just in case Andrea was waiting for him."

"And found her dead?"

"Yes, and panicked. Just as he claimed."

She saw the protest forming on my lips and held up her hand. "Hear me out, Ellie, please. It is possible that everyone has told parts of the truth. Suppose Nebels struggled with Andrea, and she fell and hit her head and was unconscious. Suppose he ran inside Mrs. Dorothy Westerfield's house while trying to decide what to do. He had done work there and knew the alarm code. And then he saw Paulie drive up."

"Why would Paulie have taken the tire jack out of the car?"

"Maybe for protection, in case he ran into Westerfield. Remember that Miss Watkins, the guidance counselor, swore Paulie had said: 'I didn't think she was dead.' "

"Joan, what are you telling me?"

"Try this scenario: Will Nebels followed Andrea to the garage and made a pass at her. There was a scuffle. She fell and was knocked unconscious. He let himself into the house, then saw Paulie drive up, get out the tire jack, and take it into the garage. A minute later, Paulie is back in the car and speeding away. Nebels isn't sure if Paulie is going to get the police. He goes into the garage again. He sees the tire jack that Paulie has dropped. Will Nebels knows he's facing prison if Andrea can tell them what happened. He kills her, takes the tire jack with him, and gets out of there. After the movie, Rob drives to the hideout and finds Andrea dead and panics."

"Joan, don't you realize you've omitted something basic?" I hoped I didn't sound as impatient as I felt with her theory. "How did the tire jack get back in the trunk of Rob Westerfield's car?"

"Ellie, Andrea was murdered on Thursday night. You discovered her body on Friday morning. Rob Westerfield wasn't questioned until Saturday afternoon. It isn't in the trial transcript, but on Friday, Will Nebels was working at the Westerfields', doing odd jobs. Rob's car was in the driveway. He always left the keys in it. Will could easily have replaced the tire jack that day."

"Where did you learn all this, Joan?"

"My cousin, Andrew, the judge, used to be in the district attorney's office. He was there when Rob Westerfield was on trial and was very familiar with the case. He's always felt that Rob Westerfield was a nasty, aggressive, worthless piece of humanity, but he also believed that he was innocent of Andrea's death."

Officer White believed that Paulie was guilty of Andrea's murder. Mrs. Hilmer was still doubtful about Paulie's innocence. Now Joan was convinced that Will Nebels was the killer.

Yet I knew with certainty that Rob Westerfield was the one who had taken my sister's life.

"Ellie, you're dismissing everything I've said." Joan's voice was quiet, her tone regretful.

"No, I'm not dismissing it. I promise you that. And as a hypothetical situation, it fits. But, Joan, Rob Westerfield was in the garage that morning when I was kneeling beside Andrea's body. I heard him breathing and I heard—it's so hard to explain. A giggle is as close as I can get to describing it. It's an odd gasping sound, and I had heard it before, one of the other times I was in his presence."

"How often would you have been in his presence, Ellie?"

"A couple of times when Andrea and I walked downtown after school or on Saturday, when he'd suddenly materialize. How much did Andrea tell you about him?"

"Not much at all. The first time I remember seeing him was at one of the high school games. She was in the band, of course, and really outstanding—she looked so good. I remember that Westerfield came up to her after a game in early October. I was standing with her. He made an outright play for her, saying how pretty she was, how he couldn't take his eyes off her—that kind of thing. He was older and very good looking, and she was flattered, of course. Plus I guess your mother had talked a lot about how important the Westerfield family was."

"Yes."

"He knew that we liked to sneak into his grandmother's garage and smoke. And I mean regular cigarettes, not pot. We thought we were hot stuff, but we weren't into anything illegal. Rob Westerfield told us to consider the place our clubhouse but to let him know when we planned to go over. Then when we did, he'd ask Andrea to get there early. You do realize that she had been friends with him—if you can call it that—for only a month or so before she died."

"Did you ever get the feeling that she had become afraid of him?"

"I got the feeling that something was terribly wrong, but she wouldn't tell me what it was. That last night she called and asked if she could come over so we could do homework together. Frankly, my mother wasn't thrilled. I was behind in algebra, and she wanted me to concentrate. She knew that Andrea and I wasted a lot of time talking when we were supposed to be studying. Also, Mom was going to her bridge club, so she wouldn't be around to make sure we were working."

"Did you finish the homework early, or do you think Andrea used you to get out of the house and meet Rob?"

"I think she intended to leave early all along, so I guess the answer is yes, I was her excuse."

And then I asked the crucial question: "Do you know if Rob ever gave Andrea a locket?"

"No, she didn't mention it to me, and if he *did* give her one, then I never saw it. Your dad gave her a locket, though, and she wore that fairly often."

Andrea had been wearing a heavy V-necked sweater that night. That was why I was so clear about seeing her clasping the locket around her neck. It was on a fairly long chain and rested at the base of the neckline.

"Then to the best of your memory she didn't have any jewelry on when she left your house?"

"I didn't say that. As I remember, she was wearing a thin gold chain. It was short, choker length."

But that's *it,* I thought, suddenly remembering another part of that evening. Her coat was downstairs, and Mother was waiting for her. Before she left the bedroom, Andrea had turned the locket around and let it fall down her back, between her shoulder blades. The effect was one of wearing a choker-length chain.

I had carefully read the description of the clothing Andrea had been wearing when her body was found. There had been no mention of that chain.

I left Joan's house a few minutes later with the sincere promise that I would call her soon. I didn't attempt to tell her that she had unwittingly verified my memory of Andrea putting on the locket.

Rob Westerfield had come back for it the morning after he killed her. I was very sure now that that locket had been too important to risk leaving on her body. Tomorrow I would describe it on the Website as I had described it to Marcus Longo twenty-two years ago.

It's another line to cast, I thought as I again drove past the Graymoor Monastery. If Rob Westerfield was worried enough to come back and get the locket, somebody out there might be interested in getting a reward to tell me why it was so important to him.

The bells of the Graymoor chapel began to chime. It was noon.

Grammar school. Praying the Angelus at noon. *And the Angel of the Lord announced to Mary* . . . And Mary's response to Elizabeth. *My soul doth magnify the Lord. . . . And my spirit doth rejoice* . . .

Maybe someday my spirit will again rejoice, I thought as I turned on the radio.

But not yet.

23

FROM THE CLERK'S DESK at the Parkinson Inn I could look into the restaurant and see that it was enjoying its usual weekend luncheon crowd. Today's group appeared to be particularly festive. I wondered if the sunny fall afternoon had a cheering effect after the several dreary days in the early part of the week.

"I'm afraid that all eight rooms are booked for the weekend, Ms. Cavanaugh," the clerk told me. "It's been that way every weekend this fall, and will be till Christmas."

Of course, that said it all. There was no use staying here during the week, then moving out for the weekend. I'd have to find another place. The prospect of driving from one inn or motel to another seeking admittance, however, was decidedly unappealing. I decided it would be a lot more efficient to go back to the apartment, get out the phone book, and start making calls to see where I could find housing for the next few months. Preferably I'd find something that wouldn't cost an arm and a leg.

The bake-and-serve corn muffin I'd had that morning was all I'd had to eat so far that day. It was then twenty of one, and I didn't particularly feel like having an American cheese, tomato, and lettuce sandwich, which, to the best of my recollection, was all that I'd find in the apartment.

I went into the restaurant and was promptly seated. Technically it was a table for two, but any person in the other seat would have to be skeletal in dimensions. That chair backed up on a sharp corner of the alcove where I'd been placed, leaving no room. Next to me was a table for six which had a reservation sign propped against the salt and pepper shakers.

In my nomadic wanderings I had been to Boston only once, when I was following up on a news story I was writing. That brief visit had left me with a permanent love of New England clam chowder, which according to the menu was the soup of the day.

I ordered it, along with a green salad and a bottle of Perrier. "I like the soup really hot, please," I told the waitress. While I waited to be served, I nibbled on crusty bread and began to analyze why I was feeling disquieted and even depressed.

It wasn't *that* hard to figure out, I decided. A few weeks ago when I came here, I'd felt like a kind of feminine Don Quixote tilting at windmills. But the sobering truth was that even the very people who I would have thought were as convinced as I was of Rob Westerfield's guilt were not taking my side.

They *knew* him. They knew what he was. And still they thought it was entirely possible he had spent his twenties and thirties in prison an innocent man, himself a victim of this crime. Sympathetic as they were to me, in their eyes I was perceived as the obsessed family member of the dead girl, fixated and unreasonable at best, manic and unbalanced at worst.

I know that in some ways I am arrogant. When I think I'm right, all the forces of heaven and hell won't budge me. Maybe that's why I'm a good investigative reporter. I have a reputation for being able to cut through the obfuscation, target what I perceive to be the truth, and then prove my case. Now, sitting in this restaurant where long ago I sat as the smallest member of a happy family, I tried to be honest with myself. Was it possible, was it *remotely* possible, that the same drive that made me a good reporter was working against me now? Was I doing a disservice not only to people like Mrs. Hilmer and Joan Lashley, but to the man I despised, Rob Westerfield?

I was so intent on my own thoughts that I was startled when a hand came across my vision. It was the waitress with the clam chowder. As I'd requested, steam was rising from the bowl.

"Be careful," she warned. "It's really hot."

Mother used to tell us that it's not appropriate to thank a waiter or waitress for service, but that lesson never took with me. To say "thank you" when something that you wanted is placed in front of you never seemed inappropriate to me, and still doesn't.

I picked up the spoon, but before I could take the first sip, the party arrived for the reserved table next to me. I looked up and my throat went dry—Rob Westerfield was standing beside my chair.

I laid down the spoon. He extended his hand, and I ignored it. He was a stunningly handsome man, even more so in person than he had been on television. There was a kind of animal magnetism about him, a suggestion of strength and confidence that is the trademark of many powerful men I have interviewed.

His eyes were a startling cobalt blue, his dark hair lightly brushed at the temples with gray, his complexion surprisingly tanned. I had seen prison pallor on other men and had the fleeting thought that since his release he must have spent several hours under a sunlamp.

"The hostess pointed you out, Ellie," he said, his voice as warm as though we were acquaintances who happened on each other every so often.

"Did she, indeed?"

"She realized who you are and was quite upset. She didn't have another table for six and thought I might not want to be seated near you."

From the corner of my eye I could see his companions taking their seats. Two of them I recognized from the television interview—his father, Vincent Westerfield, and his lawyer, William Hamilton. They were looking at me, their expressions hostile.

"Did it occur to her that I might not want to be anywhere near *you*?" I asked quietly.

"Ellie, you are totally mistaken about me. I want to find your sister's murderer and see him punished just as much as you do. Can we get together and talk quietly?" He hesitated, then, with a smile, added, "Please, Ellie."

I realized that the entire dining room had suddenly become quiet. Since everyone seemed to want to be in on our exchange, I deliberately raised my voice so that at least some of them could overhear me. "I'd love to get together with you, Rob," I said. "How about at the garage-hideout? That was a favorite place of yours, wasn't it? Or maybe the memory of bludgeoning a fifteen-year-old girl to death there might be painful even for a consummate liar like you."

I threw a twenty-dollar bill on the table and pushed back my chair.

Without the slightest indication of being upset by what I had said, Rob picked up the twenty and shoved it in the pocket of my jacket. "We have a house account here, Ellie. Anytime you come in, you're our guest. Bring your friends." Again he paused, but this time his eyes narrowed.

"If you have any," he added quietly.

I took the twenty-dollar bill out of my pocket, spotted the waitress, gave it to her, and left.

HALF AN HOUR LATER I was back in the apartment. The kettle was whistling, and I was putting together the previously rejected cheese sandwich, complete with lettuce and tomato. By then the fit of trembling that overcame me in the car had passed, and only my hands, cold and clammy, reflected the shock of seeing Rob Westerfield face to face.

Over and over in that half hour, a scene had been replaying itself in my mind. *I am on the witness stand. Flanked by his lawyers, Rob is sitting at the table reserved for the accused. He is staring at me, his eyes malevolent and sneering. I am sure that in a moment he will spring up and attack me.*

The intensity of his concentration when he was inches away

from me in the restaurant was just as absolute as it had been at the trial, and behind those cobalt blue eyes and the courteous tone, I felt and saw the same relentless hatred.

But there *is* a difference, I kept reminding myself, until I began to calm down. I'm twenty-nine, not seven. And one way or the other, I'll do him more harm now than I did then. After the trial, one of the reporters had written, "The sad and earnest child who testified in court that her big sister was really scared of Rob Westerfield carried great weight with the jury."

I took the sandwich and the tea to the table, got the phone book out of the cabinet, and opened my cellular phone. While I was eating, I decided to go through the Yellow Pages and circle places where I could inquire about a monthly rental.

Before I could begin, Mrs. Hilmer called. I started to explain to her that I was looking for a place to stay, but she cut me off. "Ellie, I just got a call from my oldest granddaughter, Janey. Remember I told you that she had her first baby last month?"

I could hear the strain in Mrs. Hilmer's voice. "Nothing is wrong with the baby, I hope," I said quickly.

"No. The baby's fine. But Janey broke her wrist and could use some help. I'm driving to Long Island this afternoon and will stay a few days. Did you make plans to go to the Parkinson Inn? After what's happened, I worry about your being alone out here."

"I stopped at the Inn, but they're all booked up for the weekend and for the next six or seven weekends as well. I'm just starting to call around to other inns and guest houses now."

"Ellie, I hope you realize that my concern is only for you. Stay in the apartment until you find something suitable, but for God's sake be sure to lock the doors."

"I will, I promise. Please don't worry about me."

"I'm taking the copies of the trial transcript and the newspapers with me. I'll be going over them while I'm in Garden City with Janey. Take down her phone number in case you want to reach me."

I jotted it down and a few minutes later heard Mrs. Hilmer's car headed down the driveway. I will confess that after the shock of seeing Rob Westerfield, I was very sorry that she had left.

"Fraidy cat, fraidy cat." That was how Andrea would tease me when, if our parents were out, we watched movies like *Friday the 13th* together on television. I always closed my eyes and snuggled against her at the scariest parts.

I remember that one night, to get back at her, I hid under her bed, and when she came into the bedroom, I reached out and grabbed her leg. *"Fraidy cat, fraidy cat,"* I chanted when she shrieked.

But Andrea wasn't here to snuggle up to now, and I'm a big girl, used to taking care of myself. I gave a mental shrug and began circling the local guest houses and inns in the Yellow Pages.

Then I started phoning the seemingly likely ones; it proved to be a dismaying task. The few that sounded possible were pretty expensive on a monthly basis, especially when I figured in the price of meals.

At the end of nearly two hours I had a short list of four places and was already looking through the newspaper at the "houses for rent" section. Oldham is pretty much a year-round community, but from the classified section I could see some rentals that appeared to be reasonable.

At three-thirty I was finished; I had six places lined up to see tomorrow. I was glad to be done because I wanted to get to the computer to write notes on my encounter with Westerfield.

There were one or two inns in the area where they said they had a room available immediately. Either one would have been all right on an interim basis, but the last thing in the world I wanted to do now was start packing. I also did not want to start emptying the refrigerator and thoroughly cleaning the apartment.

Mrs. Hilmer had made it very clear that it was my safety she was concerned about and that I was to stay here until I found something suitable. I knew she'd be gone at least three or four days, so I debated with myself, then made a decision: I would stay here for now, at least over the weekend, probably until Monday.

I opened the computer, made notes on the meeting with Westerfield, and then realized I was having a hard time concentrating. My solution was to catch an early movie and afterward have dinner somewhere nearby.

I looked up the movie listings and noted with irony that the film I wanted to see was showing at the Globe Cinema.

That was where Rob Westerfield claimed he had been when Andrea was murdered.

THE GLOBE had obviously been enlarged and updated since I was a child. It now had seven different films being shown. The lobby held a large, circular service counter where brisk sales in candy, popcorn, and sodas were being made.

Even though the early viewers were just arriving, the lobby floor was already beginning to be littered with kernels of popcorn that had spilled from the tops of overfilled paper cones.

I bought Peanut Chews—my favorite candy—and went into cinema 3, which was where the film I'd selected was being shown. It turned out to be not nearly the ballyhooed sensation (*"Now! At last! The picture you've been waiting for!"*) I'd expected, but mostly a mildly entertaining story about a woman who takes on the world, is vilified, and then, of course, conquers all and finds true love and happiness in the husband she'd kicked out three years earlier.

If they're that hard up for ideas, maybe I can sell them the story of my life, I thought as my attention continued to wander. My life minus the love interest, of course.

I was seated between two couples, senior citizens on my right, teenagers on my left. The teenagers passed the bag of popcorn back and forth, and the girl kept up a running commentary on the film.

She used to be my favorite actress, but now I don't think she's as good as . . .

There was no use trying to pay attention to what was happening on the screen. It wasn't just the kids and the popcorn and the play-by-play comments, or even the slight snore of the elderly man next to me, who by then had dozed off.

I was distracted by the fact that twenty-two years ago Rob Westerfield claimed to be in this theater while Andrea was being murdered, and no one could verify that he'd actually stayed to see the picture. Even with all the publicity the case engendered, not one person ever came forward and said, "He was sitting next to me."

Oldham was a fairly small town at that time, and the Westerfields were well known. Certainly Rob Westerfield, with his good looks and rich-boy attitude, was high profile enough to be known around town. As I sat there in that darkened movie house, I visualized him parking in the service station lot next door.

He had claimed that he spoke to Paulie Stroebel, that he told him he was leaving his car. Paulie absolutely denied that Rob spoke to him.

Then Rob made a point of talking to the ticket seller and to the ticket taker, saying something about how much he was looking forward to the film. "Real friendly," they both testified on the stand, their voices tinged with surprise. Rob Westerfield was not known for being friendly, especially to the working class.

He could easily have established his presence in the theater and then slipped out. I had rented the movie *The Guerrilla Jungle Lord* that he claimed to have seen that night. There are plenty of early scenes where the screen is so dark that someone in an end seat could easily have left without being seen. I looked around, noticed the several side exits that are only supposed to be used in emergencies, and decided to try something.

I got up, mumbled an apology for waking my sleeping neighbor, climbed over his wife, and made my way to the side exit near the back of the room.

The door opened quietly, and I found myself in a sort of alley-way between a bank and the cinema complex. Years ago, the service station, not the bank, had been here. I have copies of the diagrams and photographs that the newspapers printed during the trial, so I remembered the layout of the service station.

The enclosed garage where Paulie had been working was behind the gas pumps and faced Main Street. The parking area, where cars waiting to be serviced were kept, was behind the station. That area is now a parking lot for bank customers.

I walked down the alley, mentally replacing the bank with the service station. I could even visualize where Rob claimed he had parked his car and where it supposedly sat until the film was over at nine-thirty.

Somehow my footsteps became his, and I was in his mind—angry, bad-tempered, thwarted when the girl he thought he had under his thumb phoned to tell him she had a date with someone else.

Never mind that the someone else was Paulie Stroebel.

Meet Andrea. Show her who's boss.

Why did he take the tire jack into the hideout? I asked myself.

There were two possible reasons. One was that he was afraid that my father had learned Andrea was planning to meet him. I have no doubt that my father would have loomed in Rob's mind as a frightening and formidable figure.

The other reason was that Rob took the tire jack with him because he was planning to kill Andrea.

Fraidy cat. Fraidy cat. Oh, God, how terrified the poor kid must have been when she saw him coming at her, saw him lift his arm, brandishing that weapon. . . .

I turned and literally ran back to the other end of the alley where it joined the street. Gulping for air—because for a moment I had literally felt unable to breathe—I steadied myself and walked to my car. I'd left it in the cinema parking lot on the other side of the complex.

The air was still clear, but like last night, a sharp wind had blown up and the temperature was dropping rapidly. I shivered and quickened my steps.

When I'd looked up the film schedule, I noticed an ad for a restaurant, Villa Cesaere, not far from the theater. The ad had made it sound like the kind of place I enjoyed, so I decided to give it a try. I knew I wanted pasta, and the spicier the better. Maybe shrimp *fra diavolo,* I decided.

I simply had to get rid of the terrible inner chill that was overwhelming me.

AT NINE-FIFTEEN, fed and feeling somewhat better, I turned the car off the street and onto Mrs. Hilmer's property. Her house was in darkness, and the light at the door of the garage made for a feeble welcome.

I brought the car to a sudden stop. Something was urging me to turn around, to go to an inn or motel and spend the night there. I simply hadn't realized how insecure I would feel here tonight. I'll leave tomorrow, I thought. One more night here won't be so bad. As soon as I'm in the apartment, I'll be all right.

Of course, even that rationalization didn't make sense. While I was having dinner with Mrs. Hilmer the other evening, someone had been in the apartment. But somehow I didn't think I would find anyone waiting for me there now. My current sense of uneasiness came more from the prospect of being alone outside, so near the woods, if only for a few moments.

I turned the headlights on bright and drove slowly down the driveway. I had been carrying the duffel bag containing the trial transcript, newspapers, and my mother's jewelry in the trunk of the car all day. When I left the restaurant, I moved the bag from the trunk to the front seat so that once back at the apartment I wouldn't have to stand outside while I retrieved it.

Now I carefully scanned the area around the garage. There was no one there.

I took a deep breath, picked up the duffel bag, got out of the car, and hurried the few steps to the door.

Before I could insert the key in the lock, a car roared down the driveway and screeched to a stop. A man jumped out and lunged at me.

I stood frozen, sure I was about to see Rob Westerfield's face and hear the giggle-like sound he'd made as I was kneeling over Andrea's body.

But then a flashlight shone on me, and as he came closer, I could see that the man was wearing a uniform and that it was Officer White.

"I was given to understand that you'd moved, Ms. Cavanaugh," he said, his tone decidedly unfriendly. "What are you doing here?"

24

AFTER A FEW AWKWARD MOMENTS as I explained why I hadn't moved out yet, I insisted that Officer White come up to the apartment and phone Mrs. Hilmer at her granddaughter's house. I had left the number on a sheet of paper next to the computer. He made the call, then put me on with her.

"I'm so embarrassed, Ellie," she said. "I asked Officer White to have the police keep an eye on the house while I was away, and I told him you were leaving, but he certainly should have taken your word that you were still my guest."

You're absolutely right, I thought, but what I said was "He's right to be careful, Mrs. Hilmer." I didn't tell her that, rude as he'd been, I was actually very pleased he was here. It meant I didn't have to enter the apartment alone, and after he left, I would bolt the door.

I inquired about her granddaughter, said goodbye, and got off the phone.

"You'll be leaving tomorrow then, Ms. Cavanaugh?" Officer White asked. From his tone he might as well have said, "Here's your hat, what's your hurry?"

"Yes, Officer. Don't worry. I'll be leaving tomorrow."

"Have you had any response to that sign you carried outside Sing Sing?"

"As a matter of fact, I have," I said, giving him what Pete Lawlor calls my mysterious, self-satisfied smile.

He frowned. I had piqued his curiosity, which is exactly what I wanted to do.

"It's all over town that you had some pretty nasty things to say to Rob Westerfield at the Parkinson Inn today."

"There's no law against being honest, and there's certainly not one that says you have to make nice with murderers."

His cheekbones reddened as he stood with his hand on the doorknob. "Ms. Cavanaugh, let me give you a piece of advice from the real world. I know for a certainty that with the family money to throw around, Rob Westerfield was able to develop a very loyal following in prison. That's just the way it is. Some of those guys are on the street now. Without even talking to Westerfield about it, one of them may decide to remove a certain irritant as a favor to him, anticipating appropriate gratitude of course."

"Who will free me from this turbulent priest?" I asked.

"What are you talking about?"

"A rhetorical question, Officer. In the twelfth century, Henry the Second made that remark to some of his noblemen, and a short time later Archbishop Thomas à Becket was murdered in his cathedral. You know something, Officer White? I can't be sure if you are warning me or threatening me."

"An investigative reporter should be able to tell the difference, Ms. Cavanaugh."

With that, he was gone. It seemed to me that his footsteps were unnecessarily loud on the staircase, as if wanting me to know that he was making a kind of final exit.

I bolted the door, walked to the window, and watched him get back into his squad car and drive away.

Usually I shower in the morning, and if it's been a particularly stressful day, I shower again before I go to bed. I find it's a great way to get the knots out of shoulders and neck muscles. Tonight I decided to go even further. I filled the tub with hot water and squirted in bath oil. After six months the bottle was still almost full, showing how often I get to laze around in a tub. But tonight I needed it, and it did feel good just to lie there and soak. I stayed until the water began to cool.

I'm always amused when I read ads for seductive and provocative nightgowns and robes. My night attire is nightshirts purchased from an L. L. Bean catalogue. They're roomy and comfortable, and their companion piece is a flannel robe. Topping off that exquisite ensemble are fleece-lined bedroom slippers.

The two-door bureau with the attached mirror in the bedroom reminded me of the one my mother had painted white and antiqued for Andrea's room. As I brushed my hair in front of the mirror, I wondered idly what had become of that bureau. When Mother and I moved to Florida, we brought comparatively little furniture with us. I am certain that nothing from Andrea's inviting room accompanied us. My room at that time had been nice, too, but it was little-girl cutesy, with a Cinderella-motif wallpaper.

Then, in a flash of memory, it came to me that I once told Mother I thought the paper was babyish, and she replied, "But it's almost the same as the paper Andrea had in her room when she was your age. *She* loved it."

I guess even then I realized how different we were. I wasn't into girly things, and I never cared about dress-up clothes. Andrea, like Mother, was utterly feminine.

"You're daddy's little girl to have and hold. . . . You're the spirit of Christmas, my star on the tree . . . And you're daddy's little girl."

Unbidden, the words of that song ran through my head, and I once again envisioned Daddy in Andrea's room, holding the music box and sobbing.

It was a memory that I always tried to immediately close off. "Finish brushing your hair, girl, and go to bed," I said aloud.

With a critical eye I studied myself in the mirror. I usually wore my hair up, anchored with a comb, but now, taking a good look, I saw how long it had grown. Over the summer it became very blond, and while most of the bleaching from the sun had faded, there were still bright streaks running though it.

I often recalled the remark Detective Longo had made the first time he questioned me after Andrea's body was found. He said that my hair, like his son's, reminded him of sand when the sun is shining on it. That was such a sweet description, and streaked as my hair is now, it felt good to think that it might be true again.

I watched the eleven o'clock news, just long enough to be sure the world outside Oldham was still more or less functioning. Then, after checking the locks on the living room windows, I went into the bedroom. The wind was really blowing, so I opened the two bedroom windows a couple of inches. The cross-breeze was enough to send me scurrying under the covers, dropping my robe on the footboard and kicking off my slippers on the way.

In my apartment in Atlanta I could always fall asleep easily. But of course it was different there. I could hear faint street noises and sometimes music from the apartment of my next-door neighbor, an aficionado of hard rock who sometimes played his CDs at ear-splitting volume.

A friendly thump on our joint wall always brought a quick response, but even so I was sometimes aware of metallic vibrations as I drifted off.

I would not mind a few metallic vibrations that signified the closeness of another human being tonight, I thought as I readjusted the pillow. It seemed to me that my senses were all on high alert—probably caused by the earlier face-to-face with Westerfield.

Pete's sister Jan lives not far from Atlanta in a little town called Peachtree. Sometimes on Sunday Pete would call me and say, "Let's go for a ride to see Jan and Bill and the kids." They have a German shepherd named Rocky who is a wonderful watchdog. The instant we got out of the car, he'd be furiously barking to alert the family to our presence.

I sure wish you were paying me a visit right now, Rocky, old pal, I thought.

I did eventually manage to fall into an uneasy sleep, the kind that makes you wish you could wake up. I was dreaming that there was some place I had to go. I had to find someone before it was too late. It was dark, and my flashlight wouldn't work.

Then I was in the woods, and I could smell a campfire. I needed to find a path through the woods. There was one, I was sure of it. I'd been on it before.

It was so hot, and I was beginning to cough.

It wasn't a dream! I opened my eyes. The room was in total darkness and I could smell nothing but smoke. I was choking. I shoved back the covers and sat up. I could feel the heat building up around me. I'd burn to death if I didn't get out. Where was I? For a moment I simply couldn't orient myself.

Before I put my feet on the floor, I forced myself to think. I was in Mrs. Hilmer's apartment. The bedroom door was to the left of the bed. It was on a direct line with the headboard. Outside there was the little foyer. The apartment door was just past the foyer, on the left.

It probably took ten seconds for me to think that through. Then I was out of bed. I gasped as my feet touched the hot floorboard. I heard a crackling overhead. The roof was catching fire. I knew I only had seconds before the whole building caved in.

I stumbled forward, groping for the frame of the door. Thank God I had left it open. I felt my way along the foyer wall, passed the open space that was the frame for the bathroom door. The smoke was not quite as dense here, but then a wall of flame burst from the kitchen area of the living room. It illuminated the table, and I saw my computer, printer, and cell phone there. The duffel bag was on the floor next to the table.

I didn't want to lose them. It took a second to pull back the bolt and open the door to the stairs. Then, biting my lips from the pain of the blisters forming on my feet, coughing and gasping, I ran to the table, scooped up the computer, printer, and cell phone in one hand and the duffel bag in the other, and fled back to the door.

Behind me the flames were leaping onto the furniture, and ahead the smoke in the stairwell was thick and black. Fortunately, it was a straight staircase, and somehow I was able to stumble down it. At first the handle of the outside door seemed to be jammed. I dropped the computer, phone, and duffel bag, and yanked and twisted with both hands.

I'm trapped, I'm trapped, I thought as I felt my hair begin to singe. I gave a final desperate twist, and the handle turned. I pulled open the door, bent down and felt for my computer, and phone, and duffel bag, and stumbled out.

As I emerged, a man was running down the driveway and rushed to grab me before I fell. "Is anyone else still in there?" he shouted.

Shivering and burning at the same time, I shook my head. "My wife called the fire department," he said as he pulled me away from the blazing structure.

A car was rushing down the driveway. Only half-conscious, I realized it must have been his wife, because I heard him say, "Lynn, take her home. She's got to get out of the cold. I'll wait for the fire department." Then to me he said, "Go with my wife. We live just down the road."

Five minutes later, for the first time in over twenty years, I was sitting in the kitchen of my old house, wrapped in a blanket, a cup of tea in front of me. Through the French doors that led to the dining room I could see Mother's beloved chandelier, still in place.

And I could see Andrea and me setting the table for Sunday dinner.

"Lord Malcolm Bigbottom is our guest today."

I closed my eyes.

"It's okay to cry, you know," Lynn, the lady who now lives in my old house, said kindly. "You've had a terrible ordeal."

But I managed to blink back the tears. I felt that if I ever started shedding them, I'd never be able to stop.

25

THE FIRE CHIEF CAME to the Keltons' house and insisted on having an ambulance take me to the hospital. "You must have inhaled a lot of smoke, Ms. Cavanaugh," he said. "You need to be checked out, if only as a precaution."

Oldham County Hospital kept me overnight, which was just as well since I had no place else to go. When I was finally in bed—after the soot and grime were removed from my face and body, and my blistered feet were bandaged—I gladly accepted a sleeping pill. The room I was in was near the nurses' station, and I could hear the soft murmur of voices and the sound of footsteps.

As I fell asleep, I thought about how a few hours ago I'd been wishing for company. I never expected to have my wish granted this way.

When I was woken by a nurse's aide at seven o'clock in the morning, there wasn't a part of me that didn't ache. She checked my pulse and blood pressure and departed. I pushed back the blanket, swung my legs onto the floor, and, not sure of what would happen, tried to stand up. The soles of my feet were padded with bandages, and putting weight on them was terribly uncomfortable, but other than that I knew I was in pretty good shape.

That was when I began to realize how lucky I had been. Just a few minutes more, and I am sure I would have been overcome by smoke. By the time the Keltons arrived on the scene, it would have been impossible to save me, even had they known I was there.

Was the fire an accident? I knew it wasn't. Although I never looked inside, Mrs. Hilmer had told me that the garage under the apartment had very little in it except gardening tools.

Gardening tools don't burst into flames.

Officer White had warned me that a fellow ex-prisoner trying to curry favor with Rob Westerfield might try to get rid of me for him. I think White had the order of things reversed. I had not the slightest doubt that that fire had been ordered by Westerfield and that he had given the assignment to a former lackey in Sing Sing. It wouldn't surprise me a bit to learn that the guy who spoke to me in the prison parking lot got the assignment.

I was sure that by now Mrs. Hilmer had been notified of the fire by Officer White—I had given him her granddaughter's phone number on Long Island. I knew how distressing it was for her to learn that the garage with the apartment was gone. It had originally been a barn and had some historic value as a structure.

Mrs. Hilmer was seventy-three years old. The apartment over the garage had been her insurance that if she ever needed any kind of live-in assistance, she had separate living quarters to offer.

I'm sure as well that her granddaughter's accident made her keenly aware of how easy it is to be incapacitated.

Would insurance enable her to rebuild that structure, or would she even want the headache of having the work done? Right now Mrs. Hilmer must be thinking that no good deed goes unpunished, I thought unhappily. I would phone her, but not yet. How do you apologize for something like this?

Then I thought about the duffel bag and my computer, printer, and cell phone. I had made sure they accompanied me to the hospital room, and I remembered that the nurse said something about putting them away for me. Where were they?

There was a locker-style closet in the room. I hobbled over to it, hoping and praying that I'd find them there. I opened the door and was delighted to see them piled neatly on the floor.

I was equally delighted to see a hospital-issue chenille robe on a hanger. I was wearing one of those godforsaken hospital gowns. It was meant for someone the size of a Barbie doll, whereas I am five feet nine inches tall.

The first thing I did was unzip the duffel bag and look inside. The crumbling first page of the *New York Post* with the headline "GUILTY" was on top, just as it had been when I last opened it.

Then I reached into the bag and slid my hand down the side. My fingers groped around. I breathed a sigh of relief when I felt the leather case that I had been seeking.

Yesterday morning, just as I was getting in the car to go to Joan's house, it occurred to me that the next unauthorized visitor to the apartment might rummage around for valuables. I ran back upstairs, took the case from the drawer, and put it in the duffel bag that was already in the trunk.

Now I pulled out the case and opened it. Everything was there—Mother's engagement and wedding rings, her diamond earrings, and my modest collection of jewelry.

Gratefully, I put the case back in the bag, closed it, and picked up the computer. I carried it to the single chair, located by the window. I knew that however long I'd be in the hospital today, I'd spend my time right there.

I turned on the computer and held my breath, exhaling only when the beep sounded, the screen lit up, and I knew I hadn't lost any of the material I had stored in it.

My peace of mind somewhat restored, I hobbled back to the closet, reached for the bathrobe, and went into the bathroom. There was a small tube of toothpaste, a plastic-sealed toothbrush, and a comb on a shelf over the sink. I proceeded to attempt to tidy up.

I know that I was in shock after the fire. Now, as my thinking cleared, I began to realize how very lucky I had been to escape, not only alive, but not seriously burned. I knew also that I would have to be much more vigilant about future attempts to take my life. One thing was certain: I had to be in a place where there would be a desk clerk and other employees around.

When I'd given up trying to pull the small comb through my tangled hair, I went back into the room, settled in the chair, and, since I didn't have pen or paper, opened the computer to make a list of the things I had to do immediately.

I had no money, no clothes, no credit cards, no driver's license— all these had been lost in the fire. I would have to borrow money until I could get duplicates of my credit cards and driver's license. So who would be the lucky recipient of my pleading call?

I have friends in Atlanta, and I have school friends scattered around the country whom I could have phoned for help and received it in a minute. I crossed them off my list, though. I just didn't want to go into a long explanation as to why I was temporarily destitute.

Pete was the only one in Atlanta who knew about Andrea and about why I was here. When I took the leave of absence to come here, my explanation to my coworkers and friends had been "It's personal, guys."

I'm sure the general impression is that Ellie, who's always too busy for a blind date, is involved with somebody special and is trying to work things out with him.

Pete? The thought of having to play the helpless female to his save-the-day hero irritated me. I'd make him the court of last resort.

I'm sure I could have called Joan Lashley St. Martin, but her belief that Rob Westerfield was innocent of Andrea's death made me reluctant to go to her for help.

Marcus Longo? Of course, I thought! He'll stake me, and I'll pay him back within the week.

A breakfast tray came and was picked up an hour later, virtually untouched. Have you ever been in a hospital that actually served hot coffee?

The doctor arrived, checked my blistered feet, told me I was free to go home anytime, and departed. I had a mental image of limping around Oldham in hospital gear, asking for a handout. At precisely that psychologically low moment, Officer White appeared with a sharp-featured man he introduced as Detective Charles Bannister of the Oldham Police Department. A hospital orderly was behind them carrying folding chairs, so I gathered that this was not going to be a quick, cheery bedside visit.

Bannister expressed concern for my well-being and the hope that after the ordeal I was feeling as well as possible.

I immediately sensed that beneath the veneer of concern he had an agenda in mind, and it wasn't a friendly one.

I told him that I was quite well and grateful to be alive, a comment he accepted with a nod of his head. I was reminded of a professor I had in a philosophy course in college. After hearing a particularly stupid observation from one of the students, he would give that same kind of nod with a grave expression.

What it meant was "Now I've heard everything."

It didn't take me long to understand that Detective Bannister had one goal in mind: He was determined to prove his theory that I had made up the initial story about the intruder in the apartment. He didn't put it quite so bluntly, but the scenario he put together went pretty much as follows: After hearing about the supposed intruder, Mrs. Hilmer had been nervous. She only imagined someone had followed her to and from the library. Disguising my voice, I made the phone call warning her that I was unstable.

At that, I raised an eyebrow, but said nothing.

According to Detective Bannister, I had set the fire to gain attention and sympathy for myself, while publicly accusing Rob Westerfield of trying to kill me.

"You were in danger of being burned to death, but according to the neighbor who saw you emerge from the building, you were carrying a computer, a printer, a cell phone, and a large, heavy duffel bag. Most people in an inferno don't stop to pack, Ms. Cavanaugh."

"Just as I reached the door to the stairs, the wall at one end of the living room became a sheet of flames. It illuminated the table where I had left those things. They were very important to me, and I took that extra second to grab them."

"Why were they so important, Ms. Cavanaugh?"

"Let me tell you why, Detective Bannister." The computer was still on my lap, and I pointed to it. "The first chapter of the book I am writing about Rob Westerfield is in this computer. Pages and pages of notes that I have honed from the trial transcript of *The State versus Robson Westerfield* are also in it. I do not have backup. I do not have copies in another place."

His face remained impassive, but I noticed that Officer White's mouth was becoming a thin, angry line.

"I posted my cell phone number on the sign I was carrying when I was outside Sing Sing prison. I'm sure you've heard about my appearance there from him." I jerked my head at White. "I've already received one very interesting phone call from someone who knew Westerfield in prison. That phone is my only chance to stay in contact with him until I can get to a store, buy a new cell phone, and get the number transferred. As for the heavy duffel bag, it's in the closet. Would you care to see the contents?"

"Yes, I would."

I put the computer on the floor and stood up.

"I'll get it for you," he said.

"I prefer to keep it in my own hands at all times."

I tried not to limp as I rushed across the room. I yanked open the closet door, picked up the duffel bag, brought it back, dropped it in front of my chair, sat down, and unzipped it.

I could sense rather than see the startled reaction of the two men as they read the headline "GUILTY."

"I would prefer not to be showing these to you." I spat out the words as I yanked newspaper after newspaper from the bag and tossed them on the floor.

"My mother kept these all her life." I made no attempt to hide my anger. "They are the news accounts—starting with the discovery of my sister's body and including the moment when Rob Westerfield was sentenced to prison. They don't make *pleasant* reading, but they do make *interesting* reading, and I don't want to lose them."

The last of the newspapers was on the floor. I had to use both hands to pull out the trial transcript. I held up the cover page for them to see. "Also interesting reading, Detective Bannister," I said.

"I'm sure it is," he agreed, his face impassive. "Anything else in there, Ms. Cavanaugh?"

"If you're hoping to find a can of gasoline and a box of matches, you're out of luck." I took out the leather case and opened it. "Go through this, please."

He glanced at the contents and handed the case back to me. "Do you always carry your jewelry with you in a duffel bag with newspapers, Ms. Cavanaugh, or only when you suspect there might be a fire?"

He stood up, and White jumped to his feet. "You'll be hearing from us, Ms. Cavanaugh. Are you returning to Atlanta, or will you be staying in the area?"

"I'll be staying in the area, and I will be glad to inform you of my address. Perhaps the police department will keep a better eye on those premises than they did on Mrs. Hilmer's property. Do you think that might be possible?"

Officer White's cheekbones became stained with purple. I knew he was furious and I knew I was being reckless, but at that point I didn't care.

Bannister didn't bother to answer but turned abruptly and left with White at his heels.

I watched them go. The orderly came into the room to collect the folding chairs. His eyes widened as he took in the sight of me with the transcript on my lap, the jewelry case in my hand, the duffel bag, and scattered newspapers on the floor.

"Miss, can I help you gather them up?" he offered. "Or can I get you something? You look kind of upset."

"I am upset," I agreed. "And you can get something for me. Is there a cafeteria in the hospital?"

"Yeah. A real good one."

"Would you consider . . ." I stopped because I was on the verge of hysteria. "Would you consider treating me to a cup of very hot black coffee?"

26

THIRTY MINUTES LATER I was savoring the last sip of the excellent coffee the orderly had kindly bought for me when I had another visitor, more surprising this time. My father.

The door was partially open. He tapped on it, then walked in without waiting for a response. We stared at each other, and my throat went dry.

His dark hair was now silvery white. He was a little thinner, but held himself as erectly as ever. Glasses accentuated his keen blue eyes, and there were deep furrows in his forehead.

My mother chiding, "Ted, I know you don't realize it, but you've got to stop frowning when you concentrate. You're going to look like a prune when you get older."

He certainly didn't look like a prune. He was still a good-looking man and hadn't lost that aura of inner strength.

"Hello, Ellie," he said.

"Hello, Dad."

I can only imagine what he was thinking when he looked at me garbed in a cheap hospital bathrobe, my hair a mass of tangles, bandages on my feet. Certainly not the shining star of the song on the music box.

"How are you, Ellie?"

I'd forgotten the deep resonance in his voice. It was the sound of quiet authority that Andrea and I had respected as children. We had felt protected by it, and I, at least, was in awe of it.

"I'm very well, thank you."

"I came here as soon as I heard about the fire at Mrs. Hilmer's and learned that you'd been in that apartment."

"You needn't have bothered."

He'd been standing just inside the door. Now he pushed it shut and came over to me. He knelt down and tried to take my hands. "Ellie, for God's sake, you're my daughter. How do you think I felt when I heard that you barely got out alive?"

I pulled my hands away. "Oh, that story will change. The cops think I set the fire as a grandstand gesture. According to *them,* I want attention and sympathy."

He was shocked. "That's ridiculous."

He was so close that I caught the faint scent of his shaving cream. Was I wrong, or was it the same scent I remembered? He was wearing a shirt and tie with a dark blue jacket and gray slacks. Then I remembered that this was Sunday morning and that he might have been dressing to go to church when he heard about the fire.

"I know you mean to be kind," I said, "but I really wish you would leave me alone. I don't *need* anything from you, and I don't *want* anything from you."

"Ellie, I've seen that Website. Westerfield is dangerous. I'm desperately worried about you."

Well, at least I had one thing in common with my father. We both knew Rob Westerfield was a killer.

"I can take care of myself. I've been doing it for a long time."

He stood up. "That's not my fault, Ellie. You refused to visit me."

"I guess I did, so that means your conscience is clear. Don't let me keep you."

"I came to invite you, to *implore* you, to stay with us. That way I can protect you. If you remember, I was a state trooper for thirty-five years."

"I remember. You looked great in uniform. Oh, I did write and thank you for interring Mother's ashes in Andrea's grave, didn't I?"

"Yes, you did."

"Her death certificate gave the cause of death as 'cirrhosis of the liver,' but I think a more accurate diagnosis would be 'broken heart.' And my sister's death wasn't the only reason for that broken heart."

"Ellie, your mother left me."

"My mother *adored* you. You could have waited her out. You could have followed her to Florida and brought her home—brought *us* home. You didn't want to."

My father reached into his pocket and took out his wallet. I hoped he wouldn't dare to offer me money, but that didn't happen. He pulled out a card and laid it on the bed. "You can reach me anytime, day or night, Ellie."

Then he was gone, but the faint scent of his shaving cream seemed to linger after him. I'd forgotten that sometimes I would sit on the edge of the tub and talk to him while he was shaving. I'd forgotten that sometimes he would spin around, pick me up, and rub his face, thick with lather, against mine.

So vivid was the memory that I reached up and touched my cheek, almost expecting to feel the residue of damp suds. My cheek was wet, but it was with the tears that, for the moment at least, I could no longer deny.

27

I TRIED TO REACH Marcus Longo twice in the next hour. Then I remembered that he had said something about his wife not liking to fly alone. I realized that there was a very good chance he had flown to Denver to escort her home, and while there he'd have another adoring visit with his first grandchild.

The nurse popped her head in and reminded me that checkout time was noon. By eleven-thirty I was ready to ask if there was a social services office in the hospital, but then Joan called.

"Ellie, I just heard what happened. For heaven's sake, how are you? What can I do?"

Any pride that I had about refusing help because she didn't believe Rob Westerfield was a murdering animal evaporated. I needed her, and I knew darn well that she was as sincere in her conviction about his innocence as I was in mine about his guilt.

"Actually, you can do a lot," I said. Relief at hearing a friendly voice made my own voice tremble. "You can dig up some clothes for me. You can come and get me. You can help me find a place to stay. You can lend me some money."

"You'll stay with us—" she began.

"Negative. No. That's neither a good nor a safe idea for either one of us. You don't need your house to burst into flames because I'm around."

"Ellie, you don't believe that someone set that fire with the intent of killing you!"

"Yes, I do."

She considered that news for a moment, and I'm sure thought of her three children. "Then where can you stay that you'll be safe, Ellie?"

"An inn is my preference. I don't like the idea of a motel with separate doors to the outside." I thought of something. "Forget the Parkinson Inn. It's booked." And it's a Westerfield hangout, I reminded myself.

"I have a place in mind that I think will work," Joan said. "I also have a friend who's about your height and weight. I'll call her to borrow some clothes. What's your shoe size?"

"Nine, but I don't think I can take the bandages off my feet yet."

"Leo is a size ten. If you don't mind wearing a pair of his sneakers, they might do for now."

I didn't mind.

JOAN ARRIVED within the hour with a suitcase containing underwear, pajamas, stockings, slacks, a turtleneck sweater, a warm jacket, gloves, the sneakers, and some toiletries. I dressed, and the nurse brought in a cane I could use in walking until my blistered feet began to heal. On the way out, the billing clerk reluctantly agreed to wait for payment until I could have a copy of my medical insurance card faxed to her.

Finally we were in Joan's SUV. My hair was smoothed back and caught at the neckline with a rubber band I had acquired at the nurses' station. A cursory glance in the mirror showed that it looked tidy enough. The borrowed clothes fit quite well, and even though the sneakers looked wide and ungainly, they did a good job of protecting my painful feet.

"I made a reservation for you at the Hudson Valley Inn," Joan told me. "It's about a mile away."

"If you don't mind, I'd like to drive to Mrs. Hilmer's place. My car is still there—or at least, I hope it's there."

"Who would take it?"

"No one would take it, but it was parked about two feet from the garage. I'm keeping my fingers crossed that a beam or some debris didn't fall on it."

There wasn't a wall standing of the structure that had housed the cheery apartment Mrs. Hilmer had so generously lent me. The area around it was cordoned off, and a policeman was standing guard.

Three men in heavy rubber boots were painstakingly examining the rubble and undoubtedly trying to pinpoint the source of the blaze. They looked up when they saw us, but then went back to their probing.

I was relieved to see that my car had been moved about twenty feet toward Mrs. Hilmer's house. We got out of the SUV to examine it. It's a previously owned BMW that I bought two years ago, the first decent car I've ever had.

Of course, every inch of it was grimy with black smoke, and there were some blisters in the paint on the passenger side, but I considered myself lucky. I still had my wheels, even if I couldn't use them yet.

My shoulder bag had been in the bedroom. Along with everything else, my key ring was in it.

The cop on guard came over to us. He was very young and very polite. When I explained that I didn't have the key to the car and would contact BMW for a replacement, he assured me the car would be safe. "One of us will be on the premises for the next few days."

To see if you can pin the fire on me? I wondered as I thanked him.

Whatever lift in spirit I'd felt when I got dressed and left the hospital disappeared as Joan and I started to get back in her SUV. It was a beautiful, clear fall day, but around us the smell of smoke permeated the air. I fervently hoped that it would dissipate before Mrs. Hilmer got back. That was another thing I had to do: phone and talk to her.

I could visualize the conversation.

"I'm really sorry I caused your guest house to burn down. I certainly won't let it happen again."

I could hear the pealing of church bells in the distance, and I wondered if my father went to Mass after he visited me—he and his wife and son, the basketball star. I had thrown away his card when I was clearing out of the hospital room, but I'd noticed he still lived in Irvington. That meant he probably was still a parishioner of Immaculate Conception, the church in which I was baptized.

The godparents who were to assist my parents in reinforcing my religious education and spiritual well-being were my father's close friends, the Barrys. Dave Barry was a state trooper, too, and probably also retired by now. I wondered if he or his wife, Nancy, ever said, "Oh, by the way, Ted, any word from Ellie?"

Or was I a subject too uncomfortable to be discussed? A person to be dismissed with a shake of the head and a sigh. *"It's one of those sad things that happen in life. We just have to put it behind us and go on."*

"You're very quiet, Ellie," Joan said as she turned on the ignition. "How do you feel, really?"

"Much better than I dared hope," I assured her. "You're an angel, and with the money you are so kindly going to lend me, I am buying *you* lunch."

I could see that the Hudson Valley Inn was going to be a perfect spot for me. It was a three-story, wide-porched gingerbread kind of Victorian mansion, and the minute we stepped into the vestibule, the elderly clerk behind the desk was looking us over carefully.

Joan gave her credit card for an imprint, explaining that I'd lost my purse and it would be a few days before I would have new cards issued. That bonded Mrs. Willis, the clerk, to me for life. After introducing herself, she confided that seven years ago, in the train station, she had laid her purse beside her on the bench.

"I turned the page of the newspaper," she recalled, "and in that split second, it disappeared. What a nuisance. I was stranded. I was so upset. Someone had run up three hundred dollars on my card before I could even collect my wits and make the phone call, and . . ."

Maybe because of our shared experience, she went out of her way to give me a particularly desirable room. "It's priced as a room, but it's really a junior suite because it has a separate sitting area with a little kitchenette. And best of all it has a wonderful view of the river."

If there's anything in the world I love, it's a river view. It's not hard to figure out why that is true. I was conceived in the house in Irvington that overlooks the Hudson and lived there for the first five years of my life. I remember that when I was very little, I would pull a chair over to the window and stand on it so that I could catch a glimpse of the river shimmering below.

Joan and I walked slowly up the two flights to the room, agreed that it was exactly what I needed, and made our equally slow passage back to the quaint dining room at the rear of the inn. By then I felt as though all the blisters had given birth to septuplets.

A Bloody Mary and a club sandwich did wonders to restore a sense of normalcy to me.

Then, over coffee, Joan frowned and said, "Ellie, I hate to bring this up, but it's necessary. Leo and I went to a cocktail party last night. Everyone is talking about your Website."

"Go on."

"Some people think it's outrageous," she said frankly. "I understand it was legal for you to register it in Rob Westerfield's name, but a lot of people think that was unfair and totally unnecessary."

"Don't look so worried," I said. "I have no intention of shooting the messenger, and I *am* interested in getting reactions. What else are they saying?"

"That you should not have put those mug shots of him on the Website. That the medical examiner's testimony describing Andrea's wounds make brutal reading."

"It was a brutal crime."

"Ellie, you asked me to tell you what people are saying."

Joan looked so terribly unhappy that I was ashamed of myself. "I'm sorry. I know how miserable this is for you."

She shrugged. "Ellie, I believe Will Nebels killed Andrea. Half this town thinks Paulie Stroebel is guilty. And a lot of other people feel that even if Rob Westerfield is guilty, he has served his sentence and has been paroled, and that you ought to accept that."

"Joan, if Rob Westerfield had admitted his guilt and honestly expressed regret, I still would have hated his guts, but there wouldn't be a Website. I understand why people think the way they do, but I can't stop now."

She reached across the table, and we clasped hands. "Ellie, there's another sympathy vote out there. It's for old Mrs. Westerfield. Her housekeeper is telling everyone who will listen how upset she is about the Website and how she wishes you would at least shut it down until after a new jury has heard the evidence."

I thought of Dorothy Westerfield, that elegant woman, offering condolences to my mother on the day of the funeral, and I remembered my father ordering her from the house. He couldn't tolerate her sympathy then, and I could not allow myself to be swayed by sympathy for her now.

"We'd better change the subject," I said. "We're not going to agree."

Joan lent me $300, and we both managed a genuine smile as I paid for the lunch. "Symbolic," I said, "but it makes me feel better."

We said good-bye in the vestibule at the front door. "I hate to see you having to make that climb upstairs," she said, looking worried.

"It will be worth it just to get there. And I've got my freebie to lean on." I thumped the cane lightly to emphasize my point.

"Call me if you need anything. Otherwise, I'll talk to you tomorrow."

I hesitated about bringing up anything else controversial, but there was one more thing I had to ask her. "Joan, I know you never saw the locket that I insist Andrea was wearing, but are you still in touch with some of the girls who were in school with you and Andrea?"

"Sure. And you can bet I'll be hearing from them, given all that's going on."

"Would you ask them directly if any of them ever saw Andrea wearing the locket I described to you? Gold, heart-shaped, embossed at the edges, small blue stones in the center, and 'A' and 'R,' Andrea's and Rob's initials, engraved on the back."

"Ellie—"

"Joan, the more I think about it, the more I believe that the only reason Rob went back to the garage was that he couldn't afford to have the locket found on Andrea's body. I need to know why, and it would help if someone else confirmed that it existed."

Joan didn't comment further after that. She promised she would make inquiries and then left me to go home to her orderly life with her husband and children. Leaning heavily on the cane, I limped upstairs to the room, locked and bolted the door, carefully removed the sneakers, and sank down on the bed.

The ringing of the telephone woke me up. I was startled to see that the room was in darkness. I struggled up on one elbow, fumbled for the light, and glanced at the clock as I picked up the phone on the bedside table.

It was eight o'clock. I had been asleep for six hours. "Hello." I know I sounded groggy.

"Ellie, it's Joan. Something terrible has happened. Old Mrs. Westerfield's housekeeper went into Stroebel's delicatessen this afternoon and shouted at Paulie, telling him to admit that he'd killed Andrea. She said it was his fault that the Westerfield family was being tortured.

"Ellie, an hour ago Paulie went into the bathroom at home, locked the door, and slit his wrists. He's in intensive care in the hospital. He's lost so much blood that they don't think he's going to live."

28

I found Mrs. Stroebel in the waiting room outside the intensive care unit. She was weeping quietly, the tears running down her cheeks. Her lips were clamped together tightly, as though she was afraid that parting them would release a tidal wave of grief.

Her coat was around her shoulders, and even though her cardigan and skirt were dark blue, I could see dark stains that I was sure had been caused by Paulie's blood.

A large-framed, plainly dressed woman of about fifty was sitting protectively close to her. She looked up at me, a hint of hostility on her face.

I wasn't sure what to expect from Mrs. Stroebel. It was my Website that had triggered the verbal attack from Mrs. Westerfield's housekeeper and Paulie's despairing response to it.

But Mrs. Stroebel stood up and walked halfway across the room to meet me. "*You* understand, Ellie," she sobbed. "You understand what they have done to my son."

I put my arms around her. "I do understand, Mrs. Stroebel." I looked over her head at the other woman. She knew the question my eyes were silently asking and made a gesture with her hand which I took to mean that it was too soon to tell if Paulie would make it.

Then she introduced herself. "I'm Greta Bergner. I work with

Mrs. Stroebel and Paulie in the delicatessen. I thought you might be a reporter."

We sat together for the next twelve hours. From time to time we went in and stood at the entrance to the cubicle where Paulie was lying, an oxygen mask over his face, tubes in his arms, heavy bandages on his wrists.

During that long night, as I observed the agony on Mrs. Stroebel's face and watched her lips move in silent prayer, I found myself beginning to pray as well. At first it was instinctive, but then it became deliberate. *If you spare Paulie for her, I'll try to accept everything that happened. Maybe I won't succeed, but I swear I'll try.*

Streaks of light began to penetrate the outside darkness. At nine-fifteen a doctor came in to the waiting room. "Paulie is stabilized," he said. "He'll make it. Why don't you people go home and get some sleep."

I TOOK A CAB BACK from the hospital; along the way I had the driver stop so I could pick up the morning papers. I had only to glance at the front page of the *Westchester Post* to be grateful that in the intensive care unit Paulie Stroebel did not have access to newspapers.

The headline was "Murder Suspect Attempts Suicide."

The rest of the front page was covered with pictures of three people. The photo on the left was of Will Nebels posing for the camera, a self-righteous expression on his weak-featured face. The one on the right was of a woman in her mid-sixties with a worried frown that enhanced her severe features. The center photo was of Paulie, behind the counter of the deli, a bread knife in his hand.

The picture had been cropped so that only the hand holding the bread knife showed. There was no context for it, no baguette being sliced in preparation for a sandwich. He was looking into the camera, his eyebrows drawn together.

My guess is that Paulie had been caught by surprise when his picture was taken. Whatever, the effect was that of a surly man with disturbing eyes brandishing a weapon.

The captions under the pictures were quotes. Nebels' was "I knew he did it." The woman with severe features said, "He admitted it to me." Paulie's caption was "I'm sorry. I'm sorry."

The story was on page 3, but I had to put off reading it; the cab was pulling up to the inn. Once in my room, I turned again to the newspaper.

The woman in the photo on the front page was Lillian Beckerson, Mrs. Dorothy Westerfield's housekeeper of thirty-one years. "Mrs. Westerfield is one of the finest human beings who ever walked the face of the earth," the newspaper quoted her as saying. "Her husband was a United States senator, his grandfather was governor of New York. She's lived with this stain on her family name for over twenty years. Now, when her only grandchild is trying to prove his innocence, that woman who lied on the witness stand as a child is back trying to destroy him again on a Website."

That's me, I thought.

"Mrs. Westerfield was looking at that Website and crying yesterday afternoon. I couldn't take it anymore. I marched myself into that delicatessen and yelled at that man, asking him please to tell the truth, to admit what he had done. You know what he kept saying to me? 'I'm sorry. I'm sorry.' Now, if you were innocent, would you have said that? I don't think so."

You would if you were Paulie. I forced myself to keep reading. I'm an investigative journalist, and I could see that Colin Marsh, the guy who wrote this story, was one of those sensationalists who knows how to elicit and then manipulate provocative quotes.

He had looked up Emma Watkins, the guidance counselor who years ago swore on the stand that Paulie had sobbed, "I didn't think she was dead," when the class was told about Andrea.

Ms. Watkins told Marsh that over the years she always had been troubled by Rob Westerfield's conviction. She said that Paulie was easily agitated and that if he learned that Andrea had been joking when she said she'd go with him to the Thanksgiving mixer, he might have been upset enough to lash out.

Lash out. What a delicate way to put it, I thought.

Will Nebels, that poor excuse for a human being, that sleaze who used to like to hug teenage girls, was extensively quoted in the story. With even more flourish than he had exhibited in the earlier television interview I'd seen, he told Marsh about seeing Paulie go into the garage-hideout that night, carrying a tire jack. He ended by piously lamenting he'd never be able to make up to the Westerfield family that he didn't come forward sooner.

When I finished reading the account, I threw the paper on the bed. I was both furious and worried. The case was being tried in the press, and more and more people were going to come to believe that Rob Westerfield was innocent. I realized that if I had read the story cold, even I might have been convinced that the wrong man had been convicted.

But if Mrs. Westerfield was upset by what she read on my Website, it undoubtedly was having an effect on other people as well. I opened the computer and got busy.

"In a mistaken gesture of loyalty, Mrs. Dorothy Westerfield's housekeeper stormed into Stroebel's delicatessen and verbally attacked Paulie Stroebel. A few hours later Paulie, a gentle man already under great stress thanks to the lies perpetrated by the Westerfield money machine, attempted to commit suicide.

"My sympathy goes out to Mrs. Dorothy Westerfield, by all accounts a truly fine woman, for the pain she has suffered because of the crime committed by her grandson. I believe that she will find peace by accepting the fact that her proud family name may still be respected by future generations.

"All she needs to do is leave her vast fortune to charities that will educate future generations of students and fund medical research that will save the lives of countless human beings. Leaving that fortune to a killer compounds the tragedy that more than twenty years ago took my sister's life and that yesterday very nearly cost Paulie Stroebel *his* life.

"I understand that a Committee for Justice for Rob Westerfield has been formed.

"I invite all of you to join the Committee for Justice for Paulie Stroebel.

"Mrs. Dorothy Westerfield, you first!"

Not bad, I thought, as I transferred the text to the Website. As I was closing the computer, my cell phone rang.

"I been reading the papers." I immediately recognized the voice. It was the man who earlier claimed to have been in prison with Rob Westerfield and said he heard him confess to another murder.

"I've been hoping to hear from you." I tried to keep my tone noncommittal.

"The way I see it, Westerfield's doing a good job of making that looney Stroebel look bad."

"He's not a 'looney,' " I snapped.

"Have it your way. Here's the deal. Five thousand bucks. I give you the first name of the guy Westerfield bragged about killing."

"The *first* name!"

"It's all I know. Take it or leave it."

"Isn't there anything else you can give me? I mean when it happened, where it happened?"

"First name is all I know, and I need the money by Friday."

Today was Monday. I had about $3,000 in a savings account in Atlanta, and, much as I hated the thought, I could borrow the rest from Pete if the book advance didn't come through by Friday.

"Well?" His voice was impatient.

I knew that there was a very good chance I was being conned, but it was a chance I decided to take.

"I'll have the money by Friday," I promised.

29

BY WEDNESDAY EVENING I was reasonably back to normal. I had credit cards, a driver's license, and money. An advance on the book had been electronically transferred to a bank near the inn. The superintendent's wife in Atlanta had gone to my apartment, packed some clothes for me, and shipped them to me overnight. The blisters on my feet were healing, and I'd even had time to get my hair trimmed.

Most important, I had an appointment on Thursday afternoon in Boston with Christopher Cassidy, the scholarship student at Arbinger who, at age fourteen, had been severely beaten by Rob Westerfield.

I had already put on the Website Dr. Margaret Fisher's account of having her arm twisted by Rob Westerfield and being paid $500 by his father not to press charges.

I e-mailed the text to her before I put it on the Website. She not only okayed it but gave her professional opinion that the hair-trigger temper and violence she had experienced could very well have been the same reaction that caused him to bludgeon Andrea to death.

On the other hand, Joan had been in touch with Andrea's circle of close friends at high school, and she'd reported that not one of them ever saw her wear any locket except the one my father gave her.

Every day I was running a description of the locket on the Website, asking for any information anyone might be able to supply. So far there'd been no results. My e-mail was full of comments. Some praised what I was doing. Others vehemently objected to it. I had my share of weirdos writing as well. Two confessed to the murder. One said Andrea was still alive and wanted me to rescue her.

A couple of the letters threatened me. The one that I believed was genuine said he was very disappointed to see me escape from the fire. He added, "Cute nightshirt—L. L. Bean, wasn't it?"

Had the writer been watching the fire from the woods, or could he be the intruder who had been in the apartment and perhaps noticed the nightshirt on a hanger in the bedroom closet? Either prospect was intimidating, and if I wanted to admit it to myself, both were downright frightening.

I was in touch with Mrs. Stroebel several times a day, and as Paulie started to mend, the relief in her voice became more and more evident. However, so did the concern. "Ellie, if there is a new trial and Paulie has to testify, I am afraid he will do this again to himself. He has told me, 'Mama, in court I can't answer them so that they understand. I worried about Andrea being with Rob Westerfield. I did not threaten her.' "

Then she added, "My friends are calling me. They see your Website. They say everyone should have a champion like you. I tell Paulie about it. He would like you to visit him."

I promised I would go on Friday.

Except for the errands I'd completed, I'd been staying in the room, working on the book and having my meals sent up by room service. But at seven o'clock on Wednesday evening, I decided to go downstairs for dinner.

The dining room here was not unlike the one at the Parkinson Inn, but it had a more formal feeling. The tables were farther apart, and the table linen was white instead of checkerboard red and white. The table centerpiece at the Parkinson was a cheery, wide candle, not a prim little vase of flowers. The diners here were distinctly older—vintage senior citizens, not the exuberant groups that frequented the Parkinson.

But the food was equally good, and after debating between rack of lamb and swordfish, I succumbed to what I really felt like having and ordered the lamb.

I took from my bag a book I'd been wanting to read, and for the next hour enjoyed the combination I love—a good dinner and a good book. I was so deeply into the story that when the waitress cleared the table and then spoke to me, I looked up at her, startled.

I said yes to coffee and no to dessert.

"The gentleman at the next table would like to offer you an after-dinner drink."

I think I knew it was Rob Westerfield even before I turned my head. He was sitting not more than six feet from me, a wineglass in his hand. He raised it in a mock salute and smiled.

"He asked if I knew your name, Miss. I told him, and he wrote this note to you."

She handed me a card with Westerfield's full name embossed on the front, Robson Parke Westerfield. *My God, he's giving it the full treatment* was the thought that ran through my head as I flipped the card over.

On it he had written: "Andrea was cute, but you're beautiful."

I got up, walked over to him, tore up the card, and dropped the pieces in his wineglass. "Maybe you want to give me the locket you took back after you killed her," I suggested.

His pupils widened, and the teasing expression in his cobalt eyes disappeared. For an instant I thought he would spring up and attack me as he had attacked Dr. Fisher in the restaurant years ago. "That necklace was a big worry for you, wasn't it, jailbird?" I asked him. "Well, I think it still is, and I'm going to find out why."

The waitress was standing between the tables, her expression baffled. She obviously hadn't recognized Westerfield, which made me wonder when she had arrived in Oldham.

I jerked my head back at him. "Bring Mr. Westerfield another glass of wine, please, and put it on my bill."

SOMETIME DURING THE NIGHT the alarm was disabled on my car and the gas tank jimmied open. A very efficient way to destroy a car is to pour sand into the gas tank.

The Oldham police in the form of Detective White responded to my call about my trashed BMW. While he didn't quite ask me where I had obtained the sand, he did mention that the fire in Mrs. Hilmer's garage was definitely set. He also said that the remnants of the gasoline-soaked towels that had started the blaze were identical with the towels Mrs. Hilmer had left in the linen closet of the apartment.

"Quite a coincidence, Ms. Cavanaugh," he said. "Or is it?"

30

I DROVE A RENTED CAR to Boston for my appointment with Christopher Cassidy. I was furious that my own car had been trashed and concerned because I knew there was something else to be faced. I had thought that the intruder in the apartment probably had been looking for material that I might be using on the Website. Now I wondered if his main reason for being there was to steal items that could be used later to set the fire that almost took my life.

I knew, of course, that Rob Westerfield was behind it and that he had thugs like the one who came up to me in the parking lot at Sing Sing to do his dirty work for him. My goal was to prove to the world that an examination of his life would show a pattern of violence in the years that led up to Andrea's death. I further believed that it was his intention that I be the next victim of that violence.

Like the risk in paying $5,000 for the first name of another possible Westerfield victim, it was a chance I had to take.

Any good reporter has to be compulsively punctual. Not being able to use my own car, waiting for the police to fill out the report, and then going to the rental agency had delayed me. I still would have been comfortably early for my appointment, but then I hit bad weather.

The prediction had been for cloudy skies and possible light snow in the evening. The light snow began fifty miles outside Boston; the result was slippery roads and crawling traffic. As the minutes ticked by, I kept glancing at the clock on the dashboard, agonizing at the traffic's slow pace. Christopher Cassidy's secretary had warned me to be prompt, as he was squeezing time for me into a very full day and was leaving this evening for meetings in Europe.

It was four minutes to two when I arrived breathlessly at his office for the two o'clock appointment. During the few minutes I sat in the handsome reception room, I had to make a determined effort to collect my bearings. I felt flustered and disorganized, plus I had the beginnings of a headache.

Promptly at two o'clock Cassidy's secretary came to escort me to his private office. As I followed her in, I reviewed in my mind everything I had learned about Cassidy. I had known, of course, that he'd been a scholarship student at Arbinger Academy and that he had founded this firm. When I looked him up on the Internet, I learned that he had graduated at the top of his class from Yale, had a master's degree from the Harvard Business School, and had been honored by so many charities that it was obvious he was a generous donor.

He was forty-two years old, married, had a fifteen-year-old daughter, and was an avid sportsman.

Obviously quite a guy.

The minute I entered the room, he came out from behind his desk, walked over to me, and extended his hand. "I'm glad to see you, Ms. Cavanaugh. Is it okay if I call you Ellie? I feel as though I know you. Why don't we sit over here?" He indicated the sitting area near the window.

I chose the couch. He sat on the edge of the chair opposite me. "Coffee or tea?" he asked.

"Coffee, please, black," I said gratefully. I felt that a cup of coffee might clear my head and help me think straight.

He picked up the phone from the table at his elbow. In the brief moment he spoke to his secretary I had a chance to study him; I liked what I saw. His well-cut dark blue business suit and white shirt were conservative, but the red tie with tiny golf clubs suggested a touch of the maverick. He had broad shoulders, a solid but trim body, a good head of sable brown hair, and deep-set hazel eyes.

There was a feeling of crackling energy emanating from him, and I could sense that Christopher Cassidy never wasted a minute.

Now he came directly to the point. "When Craig Parshall phoned, he told me why you wanted to talk to me."

"Then you know that Rob Westerfield is out of prison and probably will get a new trial."

"And that he's trying to blame the death of your sister on someone else. Yes, I do know that. Blaming someone else for what he does is an old trick of his. He was pulling it when he was fourteen years old."

"That's exactly the kind of information I want to put on the Website. The Westerfields have gotten a so-called eyewitness to lie for them. As it stands now, in a second trial they have a good chance of getting an acquittal, and then the record will be expunged. Rob Westerfield becomes the martyr who spent over twenty years in prison for another man's crime. I can't let it happen."

"What do you want me to tell you?"

"Mr. Cassidy," I began.

"Anyone who despises Rob Westerfield calls me Chris."

"Chris, according to Craig Parshall, Westerfield beat you up pretty viciously when you both were sophomores at Arbinger."

"We were both good athletes. There was one starting spot on the varsity for a running back. We competed for it, and I got it. I guess he was brooding over it. A day or so later I was on my way back to the dorm from the library. I had a load of books in my arms. He came up behind up and punched me in the neck. Before I could react, he was all over me. I ended up with a broken nose and jaw."

"And no one stopped him?"

"He had picked his time. He attacked me when there was no

one else around, then tried to say I started it. Fortunately, a senior happened to be looking out the window and witnessed what happened. Of course, the school didn't want a scandal. The Westerfields have been big donors for generations. My father was ready to file charges but was offered a full scholarship for my brother who was then in the eighth grade if he'd reconsider. I'm sure now that the Westerfields paid for that so-called scholarship."

The coffee arrived. Nothing had ever tasted so good. Cassidy looked reflective as he raised the cup to his lips. Then he said, "To the credit of the school, Rob was forced to withdraw at the end of the term."

"May I tell this story on the Website? Your name would add a lot of validity to what I'm trying to do."

"Absolutely. I remember when your sister died. I read every account of the trial because of Westerfield. At the time I wished I could get on the stand and tell them what kind of animal he is. I have a daughter the age of your sister when she died. I can only imagine what your father went through, what your whole family went through."

I nodded. "It destroyed us as a family."

"I'm not surprised."

"Before he attacked you, did you have much contact with him in school?"

"I was the son of a short-order cook. He was a Westerfield. He didn't have time for me until I got in his way."

Cassidy glanced at his watch. It was time to thank him and leave. I had one question, however, that I had to get in. "What about his freshman year? Did you have much contact with him?"

"Not really. We pursued different activities. He went out for the drama club and was in a couple of productions. I saw them, and I have to admit he was very good. He wasn't the lead in either play, but he was voted best actor for one of them, so I guess that kept him happy for a while."

Cassidy stood up, and reluctantly I got up, too. "You've been very kind," I started to say, but then he interrupted me.

"You know, I just remembered something. Westerfield obviously loved the limelight and didn't want to lose his moment of glory. He wore a dark blond wig in that play, and, lest we forget how good he'd been, he used to put it on sometimes. Then he'd put on the mannerisms of the character, and I remember he even signed that character's name when he passed notes in class."

I thought of Rob Westerfield showing up at the inn last evening and giving the waitress the impression he was flirting with me. "He's still acting," I said grimly.

I GRABBED A QUICK LUNCH and was back in the car at three-thirty. The snow was continuing to fall, and the trip up to Boston began to seem like a picnic compared to the trek back to Oldham. I kept the cell phone next to me on the front seat so I wouldn't miss the call from the guy who'd been in prison with Westerfield.

He had insisted he needed the money by Friday. By now I had a hunch that his information was going to be valuable, and I was anxious that he not change his mind.

It was eleven-thirty that night when I finally got back to the inn. I was just inside my room when the cell phone rang. It was the call I was expecting, but this time the voice I heard was agitated. "Listen, I think I've been set up. I may not get out of here."

"Where are you?"

"Listen to me. If I give you the name, can I trust you to pay me later?"

"Yes, you can."

"Westerfield must've figured I might be trouble for him. He's had a ton of money since he was born. I've had nothing. If I get out of here and you pay me, I'll at least have some. If I don't, then maybe you can get Westerfield for me on a murder charge."

Now I was convinced he was genuine, that he did have information. "I swear to you I'll pay you. I swear to you I'll nail Westerfield for you."

"Westerfield told me, 'I beat Phil to death, and it felt good.' Got that? *Phil*—that's the name."

The line went dead.

31

ROB WESTERFIELD had been nineteen years old when he murdered Andrea. Within eight months, he had been arrested, indicted, tried, convicted, and sent to prison. Though he had been out on bail prior to his conviction, I could not believe that during those eight months he would have risked killing someone else.

That meant the earlier crime had been committed between twenty-two and twenty-seven years ago. I had to cover those five or six years of his life to try to find a connection between him and a dead man whose first name was Phil.

It seems incredible to think that at thirteen or fourteen, Rob might have committed a murder. Or was it? He'd been only fourteen when he viciously assaulted Christopher Cassidy.

I reasoned that in those years he had been at Arbinger in Massachusetts for a year and a half, then spent six months at Bath Public School in England, two years in Carrington Academy in Maine, and a semester or so in Willow, a nondescript college near Buffalo. The Westerfields have a house in Vail and another in Palm Beach. It seemed to me that Rob must have visited those places. He also may have gone on class trips abroad.

That was a lot of territory to cover. I knew I needed help.

Marcus Longo had been a detective with the Westchester County District Attorney's Office for twenty-five years. If anyone could track down the homicide of a man with only a first name as a clue, my money would be on him.

Fortunately, when I phoned Marcus, I reached him instead of an answering machine. As I suspected, he had flown to Colorado to pick up his wife. "We stayed a few extra days to look at some houses," he explained. "I think we found one."

His tone changed. "I was going to tell you all about the baby, but that can hold. I understand a lot of things have happened since I've been gone."

"I would have to agree with that, Marcus. May I buy you lunch? I need some advice."

"The advice is free. I buy the lunch."

WE MET AT THE DEPOT RESTAURANT in Cold Spring. There, over club sandwiches and coffee, I filled him in on my eventful week.

He stopped me regularly with questions.

"Do you think the fire was set to scare you or actually to kill you?"

"I was more than scared; I wasn't sure I'd get out alive."

"All right. And you say the Oldham police think you set it?"

"Officer White has done everything but cuff me."

"His cousin used to be in the D.A.'s office when I was there. He's a judge now and a member of the same country club as Rob's father. In fairness, he always thought Paulie Stroebel was guilty of Andrea's murder. I bet he's the one who has White riled up about you. That Website is mighty provocative to anyone who's hand-in-glove with the Westerfields."

"Then it's a success."

I looked around to make sure that I could not be overheard. "Marcus—"

"Ellie, do you realize your eyes keep darting around this place? Who or what are you looking for?"

I told him about Rob Westerfield showing up at the inn. "He didn't get there until I'd almost finished dinner," I said. "Someone called him and tipped him off. I'm sure of it."

I knew that next Marcus would either warn me to be careful or ask me to stop putting inflammatory material on the Website. I didn't give him the chance.

"Marcus, I received a call from someone who was in prison with Rob." I told him about the deal I had made to buy information and then about the phone call last night.

He listened quietly, his eyes searching my face.

He heard me out, then asked, "You believe this guy, don't you?"

"Marcus, I knew I might be suckered into losing five thousand dollars. But this is different. This man was in fear of his life. He wanted me to know about Phil because he wanted revenge on Westerfield."

"You say he referred to the sign you were holding up outside the prison?"

"Yes."

"You're assuming he was a convict, so that means he probably was released that day. You were only there once, isn't that right?"

"That's right."

"Ellie, that guy could also be a prison employee who was entering or leaving the prison while you were standing outside. Money buys favors from some guards as well as from other prisoners."

I hadn't thought about that. "I was hoping that you could get a list of the prisoners who were discharged the day after Westerfield. Then you could see if anything happened to any one of them."

"I can do that. Ellie, you realize this also could be some nut playing games."

"I know that, but I don't think so." I opened my pocketbook. "I've made a list of the schools Rob Westerfield attended, both here and in England, and the places where his family has homes. There are databases listing unsolved homicides that took place between twenty-two and twenty-seven years ago, aren't there?"

"Of course."

"Westchester County has one?"

"Yes."

"Can you access it, or get someone else to do it for you?"

"Yes, I can."

"Then it shouldn't be too hard to learn if there's a victim whose name is Phil?"

"No, it shouldn't."

"How about checking an unsolved crimes database in the areas around the schools and homes where Westerfield spent time?"

He looked at the list. "Massachusetts, Maine, Florida, Colorado, New York, England." He whistled. "That's a lot of territory. I'll see what I can do."

"One more thing. Knowing the way Rob Westerfield operates, is there a database for solved crimes that would list Phil as the victim and someone claiming innocence as serving time for it?"

"Ellie, nine out of ten people convicted at trial and behind bars claim somebody else did it. Let's start with unsolved homicides and see where we go."

"Tomorrow I'm going to put Christopher Cassidy's story about Rob on the Website. No one would question Cassidy's integrity, so his account should carry some weight. I never did get up to Carrington Academy. I'll see if I can make an appointment there for Monday or Tuesday."

"Check the student roster for the years Westerfield was there," Marcus said as he signaled for the check.

"I've thought of that. One of the schools might have had a student named Phil who tangled with Westerfield."

"That opens the territory," Marcus warned. "The students in prep school come from all over the country. Westerfield could have followed one of them home to settle a grudge."

" *'I beat Phil to death, and it felt good.'* "

Who were the people who loved Phil? I wondered. Were they still grieving? Of course they were.

The waitress was placing the tab in front of Marcus. I waited until she was gone before I said, "I can call my connection at Arbinger. He's been pretty helpful. When I go to Carrington and Willow College, I'll ask about students from Westerfield's time. Philip isn't that common a name."

"Ellie, you've told me you believe Rob Westerfield was tipped off that you were at dinner the other night?"

"Yes."

"You told me that your informant claimed to be in fear of his life?"

"Yes."

"Ellie, Rob Westerfield is worried your Website could influence his grandmother to leave her money to charity. Now he may be terrified that you could uncover another crime that might send him back to prison. Don't you realize how precarious your situation is?"

"I honestly do, but there's nothing I can do about it."

"Damn it, Ellie, yes you can! Your father was a state trooper. He's retired. You could live in his house. He could be your bodyguard. Trust me, you need one. And something else: If that guy's story is on the level, helping to put Westerfield back in prison would help your father have closure, too. I don't think you understand how tough this has been on him."

"He's been in touch with you?"

"Yes, he has."

"Marcus, you mean well," I said as we stood up, "but I don't think you understand something. My father got his closure when he let us go and never lifted a finger to bring us back. My mother needed and expected him to do that, but he did nothing. Next time he calls, tell him to watch his son play basketball and leave me alone."

Marcus gave me a hug as we separated in the parking lot. "I'll call you as soon as I start getting answers," he promised.

I drove back to the inn. Mrs. Willis was at the desk. "Your brother is waiting for you in the sunroom," she said.

32

HE WAS STANDING in front of the window, looking out, his back to me. He was a good six feet three, taller than I'd realized when I saw him on television. He was wearing khaki pants and sneakers and his school jacket. His hands were in his pockets, and he was jiggling his right foot. I had the impression that he was nervous.

He must have heard my footsteps because he turned around. We looked at each other.

"You'll never be able to deny her," my grandmother used to joke to my mother about Andrea. *"She's growing up to be the image of you."*

If she were here, she'd be saying the same sort of thing to us. In appearance, at least, we could never deny each other.

"Hello, Ellie. I'm your brother, Teddy." He walked to me, holding out his hand.

I ignored it.

"Can't I just talk to you for five minutes?" His voice had not yet fully deepened, but it was well modulated. He looked worried but determined.

I shook my head and turned to leave.

"You're my sister," he said. "You could at least give me five minutes. You might even like me if you knew me."

I turned back to him. "Teddy, you seem like a nice young man, but I'm sure you have better things to do than spend time with me.

I know you've been sent by your father. He just doesn't seem to get the fact that I never want to see or hear from him again."

"He's your father, too. Whether you believe it or not, he never stopped being your father. He didn't send me. He doesn't know I'm here. I came because I wanted to meet you. I've always wanted to meet you."

There was appeal in his voice. "Why don't we have a soda or something?"

I shook my head.

"Please, Ellie."

Maybe it was the way my name fell from his lips, or maybe I just have a hard time being downright rude. This kid hadn't done anything to me.

I heard myself saying, "There's a soda machine in the hall." I started to dig in my purse.

"I've got it. What kind do you want?"

"Plain water."

"Me, too. I'll be right back." His smile was both shy and relieved.

I sat on the brightly patterned wicker love seat, trying to figure out how to send him away. I didn't want to listen to a pitch about what a great father we had and how I should let bygones be bygones.

Maybe he *was* a great father for two of his children, Andrea and you, I thought, but I slipped between the cracks.

Teddy returned carrying the two bottles of water. I could read his mind as he eyed the love seat and the chair. He made the wise decision and chose the chair. I did not want him to sit beside me. Flesh of my flesh, bone of my bone, I thought. No, that has to do with Adam and Eve, not siblings.

Half siblings.

"Ellie, would you come and see me play basketball sometime?"

It wasn't what I expected.

"I mean, couldn't we be friends at least? I always kept hoping you'd come and visit us, but if you won't do that, maybe you and I can just get together sometimes. I read your book last year, about the cases you've worked on. It was great. I'd like to talk to you about them."

"Teddy, I'm awfully busy right now and—"

He interrupted: "I watch your Website every day. The way you write about Westerfield must be driving him crazy. Ellie, you're my sister, and I don't want anything to happen to you."

I wanted to say, "Please don't call me your sister," but the words died on my lips. I settled for "Please don't worry about me. I can take care of myself."

"Can't I help you? This morning I read in the paper about what happened to your car. Suppose somebody loosens a wheel or a brake in the one you're driving now? I'm good with cars. I could check yours out for you before you go anywhere, or I could even drive you around in mine."

He was so earnest and so concerned that I had to smile. "Teddy, you have school and, I'm sure, plenty of basketball practice. And now I honestly have to get to work"

He stood up with me. "We look a lot alike," he said.

"I know we do."

"I'm glad. Ellie, I'm getting out of your way now, but I'm coming back."

Would to God your father had had the same persistence, I thought. Then I realized that if he had, this boy would never have been born.

I WORKED FOR A COUPLE of hours, refining the way I would present Christopher Cassidy's story for the Website. When I thought I had it right, I e-mailed it to his office for his approval.

At four o'clock Marcus Longo called. "Ellie, the Westerfields have taken a page out of your book. They have a Website: comjus-rob.com."

"Let me guess what it stands for: 'Committee for Justice for Rob.'"

"You have it. I understand they've taken out ads in all the Westchester papers to advertise it. Basically the strategy is to present touching stories of people who were wrongly convicted of crimes."

"Thereby linking them to Rob Westerfield, the most innocent of them all."

"You've got it. But they've also been doing some digging about you, and they've come up with some unfortunate stuff."

"Meaning what?"

"The Fromme Center, a psychiatric facility."

"I did an undercover story on it. It was a rip-off joint. Paid a fortune by the state of Georgia, and not one legitimate psychiatrist or psychologist on staff."

"Were you a patient there?"

"Marcus, are you crazy? Of course I wasn't."

"Was there a photograph taken of you in the Fromme Center in which you were lying on a bed with your arms and legs in restraints?"

"Yes, there was, and it was taken to illustrate what had been going on there. After the state closed Fromme and moved the patients to other facilities, we did a follow-up story on the way they had kept people shackled for days at a time. Why?"

"It's on the Westerfields' Website."

"Without explanation?"

"Insinuating that you were forcibly held there." He paused. "Ellie, are you *surprised* that these people play dirty?"

"I'd be surprised if they *didn't*, frankly. I'll put the full article, including picture and text, on my Website. I'll do it under a new heading: 'Latest Westerfield Lie.' But I do understand that a lot of people who see his Website may not see mine."

"And the other way around. That's my next concern. Ellie, are you planning to put anything on the Website about the other possible homicide?"

"I'm not sure. On the one hand, someone who sees it might come forward with information about a murder victim. On the other hand, it might tip off Rob Westerfield and in some way help him cover his tracks."

"Or get rid of someone who could give damaging testimony against him. You've got to be very careful."

"That may already have happened."

"Exactly. Let me know what you decide."

I WENT ONLINE and found the new Website of "The Committee for Justice for Robson Westerfield."

It had been handsomely designed with a quotation from Voltaire under the heading: *It is better to risk saving a guilty person than to condemn an innocent one.*

The picture of a grave and contemplative Rob Westerfield was directly below the quote. It was followed by stories of people who genuinely had been imprisoned for someone else's crime. The stories were well written and pulled on heartstrings. It didn't take a great leap to figure that Jake Bern had been the author.

The personal section on the Website made the Westerfields sound like American royalty. There were pictures of Rob as a baby with his grandfather, the United States senator, and at age nine or ten with his grandmother, helping her cut the ribbon on a new Westerfield children's center. There were shots of him with his parents boarding the *Queen Elizabeth II* and dressed in tennis whites at The Everglades Club.

I guess the idea was to convey that it was beneath the dignity of this privileged young man to take a human life.

I was the star of the next page of the Website. It showed me spread out on the bed in the Fromme psychiatric center, my legs and arms shackled, wearing one of the pitifully inadequate night-shirts that were mandatory for the patients. I was only partially covered by a thin rag of a blanket.

The caption was "The witness whose testimony convicted Robson Westerfield."

I clicked off. I have a mannerism I had picked up from my father. When he was absolutely furious about something, he had a way of biting the right corner of his lip.

I was doing exactly that.

I sat for half an hour trying to calm down as I reviewed the pros and cons, and tried to figure out how to handle publicizing Westerfield's alleged confession of another murder.

Marcus Longo had talked about a territorial problem in trying to track down an unsolved homicide Rob Westerfield may have committed.

The Website was international.

Would I be exposing anyone to risk by putting the name of the supposed victim out there?

But my unidentified caller was already at risk, and he knew it.

In the end I composed a simple entry.

"Somewhere between twenty-two and twenty-seven years ago, it is alleged, Rob Westerfield committed another crime. He is directly quoted as saying when he was high on drugs in prison, *'I beat Phil to death, and it felt good.'*

"Anyone with information about this crime, please e-mail me at ellie1234@mediaone.net. Confidentiality and reward."

I looked it over. Rob Westerfield will certainly read it, I thought. But suppose he knows there is someone besides my unknown caller who has information that could hurt him?

There are two things an investigative reporter does not do: reveal sources and place innocent people in danger.

I put the entry on hold.

33

ON FRIDAY EVENING I broke down and phoned Pete Lawlor.

"Your call is being forwarded to an answering service . . ."

"This is your former coworker who has enough interest in your well-being to inquire as to your state of mind, job opportunities, and health," I said. "A response will be appreciated."

He called back half an hour later. "You must be hard up for someone to talk to."

"I am. That's why you came to mind."

"Thanks."

"May I ask where you are now."

"In Atlanta. Packing up."

"I gather a decision has been made."

"Yes. A dream job. Based in New York, but with a fair amount of traveling. Reporting from hot spots all over the globe."

"Which newspaper?"

"Negative. I'm going to be a television star."

"Did you have to lose ten pounds before they hired you?"

"I don't remember you as being cruel."

I laughed. Talking to Pete had a way of bringing a dash of amusing, everyday reality into my increasingly surreal life. "Are you joking, or do you really have a job in television?"

"It's for real. It's with Packard Cable."

"Packard. That's great."

"It's one of the newer cable networks, but growing fast. I was about to take the L.A. job even though it wasn't exactly what I wanted, but then they came to me."

"When do you start?"

"Wednesday. I'm in the process of subletting the apartment and putting stuff together to load in the car. I start driving up Sunday afternoon. Dinner Tuesday?"

"Sure. It's good to hear that melodious voice of yours. . . ."

"Don't hang up. Ellie, I've been watching your Website."

"Pretty good, isn't it?"

"If this guy is what you say he is, you're playing with fire."

I already have, I thought. "Promise you won't tell me to be careful."

"I promise. Talk to you Monday afternoon."

I WENT BACK to the computer. It was nearly eight o'clock, and I'd been working steadily. I ordered room service, and while I was waiting, I did a few stretches and a lot of thinking.

Talking to Pete had, at least for the moment, removed my tunnel vision. For the last couple of weeks I had existed in a world in which Rob Westerfield was the central figure. Now, for just a moment, I was looking past that time, past his second trial, past my ability to prove to the world the depth of his violent nature.

I could dig up and publicize every nasty, rotten thing he'd ever done. Perhaps I could track down an unsolved murder he had committed. I could tell his sorry, dirty story in the book. Then it would be time for me to begin the rest of my life.

Pete was already beginning his—a new base in New York, a new job in a different media.

I locked my hands behind my head and began to twist from side to side. My neck muscles were tight, and it felt good to try to stretch them. What was not so good was the dismaying realization that I missed Pete Lawlor terribly and would not want to return to Atlanta unless he was there.

I SPOKE TO MRS. STROEBEL on Saturday morning. She told me that Paulie was no longer in intensive care and probably would be discharged after the weekend.

I promised to drop by later for a visit, at about three o'clock. When I arrived, Mrs. Stroebel was sitting by Paulie's bed. As soon as she looked up at me, I could see from the concern on her face that there was a problem.

"He developed a high fever around lunchtime. There is an infection in one of his arms. The doctor tells me it will be all right, but I worry. Ellie, I worry so."

I looked down at Paulie. His arms were still heavily bandaged, and he had several IVs dripping from overhead pulleys. He was very pale and kept turning his head from side to side.

"They are giving him an antibiotic plus something to calm him down," Mrs. Stroebel said. "The fever makes him restless."

I pulled up a chair and sat beside her.

Paulie began to mumble. His eyes flickered open.

"I am here, Paulie," Mrs. Stroebel said soothingly. "Ellie Cavanaugh is here with me. She came to pay a visit."

"Hi, Paulie." I stood up and leaned over the bed so that he could see me.

His eyes were glazed with fever, but he tried to smile. "Ellie, my friend."

"You bet I am."

His eyes closed again. A moment later he began to mutter incoherently. I heard him whisper Andrea's name.

Mrs. Stroebel clasped and unclasped her hands. "That's all he talks about. It preys on his mind so much. He is so afraid they will make him go back to court. No one understands how much they frightened him last time."

Her voice was rising, and I could see that Paulie was becoming agitated. I squeezed her hand and nodded at the bed. She understood what I meant.

"Of course, Ellie, thanks to you, everything will be fine," she said brightly. "Paulie knows that. People come into the store and tell me that they look at your Website where you show what a bad person Rob Westerfield is. Paulie and I looked at the Website last week. It made us very happy."

Paulie seemed to calm down a little, then he whispered, "But, Mama . . . suppose I forget and . . ."

Mrs. Stroebel seemed suddenly flustered. "No more talk, Paulie," she said abruptly. "Go to sleep. You must get better."

"Mama—"

"Paulie, you must be quiet now." She laid a gentle but resolute hand on his lips.

I had the distinct feeling that Mrs. Stroebel was uneasy and wanted me to leave, so I got up to go.

"Mama . . ."

Mrs. Stroebel sprang up with me, blocking access to the bed, as though she were afraid that I would get too close to Paulie.

I couldn't imagine what was upsetting her. "Tell Paulie good-bye for me, Mrs. Stroebel," I said hurriedly. "I'll call you tomorrow to see how he's doing."

Paulie was beginning to talk again, tossing restlessly and mumbling incoherently.

"Thank you, Ellie. Good-bye." Mrs. Stroebel began propelling me to the door.

"Andrea . . ." Paulie shouted, *"don't go out with him!"*

I spun around.

Paulie's voice was still clear, but now his tone was frightened and pleading. "Mama, suppose I forget and tell them about the locket she was wearing? I'll *try* not to tell, but if I forget, you won't let them put me in prison, will you?"

34

"THERE IS AN EXPLANATION. You must believe me. It is not what you think," Mrs. Stroebel sobbed to me as we stood in the corridor outside Paulie's room.

"We have to talk, and you have to be absolutely honest with me," I said. We couldn't do it then, though—Paulie's doctor was coming down the hall.

"Ellie, I will call you tomorrow morning," she promised. "I am too upset now." Shaking her head as she turned away, Mrs. Stroebel struggled to regain her composure.

I drove back to the inn on automatic pilot. Was it possible, was it *remotely* possible, that all this time I had been wrong? Had Rob Westerfield—and, indeed, his whole family—been victimized by a terrible miscarriage of justice?

He twisted my arm. . . . He came up behind me and punched me in the neck. . . . He said, "I beat Phil to death, and it felt good."

Paulie's response to the verbal attack of Mrs. Westerfield's housekeeper had been to hurt himself, not someone else.

I could not believe that Paulie had been Andrea's murderer, but I was sure that years ago Mrs. Stroebel had kept him from telling something he knew.

The locket.

As I drove into the parking lot of the inn, I was overwhelmed with a crushing sense of the irony of what was happening. No one, absolutely no one believed that Rob Westerfield had given Andrea a locket and that she had been wearing it the night she died.

But now the existence of the locket had been validated by the one person who would be terrified to publicly admit any knowledge of it.

I looked around as I got out of the car. It was a quarter past four, and the shadows were already long and slanting. What was left of the sun was passing in and out of clouds, and a light wind was blowing the remaining leaves from the trees. They made a rustling sound along the driveway, and in my edgy frame of mind they sounded to me like footsteps.

The parking lot was almost full, and then I remembered that I'd noticed preparations for a wedding reception when I left this afternoon. To find a space I had to drive around the bend to the farthest section of the parking area, putting me out of sight of the inn. It was getting to be a chronic state of mind, the feeling that someone might be hanging around, watching me.

I didn't run, but I moved quickly as I made my way through a row of parked cars toward the safety of the inn. As I passed an old van, the door suddenly slid open, and a man jumped out and tried to grab my arm.

I began to run and got about ten feet but then tripped on one of the extra-large moccasins I'd bought to accommodate my bandaged feet.

As one of the shoes flew off, I felt myself falling forward and frantically tried to regain my balance, but it was too late. My palms and body caught the worst of the fall, and literally every ounce of breath was knocked out of me.

The man was immediately down on one knee beside me. "Don't scream," he said urgently. "I'm not going to hurt you; *please don't scream!*"

I couldn't have screamed. Nor could I have gotten away from him and run to the inn. My entire body was shaking in reaction to the severe impact with the hard surface of the ground. My mouth open, I gulped air in great shuddering gasps.

"What . . . do . . . you . . . want?" At last I was able to get out those few words.

"To talk to you. I was gonna e-mail you, but I didn't know who else might see it. I want to sell you some information about Rob Westerfield."

I looked up at him. His face was very close to mine. He was a man somewhere in his early forties, with thin, not particularly clean hair. He had a nervous way of sliding his eyes around like someone who expects to have to make a run for it at any moment. He was wearing a visibly worn lumber jacket and jeans.

As I began to struggle to my feet, he retrieved my moccasin and handed it to me. "I'm not going to hurt you," he repeated. "It's risky for me to be seen with you. Hear me out. If you're not interested in what I have to say, I'm out of here."

It wasn't rational perhaps, but for some reason I believed him. If he had wanted to kill me, he'd already had all the chance he needed.

"Are you willing to listen?" he asked impatiently.

"Go ahead."

"Would you sit in my van for a couple of minutes? I don't want no one to see me. The Westerfields' people are all over this town."

I could vouch for that, but I wasn't about to get in his van. "Say what you have to say out here."

"I have something that maybe might stick Westerfield with a crime he committed years ago."

"How much do you want?"

"A thousand bucks."

"What have you got?"

"You know that Westerfield's grandmother was shot and left for dead about twenty-five years ago? You wrote about it on your Website."

"Yes, I did."

"My brother, Skip, he went to prison for that job. He got twenty years. He died after he'd served half his time. Couldn't take it. He was always kind of sickly."

"Your brother was the one who shot Mrs. Westerfield and burglarized her home?"

"Yeah, but Westerfield planned it, see, and hired Skip and me to do the job."

"Why did he do it?"

"Westerfield was heavy into drugs. That's why he dropped out of college. He owed people big time. He'd seen his grandmother's will. She'd left one hundred thousand dollars directly to him. The minute she croaked, it would be in his pocket. He promised us ten thousand dollars to do the job."

"Was he *with* you that night?"

"Are you kidding? He was in New York at a dinner with his mother and father. He knew how to cover his bases."

"Did he pay your brother or you?"

"Before the job he gave my brother his Rolex as security. Then he reported it stolen."

"Why?"

"To cover his tracks after my brother was arrested. Westerfield claimed he met us in a bowling alley the night before the old lady was hit. He said Skip kept eyeing his watch, so he put it in his bag when he started bowling. He told the cops that, when he went to get his watch out of the bag later, it wasn't there and we weren't around. He swore that was the only time he ever saw Skip or me."

"How could you have known about his grandmother without him telling you?"

"There'd been a big write-up about her in the paper. She gave a wing to a hospital or something."

"How did your brother and you get caught?"

"I didn't. My brother was picked up the next day. He had a record and was nervous about having to shoot the old lady. That was the reason he was there, but Westerfield wanted it to look like a burglary. Rob didn't give us the combination of the safe because only the family knew it, and that would have given him away. He told Skip to bring a chisel and knife and scratch up the safe like he tried to force it open and couldn't. But Skip cut his hand and took off his glove to wipe it. He must have touched the safe because they found his fingerprint on it."

"Then he went upstairs and shot Mrs. Westerfield."

"Yeah. But nobody could prove I was there. I was the lookout and drove the car. Skip told me to keep my mouth shut. He took the rap, and Westerfield got off scot-free."

"So did you."

He shrugged. "Yeah, I know it."

"How old were you?"

"Sixteen."

"How old was Westerfield?"

"Seventeen."

"Didn't your brother try to implicate Westerfield?"

"Sure. Nobody believed him."

"I'm not certain about that. His grandmother changed her will. That hundred-thousand-dollar direct grant was taken out of it."

"Good. They let Skip plead to attempted murder with a twenty-year sentence. He could have gotten thirty but he was willing to plead to a max of twenty. The D.A. agreed to the deal so that the old lady wouldn't have to testify at a trial."

The last of the sun had gone totally behind the clouds. I still felt shaken from the fall, and now I was cold, too.

"What's your name?" I asked.

"Alfie. Alfie Leeds."

"Alfie, I believe you," I said. "But I don't know why you're telling me this now. There's never been a shred of evidence to prove that Rob Westerfield was in on that crime."

"I have proof he was involved."

Alfie reached into his pocket and pulled out a folded sheet of paper. "This is a copy of the diagram Rob Westerfield gave us so that my brother could get into the house without setting off the alarm."

From another pocket he took out a pencil flashlight.

Standing out in the windy parking lot was no place to study a diagram. I looked at the guy again. He was an inch shorter than I am, and he didn't look particularly strong. I decided to take a chance. "I'll get in the van, but only if I sit in the driver's seat," I told him.

"Have it your way."

I opened the driver's door and looked around. There was no one else there. The backseat had been flattened down and contained what looked like paint cans, a drop cloth, and a ladder. He had gone around to the passenger side. I slid in behind the wheel but did not fully close the door. I knew that if this was a setup, I still could get out pretty fast.

In my job as an investigative reporter I've had to meet a number of unsavory characters in places I wouldn't have chosen to visit otherwise. As a result, my sense of self-preservation has become well developed. I decided that allowing for the fact that I was cloistered with a man who'd been part of a murder plot, I was as safe as I could get.

When we were both inside the van, he handed me the paper. The thin beam of the flashlight was enough to enable me to recognize the Westerfield house and driveway. The garage-hideout was even depicted. Below the buildings there was a precise layout of the interior of the mansion.

"See, it shows where the alarm is and gives the code to disarm it. Rob wasn't worried that disarming the alarm would draw attention to himself because a lot of handymen and other employees knew the code too. There's the layout of the ground floor, the library with the safe, the stairs to the old lady's bedroom, and the section off the kitchen that was the maid's apartment."

There was a name printed on the bottom of the page. "Who's Jim?" I asked.

"The guy who drew this. Westerfield told Skip and me that he did some work on the house. We never met him."

"Did your brother ever show this to the police?"

"He wanted to use it, but the lawyer they gave him said forget it. He said Skip had no proof Westerfield gave it to him, and the fact that he even had it just made Skip look bad. He said being that the safe was downstairs and the way the old lady's bedroom is so clearly marked only helped prove that Skip was planning to kill her."

"Jim could have corroborated your brother's story. Did anyone try to find him?"

"I guess not. I've kept the map all these years, and when I saw your Website, I figured this is one more thing you might investigate and hang on Westerfield. Have we got a deal? Will you give me a thousand bucks for it?"

"How can I be sure that this isn't something you drew up yourself to get money from me?"

"You can't. Give it back."

"Alfie, if the lawyer had looked into this guy, Jim, and had told the D.A. about him and had shown the D.A. the sketch, they would have had to investigate the information seriously. Your brother might have gotten a better sentence in exchange for his cooperation, and Westerfield might have paid for his crime too."

"Yeah, but there was another problem. Westerfield hired both my brother and me to do the job. The lawyer told my brother that if the cops would end up arresting Westerfield, he could make his own deal and tell the D.A. that I was involved. Skip was five years older than me and felt guilty about getting me into it."

"Well, the statute of limitations has run out for both you and Rob. But wait a minute. You say this is a copy of the original. Where is the original?"

"The lawyer tore it up. He said he didn't want it to fall in the wrong hands."

"He tore it up!"

"He didn't know Skip had made a copy and given it to me."

"I want this," I said. "I'll have the cash for you in the morning."

We shook hands. His skin felt somewhat grimy, but it was also calloused, which said to me that Alfie did hard, heavy work.

As he carefully folded the paper into neat squares and put it in his inside pocket, I couldn't help saying, "With this kind of evidence I just can't understand why your brother's lawyer didn't try to make a deal with the district attorney. It wouldn't have been hard to follow up on an employee named Jim who drew this diagram. The cops could have squeezed him to give up Rob, and you would have been tried in Juvenile Court. I wonder if your brother's lawyer sold out to the Westerfields."

He smiled, baring stained teeth. "He's working for them now. He's that Hamilton guy, the one who's all over television saying he's going to get a new trial and acquittal for Rob."

35

WHEN I GOT BACK to the room, there was a message to call Mrs. Hilmer. I'd spoken to her several times since the fire, and she'd been simply wonderful to me. Her whole concern was about my being okay and she was distressed over my almost being trapped in the fire. You would have thought I'd done her a favor by being the reason the garage and apartment had been reduced to rubble. I agreed to have Sunday dinner with her.

I'd barely hung up when Joan called. I'd also been speaking to her, but we hadn't seen each other during the week and I was anxious to return the money and clothes I'd borrowed. I'd had the slacks, sweater, and jacket cleaned and the lingerie laundered, and I bought a bottle of champagne for Joan and Leo and another for the friend who was my size.

Of course that was not Joan's reason for calling. She and Leo and the kids were going out for dinner to Il Palazzo and wanted me to join them.

"Great pasta, great pizza, a fun place," she promised. "I really think you'd enjoy it."

"You don't have to sell me. I'd love to go."

In fact, I needed to get out. After my parking lot encounter with Alfie, the paramount thought in my mind was of all the people whose lives had been altered or destroyed by Rob Westerfield and by the Westerfield fortune.

Andrea, first of course. Then Mother. Then Paulie, who was so afraid he'd be tricked into revealing he knew something about the locket. Whatever his knowledge of the locket turned out to be, I would stake my life that it did not tie him to Andrea's death.

Mrs. Stroebel, hardworking and honest, also had been caught in the Westerfield web of misery. It must have been agony for her when Paulie was on the witness stand during the trial. Suppose just one person had believed me when I said that Rob had given Andrea a locket, and then Paulie had been asked about it in court. He easily could have incriminated himself.

I believed everything that Alfie Leeds had told me. I had no doubt that his brother had been a potential killer. He was willing to take Mrs. Westerfield's life and had left her for dead. Bad as he was, though, he was entitled to a lawyer who truly represented him. The lawyer he was assigned sold him out to the Westerfields.

I could visualize William Hamilton, *Juris Doctor,* seeing that case as his chance to break into the big time. He probably went to Rob's father, showed him the diagram, and was properly rewarded for his cooperation.

Alfie was a victim, too. He'd been protected by his big brother and no doubt was left feeling guilty that he couldn't find a way to nail Rob Westerfield. And then he spent all those years sitting on evidence that he was afraid to show anyone.

The hardest to swallow for me, of course, was the knowledge that if Rob Westerfield had been convicted of planning the attempted murder of his grandmother, he would never have met Andrea.

Now I had another person on my list of people I wanted to nail to the wall: William Hamilton, Esquire.

Anyhow, those were the sad and furious thoughts that were running through my head when Joan called. I definitely needed a break. We agreed to meet at seven o'clock at Il Palazzo.

Tilting at windmills, I told myself as I drove the short distance into the heart of town. I had the feeling that I was being followed. Maybe I should call Officer White, I thought sarcastically. He's terribly worried about me. He'll be here right away, sirens blazing.

Oh, give him a break, I snapped at myself. He's honestly convinced that I'm back in this town to make trouble and that I'm obsessed because Rob Westerfield is a free man.

Okay, Officer White, I'm obsessive on that score, but I didn't burn my feet or ruin my car to prove my point.

JOAN AND LEO and their three boys were seated at a corner table when I got to Il Palazzo. I vaguely remembered Leo. He had been a senior at Oldham High when Joan and Andrea were sophomores.

It's inevitable that when people from those days see me for the first time, the first thing they think about is Andrea's death. Then they invariably either comment on it or make an obvious effort to ignore it.

I liked the way Leo handled his greeting to me. He said, "I remember you, of course, Ellie. You were over at Joan's house with Andrea a couple of times when I stopped by. You were a solemn little kid."

"And now I'm a solemn *big* kid," I told him.

I liked him immediately. He was about six feet tall, solidly built, with light brown hair and intelligent dark eyes. His smile was like Joan's, warm and all-embracing. He conveyed the immediate feeling of trustworthiness. I knew he was a stockbroker, so I made a mental note to talk to him if I ever had any money. I was sure I'd be comfortable taking his advice on where to invest it.

The boys' ages were ten, fourteen, and seventeen. The oldest, Billy, was a senior in high school and almost immediately told me his team had played basketball against Teddy's team.

"Teddy and I talked about the colleges we're applying to, Ellie," he said. "We're both trying for Dartmouth and Brown. I hope we end up at the same one. He's a nice guy."

"Yes, he is," I agreed.

"You didn't tell me you'd met him," Joan said quickly.

"He stopped in to see me at the inn for a few minutes."

There was a satisfied look in her eye. I wanted to tell her not to set aside any dates for a grand reunion of the Cavanaughs, but then the menus arrived and Leo was smart enough to change the subject.

I did a fair amount of babysitting in my teenage years, and I like being around kids. My job in Atlanta certainly didn't expose me to many of them, so it had been a while. It was a treat to be with these three boys. Pretty soon, over mussels and pasta, they were talking to me about their activities, and I promised Sean, the ten-year-old, that I'd play chess with him.

"I'm good," I warned him.

"I'm better," he assured me.

"We'll see about that."

"How about tomorrow? It's Sunday. We'll be home."

"Oh, sorry, but tomorrow I have plans. Soon, though." Then I remembered something and looked at Joan. "I didn't put the suitcase I wanted to return to you in the car."

"Bring it tomorrow, and we'll have a game of chess," Sean suggested.

"You have to eat," Joan said. "Brunch about eleven-thirty?"

"Sounds great," I told her.

The bar at Il Palazzo was a glass-paneled section of the dining room, directly off the entrance hall. When I arrived, I hadn't paid attention to anyone in the bar. But I had noticed that during dinner Joan sometimes glanced past me, her expression troubled.

We were sipping coffee when I learned the reason for her concern.

"Ellie, Will Nebels has been at the bar since before you got here. Someone must have pointed you out to him. He's on his way over, and from the look of him, I'd say he's drunk."

The warning wasn't fast enough. I felt arms around my neck, a sloppy kiss on my cheek. "Little Ellie, my goodness, little Ellie Cavanaugh. Do you remember how I fixed your seesaw for you, honey? Your daddy was never any good at fixing stuff. Your mama used to call me all the time. 'Will, this needs to be done. Will—' "

He was kissing my ear and the back of my neck.

"Get your hands off her," Leo said, his voice clipped. He was on his feet.

I was literally pinned down. Nebels's full weight was on me now. His arms were resting on my shoulders; his hands were sliding down, groping inside my sweater.

"And pretty little Andrea. With my own eyes I seen that retard go in that garage carrying that tire jack. . . ."

A waiter was pulling at him from one side, Leo and Billy from the other. I kept trying to push his face away, but to no avail. He was kissing my eyes. Then his moist, beery mouth was pressing against my lips. My chair started to tilt back as we struggled. I was terrified that I was going to slam the back of my head against the floor and end up with him sprawled over me.

But men from nearby tables came rushing over, and strong hands caught the teetering chair before it reached the floor.

Then Nebels was forcibly dragged away and the chair lifted up. I dropped my face into my hands. For the second time in six hours I was trembling so violently that I could not respond to the concerned inquiries coming from all sides of me. The couple of pins that anchored my hair had pulled loose, and it was spilling around my shoulders. I felt Joan stroking it, and wanted to beg her to stop—compassion at that moment would undo me. Maybe she sensed my feeling because she withdrew her hand.

I could hear the manager sputtering apologies. You *ought* to apologize, I thought. You should have stopped serving that drunk long ago.

That flash of anger was all I needed to get me back on course. I raised my head and began to smooth back my hair. Then I glanced around the table at the concerned faces, and shrugged. "I'm okay," I told them.

I looked at Joan and knew what she was thinking. She might as well have been shouting it.

"Ellie, now do you understand what I said about Will Nebels? He's admitted he was in Mrs. Westerfield's house that night. He was probably drunk. What do you think he would have done if he saw Andrea go into that garage alone?"

A HALF HOUR LATER, after a fresh cup of coffee, I absolutely insisted on driving myself home. But on the way I wondered if I had been foolish. I was now positive that I was being followed and was not about to risk being alone again in that parking lot. I therefore did not turn off at the inn but drove past it and called the police on my cell phone.

"We'll send a car," the cop at the desk told me. "Where are you?"

I told him.

"All right. Circle back and turn into the driveway of the inn. We'll be right behind whoever is tailing you. Under no circumstances get out of the car until we come for you."

I drove slowly, and the car behind me slowed down as well. Now that I knew a squad car was coming, I was glad the car on my tail was still there. I wanted the police to find out who was in that car and why I was being followed.

I was approaching the inn again. I turned into the driveway, but the car behind me kept going. A moment later I saw a domelight flashing and heard the wail of the police siren.

I pulled over to the side of the driveway and stopped. Two minutes later the squad car, its light no longer flashing, drove up behind me. A cop got out and came up to the driver's door of my car. As I rolled down the window, I could see that he was smiling.

"You *were* being followed, Ms. Cavanaugh. The kid says he's your brother and was making sure you got back here safely."

"Oh, for goodness sake, tell him to go home!" I said. Then I added, "But thank him for me, please."

36

I'D PLANNED TO CALL Marcus Longo on Sunday morning, but he beat me to it. When the phone rang at nine o'clock, I was at the computer, with my second cup of coffee on the table beside it.

"I have you pegged as an early starter, Ellie," he said. "I hope I'm right."

"As a matter of fact, I slept late this morning," I said. "Seven o'clock."

"That's about what I would have expected of you. I've been in touch with the office at Sing Sing."

"To see if they learned of any recently discharged convict or prison guard who might have had a fatal accident?"

"That's right."

"You've heard something?"

"Ellie you were outside Sing Sing on November first. Herb Coril, a convict who at one time was in the same cell block as Rob Westerfield, was discharged that morning. He was staying at a halfway house in lower Manhattan. He hasn't been seen since early Friday evening."

"I got that last call on Friday night about ten-thirty," I said. "Whoever called me was afraid for his life."

"We can't be sure it's the same person, and we can't be sure that Coril didn't just break the conditions of his release and take off."

"What's your guess?" I asked.

"I've never been strong on coincidences, especially one like this."

"Neither am I."

I told Marcus about my meeting with Alfie.

"I only hope nothing happens to Alfie before you get that diagram," Marcus said grimly. "I'm not surprised to hear this. We all thought that Rob Westerfield planned that job. I know what that must be doing to you."

"You mean the fact that Rob might have been in prison and therefore not around here to meet Andrea? That's all I've been thinking about, and it's been torturing me."

"You do understand that even with the copy of the diagram and Alfie making a statement to the D.A., you'll never get a conviction. Alfie was involved himself, and the diagram is signed by someone named Jim whom nobody has ever met."

"I know."

"The statute of limitations on that crime has run out for all of them—Westerfield, Alfie, and Jim, whoever that is."

"Don't forget Hamilton. If I could prove that he destroyed evidence that might have gotten his client a lighter sentence by implicating Westerfield, the ethics committee would be all over him."

I promised to let Marcus see the diagram that Alfie was bringing me. Then I said good-bye and tried to get back to work. It was slow, though, and after getting only a little more done, I realized it was time to drive to Joan's for brunch.

This time I remembered the suitcase and the plastic cleaner's bag with the slacks, sweater, and jacket.

Even before I was near the Franciscan Friars monastery at Graymoor, I knew that I was going to stop there. All week a memory had been slowly emerging from my subconscious. I had visited the place with Mother after Andrea died. She had called Father Emil, a priest she knew. He was going to be at Saint Christopher's Inn that day, and they arranged to meet there.

Saint Christopher's Inn, on the grounds of the monastery, is the friars' home for destitute men who are alcoholics or drug addicts. I had a vague memory of sitting with a lady, a secretary probably, while Mother was in the office. Then Father Emil took us into the chapel.

I remembered that there was a book on the side of the chapel where people could write petitions. Mother wrote something and then gave the pen to me.

I wanted to go there again.

The friar who admitted me introduced himself as Fr. Bob. He didn't question my request. The chapel was empty, and he stood at the door as I knelt for a few minutes. Then I looked around and saw the stand with the ledger-sized book.

I went over to it and picked up the pen.

Suddenly I remembered what I had written that last time: *Please let Andrea come back to us.*

This time I could not force myself to stop crying.

"There have been many tears shed in this chapel." Fr. Bob was standing beside me.

We talked for an hour. When I got to Joan's, I was on speaking terms with God again.

JOAN AND I respectfully disagreed with each other about Will Nebels's performance the night before.

"Ellie, he was just plain drunk. How many people shoot off at the mouth when they've had too much to drink? My point is that's not when they lie—it's when they're more likely to let slip the truth."

I had to admit that Joan was right on that point. I'd investigated and written about two cases in which the killer would never have been caught if he hadn't loaded up on scotch or vodka and poured his heart out to someone who immediately called the cops.

"That's not the way I see it, though," I explained to her and Leo. "To me, Will Nebels is a spineless, gutless loser. Think of him as the stuff you pour into a gelatin mold. You plan the shape you want, and then, you have it. He wasn't too drunk to remember that he once fixed my seesaw and that my father wasn't born with a tool in his hand."

"I agree with Ellie," Leo said. "Nebels is more complex than he appears to be on the surface." Then he added, "That, of course, doesn't mean that Joan isn't right. If Nebels did see Paulie Stroebel go into that garage that night, he got smart enough to figure that the statute of limitations had run out and that it was safe for him to make a buck out of it."

"Only he didn't figure this one out himself," I said. "They came to him. He agreed to tell the story they needed, and they paid him to tell it."

I pushed my chair back. "Brunch was wonderful," I said, "and now I feel like winning a chess game from Sean."

For a moment I paused to look out the window. It was the second beautiful Sunday afternoon I'd been in this room at this exact same time. I was aware again of the spectacular view of the river and the mountain from this spot.

In my world, which was so far from peaceful, to experience that view was like being at an oasis.

I won the first chess game. Sean won the second. We agreed to a rematch "really soon."

BEFORE I STARTED HOME I phoned the hospital and spoke to Mrs. Stroebel. Paulie's fever had broken, and he was feeling much better. "He wants to talk to you, Ellie."

Forty minutes later I was at his bedside. "You look a lot better than you did yesterday," I told him.

He was still very pale, but his eyes were clear and he was propped up with an extra pillow. He smiled shyly. "Ellie, Mama said you know that I saw the locket, too."

"When did you see it, Paulie?"

"I worked at the service station. My first job there was just to wash and clean the cars after they were fixed. When I cleaned Rob's car one day, I found the locket stuck in the front seat. The chain was broken."

"You mean the day Andrea's body was found?" But that doesn't make sense, I thought. If Rob went back for the locket that morning, he never would have left it in his car. Or could he really have been that stupid?

Paulie looked at his mother. "Mama?" he appealed.

"It's all right, Paulie," she said soothingly. "You've had a lot of medicine, and it's hard to keep track of everything. You told me you saw the locket twice."

I looked sharply at Mrs. Stroebel, trying to decide if she was prompting him. But Paulie nodded.

"That's right, Mama. I found it in the car. The chain was broken. I gave it to Rob, and he gave me a ten-dollar tip. I put it with the money I was saving for your fiftieth birthday present."

"I remember, Paulie."

"When was your fiftieth birthday, Mrs. Stroebel?" I asked.

"It was May first, the May before Andrea died."

"The May before Andrea died!" I was absolutely shocked. Then he *didn't* buy the locket for her, I thought. It was one that some girl may have lost in the car, and he had it initialed and gave it to Andrea.

"Paulie, do you remember the locket clearly?" I asked.

"Yes. It was nice. It was shaped like a heart and it was gold and it had little blue stones in it."

That was exactly the way I had described it on the witness stand.

"Paulie, did you ever see the locket again?" I asked.

"Yes. Andrea was so nice to me. She came up and told me how good I was at football and that I'd won the game for the team. That was when I decided to ask her to go to the mixer with me.

"I walked over to your house, and I saw her going through the woods. I caught up with her outside Mrs. Westerfield's house. She was wearing the locket, and I knew Rob must have given it to her. He's not nice. He gave me that big tip, but he's not nice. His car always had dents in it because he drove so fast."

"Did you see him that day?"

"I asked Andrea if I could talk to her, but she said not then, that she was in a hurry. I went back into the woods and watched her go into the garage. A few minutes later, Rob Westerfield went in."

"Tell Ellie when that was, Paulie."

"It was one week before Andrea died in that garage."

One week before.

"Then a couple of days before she died, I talked to her again. I told her Rob was a very bad person and that she shouldn't meet him in the garage and that I knew her father would be very angry if he knew she went there with him."

Paulie looked directly at me. "Your father was always so nice to me, Ellie. He always gave me a tip for filling the gas tank, and he always talked to me about football. He was very nice."

"When you warned Andrea about Rob, was that the time you asked her to go to the mixer with you?"

"Yes, and she said she would, and she made me promise not to tell her father about Rob."

"And you never saw the locket again?"

"No, Ellie."

"And you never went to the garage again?"

"No, Ellie."

Paulie closed his eyes, and I could see that he was becoming very tired. I covered his hand with mine.

"Paulie, I don't want you to worry anymore. I promise you that it's going to be all right, and before I'm finished, everyone will know how nice and kind and good you are. And you're smart, too. When you were a kid, you could see how rotten Rob Westerfield was. A lot of people around here still can't see through him."

"Paulie thinks with his heart," Mrs. Stroebel said softly.

Paulie opened his eyes. "I'm so sleepy. Did I tell you all about the locket?"

"Yes, you did."

Mrs. Stroebel walked me to the elevator. "Ellie, even at the trial they were trying so hard to blame Paulie for Andrea's death. I was so frightened. That was why I told him he must never talk about the locket."

"I understand."

"I hope you do. A special child will always need to be protected, even as a grown-up. You heard the Westerfield lawyer on television telling everyone that in a new trial he would prove Paulie killed Andrea. Can you imagine Paulie on the witness stand with that man hammering at him?"

That man. William Hamilton, Esquire.

"No, I can't."

I kissed her cheek. "Paulie is lucky he has you, Mrs. Stroebel."

Her eyes lowered to meet mine. "He's lucky he has you, Ellie."

37

AT SEVEN O'CLOCK I was on my way to having dinner with Mrs. Hilmer. Of course that meant I had to pass our old house. Tonight it was brightly lit, and with the moon shining over the woods behind it, it could have been on the cover of a magazine. It was the house Mother had visualized, a perfect example of a lovingly restored and expanded farmhouse.

The windows of my room were over the front door, and I could see the outline of a figure moving between them. The Keltons, who now owned the house, were a couple in their early fifties. They were the only people from the house I saw the night of the fire, but they might have adolescent children who had slept through the wailing of the police and fire vehicles. I wondered if whoever had my room liked to wake up early and lie in bed watching the sunrise, the way I had.

Mrs. Hilmer's house was well lit, too. I turned into her driveway, which now had only one destination. My headlights picked up the charred remains of the garage and apartment. For some incongruous reason I thought of the candlesticks and decorative fruit bowl that had graced the apartment's dining room table. They were not valuable, but they obviously had been chosen with taste and care.

Everything in the apartment had been chosen with care. If

Mrs. Hilmer chose to rebuild, those were the kinds of items that required time and effort to replace.

With that thought in mind, I entered her home with apologies on my lips, but she would have none of it. "Will you stop worrying about the garage?" she sighed as she pulled my face down for a kiss. "Ellie, that fire was deliberately set."

"I know it. You don't think I was responsible, do you?"

"Good Lord, no! Ellie, when I got back and Brian White came marching in here practically accusing you of being a pyromaniac, I gave him a real piece of my mind. If it makes you feel better, he as much as told me that I only imagined I was followed back and forth to the library that day. I set him straight on that, too. But I tell you, Ellie, it's terrible to think that whoever got into the apartment when you were here for dinner that night actually stole towels from it to make it look as if you set the fire."

"I took towels from the linen closet every day. I never noticed that five or six bath towels were missing."

"How could you? The shelves were stacked with them. I went through a period of not being able to resist a bargain, and now I have enough towels to last me till kingdom come. Well, dinner is ready, and you must be hungry. Let's go right to the table."

Dinner consisted of shrimp creole, followed by a Bibb lettuce salad. It was delicious. "Two good meals in one day," I said. "I'm getting spoiled."

I asked about her granddaughter and learned that her broken wrist was mending nicely.

"It was wonderful to spend time with Janey, and the new baby is adorable. But, Ellie, let me tell you, after a week I was ready to go home. The spirit is willing, but it's a long time since I had to get up to heat a bottle at five A.M."

She said she had been watching my Website, and I could see that any feeling of sympathy she had for Rob Westerfield was crumbling. "When I read that statement from the psychologist, telling how Rob twisted her arm in the restaurant, I was shocked.

As I buttoned it, I realized I had not thought to ask her if the name Phil meant anything to her.

"Mrs. Hilmer, in prison, apparently while he was high on drugs, Rob Westerfield may have confessed to beating a man named Phil to death. Did you ever know or hear about anyone by that name from around here who might have disappeared or been the victim of a homicide?"

"Phil," she repeated, looking past me and frowning in concentration. "There was Phil Oliver who had a terrible run-in with the Westerfields when they wouldn't renew his lease. But he moved away."

"Do you know what became of him?"

"No, but I can find out. He and his family had a couple of good friends here who are probably still in touch."

"Will you check for me?"

"Of course."

She opened the door, then hesitated. "I know something or read something about a young person named Phil who died a while ago . . . I can't remember where I heard about it, but it was very sad."

"Mrs. Hilmer, think. This is so terribly important."

"Phil . . . Phil . . . Oh Ellie, it's just not coming to me."

Of course I had to settle for that. But when I left Mrs. Hilmer a few minutes later, I urged her to stop actively trying to remember the connection, and let her subconscious work on it.

I was closing in on Rob Westerfield. I could feel it in my bones.

The car that was following me tonight was much more subtle than the one Teddy had driven. He rode without lights. I only became aware of his presence when I had to stop to let traffic pass before I could turn into the driveway of the inn, and he was forced to stop directly behind me.

I turned, trying to get a look at the driver. The car was heavy and dark, and I knew it wasn't Teddy.

Another car was coming up the driveway, leaving the inn, and its headlights illuminated the face in the car behind me.

Tonight it was my father who wanted to be sure that I got back to the inn safely. For a split second we looked at each other, then I turned left into the driveway and he kept going down the road.

38

ALFIE PHONED ME at seven o'clock Monday morning. "You still wanna buy it?"

"Yes, I do. My bank is Oldham-Hudson on Main Street. I'll be there at nine o'clock, and you can meet me in the parking lot at five after nine."

"Okay."

As I was leaving the bank, he drove up and parked next to my car. From the street no one would have been able to see what was taking place.

He opened the window. "Let's have the money."

I handed it to him.

After he had counted it, he said, "Okay, here's the diagram."

I examined it carefully. In the daylight it seemed even more chilling when I considered that it had been commissioned by the seventeen-year-old grandson of the potential victim. I knew that I would pay anything Alfie asked to have his permission to put it on my Website.

"Alfie, you know that the statute of limitations has expired. If the cops knew about this, you wouldn't get into any trouble. But if I show it on the Website and write about what you told me, it might make the difference between Mrs. Westerfield leaving her money to charities or to Rob."

I was standing outside the van. He was sitting in it, his hand on the wheel. He looked like what he had become: a hardworking guy who never had much of a break.

"Listen, I'd rather take my chances on Westerfield coming after me than think of him rolling in big bucks. Go for it."

"You're sure?"

"I'm sure. It kind of makes it up to Skip."

AFTER THE EXPERIENCE of driving to Boston and getting caught in heavy traffic, I allowed plenty of travel time for the drive to Maine when I rescheduled my appointment with Jane Bostrom, director of admissions at Carrington Academy.

That was why I was in Rockport long enough to stop for a grilled cheese sandwich and Coke at a coffee shop a mile from the school. I now felt prepared to take her on.

When I was escorted into her office, her greeting to me was cordial but reserved, and I was certain that she was going to be less than cooperative in releasing information to me. She was at her desk and offered me the seat facing it. Like many executives she had a visiting area with a couch and several chairs, but I was not invited to join her there.

She was younger than I had expected, about thirty-five, with dark hair and large gray eyes that seemed to be somewhat wary. From our brief conversation on the phone it was evident that she was proud of her school and was not about to have an investigative reporter trash it because of one student.

"Dr. Bostrom," I said, "let me put my cards on the table. Rob Westerfield spent his junior and senior years in Carrington. He was kicked out of his former prep school because he viciously assaulted another student. He was fourteen years old when that incident occurred.

"At seventeen he planned the murder of his grandmother. She was shot three times, and it is a miracle that she survived. At nineteen he bludgeoned my sister to death. I am at present tracking down the probability that there is at least one more person whose life he has taken."

I watched as her expression became dismayed and distressed. She took a long moment before she spoke. "Ms. Cavanaugh, that information about Rob Westerfield is horrifying, but please understand something. I have his file in front of me, and there is absolutely nothing in it that indicates a serious behavior problem while he was here."

"I find it hard to believe that with the violent history I've been uncovering, he was able to spend two years without a major infraction on his record. May I ask how long you have been employed at Carrington, Dr. Bostrom?"

"Five years."

"Then of course the only thing you have to go by is a record that may have been tidied up."

"I am going by the record in front of me."

"May I ask if the Westerfields have made any significant contributions to Carrington Academy?"

"At the time Rob was a student, they helped to renovate and refurbish the athletic center."

"I see."

"I don't know what you see, Ms. Cavanaugh. Please try to understand that many of our students have had an emotionally rough time and need guidance and compassion. Sometimes they've been pawns in nasty divorces. Sometimes one or the other parent simply walked out of their lives. You'd be amazed at what that can do to a child's sense of worth."

Oh, no, I wouldn't be amazed at all, I thought. In fact, I understand perfectly.

"Some of our students are young people who can't seem to get along with their peer group or with adults or both."

"That would seem to have been Rob Westerfield's problem," I

said. "But unfortunately for the rest of us, his family has always tried to either cover up for him or buy him out of trouble."

"Please understand that we run a tight ship here. We believe that an important step in healing an emotional problem is helping to build a sense of self-worth. Our students are expected to keep up their marks, take part in sports and other activities, and volunteer for the community programs that our school sponsors."

"And Rob Westerfield achieved all these goals willingly and joyfully?"

I could have bitten my tongue. Jane Bostrom had given me the courtesy of an interview, and she was answering my questions. However, it was clear that if there had been any big problems at this school with Rob Westerfield, they had not been put on his record.

"Rob Westerfield apparently achieved those goals to our school's satisfaction," she said stiffly.

"Do you have a list of the student body while he was enrolled here?"

"Of course."

"May I see it?"

"For what purpose?"

"Dr. Bostrom, when he was high on drugs in prison, Rob Westerfield made a statement to another convict. He said, 'I beat Phil to death, and it felt good.' Since he assaulted a fellow student at his previous prep school, it is not unlikely that while he was here, he had an encounter with a student named Phil or Philip."

Her eyes darkened and became progressively more concerned as she absorbed the implications of what I was saying. Then she stood up.

"Ms. Cavanaugh, Dr. Douglas Dittrick has been with Carrington for forty years. I'm going to invite him to join us. I'll also send for the student roster for those years. I think we'd better go into the conference room. It will be easier to spread out the lists on the table there and go through them carefully."

• • •

DR. DITTRICK SENT WORD that he was in the middle of a lecture and would join us in fifteen minutes. "He's a great teacher," Jane Bostrom told me as we opened the rosters. "I think if the roof was falling down, he wouldn't budge until he finished his lecture."

She seemed more comfortable with me by then, and certainly willing to help. "We want to watch for 'Philip' as the middle name as well as the first," she warned. "We have many students who are known by their middle names when they've been named after fathers and grandfathers."

The student body totalled about six hundred during Rob Westerfield's time at Carrington. I quickly realized that Philip was not a common name. The usuals, James and John and Mark and Michael, showed up regularly on the lists.

And a host of others: William, Hugo, Charles, Richard, Henry, Walter, Howard, Lee, Peter, George, Paul, Lester, Ezekiel, Francis, Donald, Alexander . . .

And then a Philip.

"Here's one, I said. "He was a freshman when Westerfield was a sophomore."

Jane Bostrom got up and looked over my shoulder. "He's on our board of trustees," she said.

I kept looking.

Professor Dittrick joined us, still wearing his academic gown. "What's so important, Jane?" he asked.

She explained and introduced me. Dittrick was about seventy, of medium build with a scholarly face and a firm handshake.

"I remember Westerfield, of course. He'd only been graduated two years before he killed that girl."

"She was Ms. Cavanaugh's sister," Dr. Bostrom interjected quickly.

"I'm very sorry, Ms. Cavanaugh. That was a terrible tragedy. And now you're looking to see if someone named Phil who was here around his time became a homicide victim."

"Yes. I do realize it may seem farfetched, but it's an avenue I have to explore."

"Of course." He turned to Dr. Bostrom. "Jane, why don't you see if Corinne is free and ask her to come over. She wasn't the director of the theater twenty-five years ago, but she was on staff then. Ask her to bring playbills from those performances Westerfield was in. I seem to remember that there was something funny about the way he was listed in the program."

Corinne Barsky arrived twenty minutes later. A vivacious, slender woman of about sixty with dark snapping eyes and a rich, warm voice, she was carrying the playbills that had been requested.

By then we had isolated two former students with the first name Philip and one with Philip as a middle name.

The first one we'd found, as Dr. Bostrom had told me, was a current trustee of the school. Dr. Dittrick remembered that the student with the middle name Philip had attended his twentieth class reunion two years ago.

That left only one to check. Dr. Bostrom's secretary ran his name through the computer. He lived in Portland, Oregon, and made annual contributions to the alumni fund. The latest was last June.

"I'm afraid I've wasted a lot of your time," I apologized. "If I can have a quick look at the playbills, I'll be on my way."

In each of them Rob Westerfield played the male lead. "I remember him," Corinne Barsky told me. "He was genuinely good. Very full of himself, very arrogant toward the other students, but a good actor."

"Then you had no problems with him?" I asked.

"Oh, I remember him having a row with the director. He wanted to use what he called his stage name instead of his own name in the show. The director refused."

"What was his stage name?"

"Give me a minute, I'll try to remember."

"Corinne, wasn't there some kind of flap about Rob Westerfield and a wig?" Dr. Dittrick asked. "I'm sure I remember something about that."

"He wanted to wear a wig he used in a performance at his previous school. The director wouldn't allow that, either. During the play Rob would come out of the dressing room wearing his own wig and only switched to the appropriate one at the last second. I understand that he wore his wig around campus as well. He got detention any number of times because of it, but he kept on doing it."

Dr. Bostrom looked at me. "That wasn't in his file," she said.

"Of course his file was sanitized," Dr. Dittrick said impatiently. "How else do you think the athletic center got a total renovation at that time? All it took was President Egan's suggestion to Westerfield's father that Rob might be happier in school elsewhere."

Dr. Bostrom looked at me, alarmed. "Don't worry. I'm not going to print that," I told her.

I looked around for my shoulder bag and fished out my cell phone. "I'm going to get out of your way," I promised them, "but there's one call I'd like to make before I leave. I've been in contact with Christopher Cassidy who was a student at Arbinger with Westerfield. In fact, he's the one Rob beat up in his sophomore year. Mr. Cassidy told me that Rob sometimes used the name of a character he played on stage. He was going to try to find out what it was."

I looked up the number and dialed it.

"Cassidy Investment Firm," the operator said briskly.

I was in luck. Christopher Cassidy was back from his trip, and I was put through to him immediately. "I checked around," he said, sounding triumphant. "I have the name Westerfield used, and it is from one of the plays he was in."

"I remember the name," Corinne Barsky was saying, excitement in her voice.

Cassidy was in Boston. Barsky was a few feet away from me in Maine. But they said it together.

"It's Jim Wilding."

Jim, I thought! Rob had drawn the diagram himself.

"Ellie, I have to take another call." Cassidy apologized.

"Go ahead. That's all I needed to know."

"What you wrote about me for the Website is great. Put it on. I'll back you one thousand percent."

He clicked off.

Corinne Barsky had opened one of the playbills. "You may be interested in this, Ms. Cavanaugh," she said. "The director used to have every member of the cast sign a playbill next to where they are listed in the cast."

She held it up and pointed. With defiant emphasis Rob Wester-field had signed not his own name but "Jim Wilding" instead.

I stared at it for a long minute. "I need a copy of this," I said. "And please take very good care of the original. In fact, I wish you'd lock it in a safe."

TWENTY MINUTES LATER I was sitting in my car, comparing the signature on the diagram with the one on the playbill.

I'm no handwriting expert, but when I compared the way the name "Jim" was signed on both documents, the signatures seemed identical.

I began the long drive back to Oldham, exulting in the prospect of exhibiting them on the Internet side by side.

Mrs. Dorothy Westerfield would have to face the truth. Her grandson had planned her death.

I must confess I thoroughly enjoyed the benevolent feeling that I was about to make a number of charities, medical facilities, li-braries, and universities very, very happy.

39

I KEEP MY CELL PHONE on the other pillow. Tuesday morning it began to ring and woke me up. As I gave a sleepy "Hello," I glanced at my watch and was shocked to see that it was nine o'clock.

"Must have had a night on the town."

It was Pete.

"Let's see," I said. "Driving from Maine to Massachusetts and across New York State. It was the most exciting night of my life."

"Maybe you're too tired to come down to Manhattan."

"Maybe you're trying to wiggle out of the invitation to come to Manhattan," I suggested. By now I was awake and on the verge of being disappointed and angry.

"My suggestion was going to be that I drive to Oldham, pick you up, and we'll find a place for us to have dinner."

"That's different," I said cheerfully. "I have a great spot in mind, and it's only fifteen minutes from the inn."

"Now you're thinking. Give me directions."

I did, and he congratulated me. "Ellie, you're one of the few women I know who can give lucid directions. Is it something I taught you? Never mind answering. I can be there around seven."

Click.

I sent for room service, showered, washed my hair, and phoned a nearby nail salon to make an appointment for four o'clock. I had broken several nails when I fell in the parking lot and wanted to do something about them.

I even took time to study my limited wardrobe and decide on the leaf brown pantsuit with the caracul collar and cuffs. The suit had been an impulse buy at the end of the season last year, expensive even at half price, and I had yet to wear it.

Parading it out for Pete seemed like a good idea.

Actually, it was comforting to have something to anticipate at the end of the day. I knew it was not going to be easy to spend the afternoon writing Alfie's story about the break-in and tying the incriminating diagram to Rob Westerfield's use of the name Jim in school.

By not easy, I meant emotionally not easy, because of the unbearable certainty that if Rob Westerfield had been convicted of that crime, Andrea would not have met him.

He'd have been in prison. She would have grown up and gone to college, and, like Joan, probably gotten married and had a couple of children. Mother and Daddy would still be in that wonderful farmhouse. Daddy would have come to love it as much as she did and by now realized what a great buy it had been.

I would have grown up in a happy home and gone to college. Choosing to study journalism had nothing to do with Andrea's death, so I probably would be in the same kind of job. It's the career that held a natural attraction for me. I still wouldn't be married. I think I always wanted a career before a commitment.

If Rob had been convicted, I would not have spent my life grieving for my sister and yearning for what I had lost.

Now, even if I manage to convince Rob's grandmother and the rest of the world of his guilt, he still will get away with it. The statute of limitations has run out on that crime.

And even if his grandmother changes her will, his father has plenty of money, at least plenty by normal standards, so Rob will live well.

Disgusting liar that he is, in a second trial Will Nebels's story might throw enough doubt in jurors' minds to give Westerfield an acquittal.

Then his record will be expunged.

I beat Phil to death, and it felt good.

There is only one way I can get Rob Westerfield back behind bars and that is to track down Phil, that other person whose life he extinguished. Fortunately, there is no statute of limitations for murder.

BY THREE-THIRTY I was ready to transfer everything to the Website: Christopher Cassidy's story of being beaten by Rob Westerfield in prep school; Rob's insistence on being called "Jim" because of the character he had played on stage; Rob's role in planning the attempt on his grandmother's life.

I wrote that William Hamilton, Esq., was the court-appointed lawyer who had destroyed the original diagram implicating Westerfield in the crime. I ended the piece with the diagram and playbill displayed side by side. On screen the "Jim" signatures were startling in their similarity.

I kissed my fingers in a salute to the story, pressed the appropriate keys on the computer, and an instant later it was out there on my Website.

40

IT WAS A QUARTER OF FIVE when I got back to the inn. The multibillion-dollar cosmetic industry would go broke if it relied on people like me. What little makeup I had was lost in the fire. I had picked up a compact and lipstick at a drugstore a day or two later, but it was time to spend half an hour replacing items like mascara and blush.

Even though I had slept till nine o'clock this morning, I was still sleepy and wanted to take a nap before it was time to dress for my date with Pete.

I wondered if seeing the finish line felt like this. The athlete runs the marathon and knows the end of the race is near. I've heard that there is an interval of a few seconds when the runner actually slows, regroups, and then goes into the final sprint toward victory.

That was the way I felt. I had Rob Westerfield on the ropes, and I was convinced that I was about to learn the truth of what he had done to Phil and where it had happened. If I was right, it would send him back to prison.

I beat Phil to death, and it felt good.

And then when he had been brought to real justice, when the Committee for Justice for Rob Westerfield had been dissolved and slunk away into oblivion, then and only then, like a newly hatched chicken, would I take my own tentative steps into the future.

Tonight I was meeting someone I wanted to see and who

wanted to see me. Whither do we wander? I didn't know and wasn't looking ahead that far. But for the first time in my life I was beginning to anticipate the future with my debt to the past nearly paid. It was a hopeful, satisfying feeling.

Then I walked through the door of the inn, and my half-brother Teddy was standing there waiting for me.

This time he was not smiling. He looked uncomfortable, yet determined, and his greeting to me was abrupt. "Ellie, come inside. We have to talk."

"I invited your brother to wait in the sunroom, but he was afraid that he might miss you," Mrs. Willis said.

You're absolutely right, I *would* have missed him, I thought. I would have been upstairs like a shot if I had known he was waiting.

I didn't want her to hear whatever he was going to say, so I walked ahead of him into the sunroom. This time he closed the door, and we stood facing each other.

"Teddy," I began, "you have to listen to me. I know you mean well. I know your father means well. But you can't be trailing after me. I am perfectly fine, and I can take care of myself."

"No, you can't!" His eyes were flashing, and in that moment he looked so like my father that I was transported back to the dining room at home, and Daddy was telling Andrea that *she was forbidden to ever have anything to do with Rob Westerfield.*

"Ellie, we saw what you put on the Website this afternoon. Dad is beside himself with worry. He said that the Westerfields now have to stop you, and they *will* stop you. He said you've become a terrible danger to them, and in the process you've put yourself in great danger. Ellie, you can't do this to Dad or to yourself. Or to me."

He was so upset, so vehement, that I felt sorry for him. I put my hand on his arm. "Teddy, I don't want to upset you or your father. I'm doing what I have to do. I don't know how many ways to say it to you, but please, just leave me alone. You've gotten along without me all your life, and your father has gotten along without me since

I was a small child. What is all this about? I tried to tell you the other day—you don't *know* me. You have no reason to *worry* about me. You're a nice kid, but let's leave it at that."

"I'm not just a nice kid. I'm your brother. Whether you like it or not, I'm your brother. And stop saying 'your father' to me. You think you know everything, but you don't, Ellie. Dad never stopped being your father. He's always talked about you, and I always wanted to hear about you. He told me what a great little kid you were. You don't even know it, but he went out to your college graduation and sat in the audience. He got a subscription to the *Atlanta News* when you started working there, and he's read every article you've ever written. So stop saying he's not your father."

I didn't want to hear it. I kept shaking my head. "Teddy, you just don't understand. When my mother and I went to Florida, he let us go."

"He told me you thought that, but it isn't true. He didn't just let you go. He wanted you back. He tried to *get* you back. The few times you visited him after he and your mother broke up, you never said one word to him and you wouldn't even eat. What was he supposed to do? Your mother told him there was too much grief to contain under one roof, that she only wanted to remember the good parts and go on to a new life. And she did."

"How do you know all this?"

"Because I asked him. Because I thought he'd have a heart attack when he saw the last item you put on the Website. He's sixty-seven years old, Ellie, and he has high blood pressure."

"Does he know you're here?"

"I told him I was coming. I'm here to beg you to come home with me, and if you won't do that, at least to check out of here and go someplace where nobody except us knows where you are."

He was so earnest, so concerned, so caring that I almost put my arms around him. "Teddy, there are things you don't understand. I knew Andrea might have gone to meet Rob Westerfield that night, and I didn't tell on her. I've had to carry that blame all my life. Now when Westerfield gets his new trial, he's going to convince a lot of people that Paulie Stroebel killed Andrea. I didn't save her, but I have to try to save Paulie."

"Dad told me it was *his* fault that Andrea died. He was late getting home. One of the guys he worked with had gotten engaged, and he had a beer with him to celebrate. He was starting to get suspicious and worried that Andrea was still seeing Westerfield behind his back. He told me that if he had been home earlier, he would never have allowed her to go to Joan's house that night—so instead of being in that garage, she would have been at home, safe."

He believed what he was telling me. Was my memory so distorted? Not completely. It wasn't that simple. But was my abiding sense of guilt—"If only Ellie had told us"—only a part of the total picture? My mother let Andrea go out after dark alone. My father suspected Andrea was still seeing Rob but had not yet actually confronted her. My mother had insisted on moving to what was then a rural and isolated community. My father may have been too strict with Andrea; his attempts to protect her may have made her rebellious. I was the confidante who knew of the secret meetings.

Did the three of us *choose* to harbor guilt and grief within our own souls, or did we *have* any choice?

"Ellie, my mother is a very nice lady. She was a widow when she met Dad. She knows what it is to lose someone. She wants to meet you. You'd like her."

"Teddy, I promise I will meet her someday."

"Someday *soon*."

"When I've seen this through. It's not going to take much longer."

"You will talk to Dad? You will give him a break?"

"When this is over, we'll have lunch or something. I promise. And listen, I'm going out tonight with Pete Lawlor, someone I worked with in Atlanta. I don't want either one of you following me around. He's picking me up here and will deposit me back here safely, I promise."

"Dad will be relieved to hear that."

"Teddy, I have to get upstairs. There are a couple of calls I have to make before I go out."

"I've said what I have to say. No, maybe I haven't. There's something else Dad told me that you should know. He said, 'I've lost one little girl. I can't lose another.' "

41

IF I HAD EXPECTED a hint of romance in our meeting, it was quickly dismissed. Pete's greeting to me was "You look great," accompanied by a quick kiss on the cheek.

"And you're so gussied up, you look as though you won a fifteen-minute shopping spree in Bloomingdale's," I told him.

"Twenty minutes," he corrected. "I'm starving, aren't you?"

I had made a reservation at Cathryn's, and while we were driving over, I said, "Big request."

"Let's have it."

"Tonight I would like not to talk about what I've been doing these past weeks. You watch the Website, so you really know what's going on anyhow. But I need to get away from it for a few hours. So tonight is *your* night. Tell me every single place you've been since I saw you in Atlanta. I want every detail about the interviews you've had. Then tell me why you're so pleased about the job you're taking. You can even tell me if you had a hard time choosing between that very nice, and obviously new, red tie or another one."

Pete has a way of raising one eyebrow. He did that now. "You're serious?"

"Absolutely."

"The minute I saw this tie, I knew I had to have it."

"Very good," I encouraged. "I want to hear more."

At the restaurant we looked at the menu, ordered smoked

salmon and a seafood pasta, and agreed to split a bottle of Pinot Grigio. "It's handy that we both like the same entrées," Pete said. "Makes it easier with the wine selection."

"The last time I was here I had the rack of lamb," I told him.

He looked at me.

"I love to irritate you," I admitted.

"It shows."

Over dinner he did open up to me. "Ellie, I knew the paper was on the way out. That happens to any business that's family owned when the present generation is only interested in the dollar sign. Frankly, I was getting itchy anyway. In this business, unless you can see that you have a good reason to stay with a company, you've got to be aware of other opportunities."

"Then why didn't you leave sooner?" I asked.

He looked at me. "I'll take a pass on that one. But when it became inevitable, I knew two things for sure. I wanted either to get with a solid newspaper—such as *The New York Times,* the *L. A. Times,* the *Chicago Trib,* or the *Houston Chronicle*—or to try something else altogether. The newspaper jobs were there, but then that 'something else' opened up, and I went for it."

"A new cable news station."

"Exactly. I'm in on the ground floor. It has risks, of course, but substantial investors are committed to making it happen."

"You said it involved a lot of traveling?"

"By a lot I mean the kind anchormen do when they're onto a big story."

"You're not telling me you're an anchorman!"

"Perhaps that's too grandiose a word. I'm on the news desk. Short, clipped, and hard-hitting is in these days. Maybe it will work; maybe it won't."

I thought about it. Pete was smart, intense, and got to the point quickly. "I think you'll actually be good at it," I told him.

"There's something so touching about the way you lavish praise on me, Ellie. Don't go overboard, please. It might go to my head."

I ignored that. "Then you're going to be based in New York City and you're moving there?"

"I already have. I found an apartment in SoHo. It's not great, but it's a start."

"Won't that be kind of a big change for you? Your whole family is in Atlanta."

"My grandparents were all New Yorkers. I used to visit them a lot when I was a kid."

"I see."

We waited silently while the table was cleared. Then when we'd ordered espresso, Pete said, "All right, Ellie, we've played the game by your rules. Now I get *my* two cents in. I want to hear everything you've been up to, and I mean *everything*."

By now I was ready to talk about it, so I told him all, including Teddy's visit. When I was finished, Pete said, "Your father's right. You've got to move in with him or at least not be visible around Oldham."

"I think he may be right about that," I admitted reluctantly.

"I have to go to Chicago in the morning for a meeting with the board of Packard Cable. I'll be gone until Saturday. Ellie, please go down to New York and stay in my apartment. You can be in touch with Marcus Longo and Mrs. Hilmer and Mrs. Stroebel from there, and you can keep up your Website as well. But at the same time, you'll be safe. Will you do that?"

I knew he was right. "For a few days, until I can figure out where to go, yes, I will."

When we got back to the inn, Pete left his car in the driveway and walked me inside. The night clerk was on duty. "Has anyone been looking for Ms. Cavanaugh?" Pete asked him.

"No, sir."

"Any messages for her?"

"Mr. Longo and Mrs. Hilmer returned her calls."

"Thank you."

At the foot of the stairs, he put his hands on my shoulders.

"Ellie, I know you've had to see this through, and I've understood. But now you can't go it alone anymore. You need us around you."

"Us?"

"Your father, Teddy, me."

"You've been in touch with my father, haven't you?"

He patted my cheek. "Of course I have."

42

I DREAMT A LOT that night. It was an anxiety-ridden dream. Andrea was slipping through the woods. I was trying to call her back, but I couldn't make her hear me and watched in despair as she ran past old Mrs. Westerfield's house and into the garage. I was trying to shout a warning, but then Rob Westerfield was there and waving me away.

I woke to the faint sound of my own voice trying to call for help. Dawn was just breaking, and I could see that it was going to be another of those gray, cloudy, cold days we get in early November.

Even as a child I found the first two weeks of November unsettling, but after the middle of the month, the festive feeling of Thanksgiving was in the air. But those first two weeks seemed long and dreary. Then, after Andrea died, they became forever linked with the memories of the last days we spent together. The anniversary of her death was only a few days away.

Those were the thoughts in my mind as I lay in bed, wishing for an hour or two more of sleep. The dream wasn't hard to analyze. The imminent anniversary of Andrea's death and the fact that I was acutely aware that Rob Westerfield would be enraged by the latest information on my Website were playing on my mind.

I knew that I needed to be very careful.

At seven o'clock I sent for room service; then I began to work on my book. At nine o'clock I showered, dressed, and phoned Mrs. Hilmer.

I was hoping against hope that her call had been to say she remembered why the name "Phil" was familiar to her. But even as I asked her that question, I realized it was terribly unlikely that she would come up with anything that could be connected to Rob Westerfield's vicious boast.

"Ellie, that name is the only thing I've been able to think about," she said, sighing. "I called you last night to tell you that I checked with my friend who's in contact with Phil Oliver. I told you about him. Phil Oliver is the man who lost his lease and had a pretty ugly confrontation with Rob Westerfield's father. My friend told me that he's down in Florida, likes it well enough, but is still pretty bitter about the way he was treated. He reads your Website and loves it. He says if you want to start a Website to let the world know the kind of man Rob's father is, too, he'll be happy to talk to you."

Interesting, I thought, but not helpful information right now.

"Ellie, the one thing I'm sure of is that whatever I heard or read about 'Phil,' it was only recently. And if this is any help, it made me sad."

"Sad?"

"Ellie, I know I'm not making sense, but I'm working on it. I'll get back to you the minute I piece it together."

Mrs. Hilmer had been calling me on the phone at the inn. I didn't want to explain that I was checking out, or go into detail about Pete and his apartment in New York. "You have my cell phone number, don't you, Mrs. Hilmer?"

"Yes, you gave it to me."

"I'm going to be in and out so much. Will you call me on that number if you come up with the connection?"

"Of course."

• • •

MARCUS LONGO was the next one on my list to call. I thought he sounded subdued, and I was right.

"Ellie, what you put on the Website yesterday is inviting a massive lawsuit from both Westerfield and his lawyer, William Hamilton."

"Good. Let them sue me. I can't wait to depose them."

"Ellie, being right isn't always a provable or successful legal defense. The law can be very tricky. The drawing you claim is evidence of Rob Westerfield's part in the attempted murder of his grandmother was provided by the brother of the man who shot her. And he admits that he was the driver of the getaway car. He's hardly a stellar witness. How much did you pay him for that information?"

"One thousand dollars."

"Do you know how that would look in court? If not, let me explain it to you. You put up a sign outside Sing Sing. You advertise on the Website. In so many words it says, 'Anyone who knows of a crime Rob Westerfield may have committed can make a quick buck.' This guy could be an out-and-out liar."

"Do you think he is?"

"What I think doesn't matter."

"Oh, but it does, Marcus. Do you believe Rob Westerfield planned that crime?"

"Yes, I do, but then I always thought he planned it. That has nothing to do with the multimillion-dollar slander suit you may be facing."

"Let them sue. I hope they do. I have a couple of thousand dollars in the bank and a car with sand in the gas tank that probably needs a new engine, and I may make some decent money on my book. They're welcome to try to get it."

"It's your show, Ellie."

"Two things, Marcus. I'm checking out of here today and going to stay at a friend's apartment."

"Not around here, I hope."

"No, in Manhattan."

"That is a great relief for me. Does your father know that?"

If not, I bet you'll tell him, I thought. I wondered how many of my friends in Oldham were in contact with my father. "I'm not sure," I said honestly. For all I knew, Pete may have called him last night the minute he left me.

I was going to ask Marcus if he had any success in following up on a homicide with someone named "Phil" as the victim, but he anticipated the question. "So far, zero, blank, nothing to tie Westerfield to another crime," he said. "But I still have a lot of searching to do. We're also following up on that name Rob liked to use in school."

"Jim Wilding?"

"Yes."

We agreed to stay in close touch.

I HADN'T SPOKEN to Mrs. Stroebel since Sunday afternoon. I called the hospital, hoping to hear that Paulie had been discharged, but he was still there.

Mrs. Stroebel was with him. "Ellie, he's much better. I stop in around this time each day, then go to the store and come back around noon. Thank God for Greta. You met her the day Paulie was brought in here. She is so good. She is keeping everything going."

"When will Paulie be able to go home?"

"I think tomorrow, but, Ellie, he wants to see you again. He is trying to remember something you said to him that he says was not correct. He wants to straighten it out, but he doesn't know what it is. You understand—he's had so much medication."

My heart sank. Something *I* said? Dear God, was Paulie confused again, or was he going to retract anything he had told me? I was glad I had held off putting on the Website his story connecting Rob to the locket.

"I can come over and see him," I offered.

"Why don't you come around one o'clock? I will be here then, and I think that makes him more comfortable."

More comfortable, I thought, or do you mean you want to be sure he won't say anything that will incriminate him? No, I didn't believe that. "I'll be there, Mrs. Stroebel," I said. "If I arrive before you, I'll wait for you to come before I visit Paulie."

"Thank you, Ellie."

She sounded so grateful that I was ashamed of myself for thinking she might be trying to prevent Paulie from being honest with me. She had been the one to call me, and her life was now split between keeping up the deli and visiting her ailing son. God tempers the wind to the shorn lamb. He does it best when he sends someone like Paulie a mother like Anja Stroebel.

I MANAGED TO GET two hours' work in, then I checked Rob Westerfield's Website. It still had the picture of me shackled to the bed, and more names had been added to the Committee for Justice for Rob Westerfield. But nothing had been added to refute my story of his involvement in the attempted murder of his grandmother.

I took that to be a sign of consternation in the ranks. They were still debating what to do about it.

At eleven o'clock the phone rang. It was Joan. "Want to have a quick lunch around one o'clock?" Joan asked. "I have some errands to do and just realized I'll be passing your door."

"I can't. I promised to visit Paulie at the hospital at one o'clock," I said, then hesitated. "But Joan—"

"What is it, Ellie? Are you all right?"

"Yes, I'm fine. Joan, you told me you have a copy of the obituary notice my father put in the paper for my mother."

"Yes, I do. I offered to show it to you."

"Can you put your hand on it easily?"

"Yes, I can."

"Then if you're passing the inn, would you mind dropping it off at the desk? I'd really like to see it."

"Consider it done."

WHEN I GOT TO THE HOSPITAL, there was a buzz of activity in the lobby. I saw a group of reporters and cameramen clustered together at the far end of the room, and I quickly turned my back to them.

The woman next to me on the line to get a visitor's pass told me what had happened. Mrs. Dorothy Westerfield, Rob's grandmother, had been rushed into the emergency room, suffering from a heart attack.

Her lawyer had issued a statement to the media that last evening, as a permanent memorial to her late husband, U. S. Senator Pearson Westerfield, Mrs. Westerfield had changed her will and would be leaving her estate to a charitable foundation that would be charged with dispersing all of it within ten years.

The statement said that the only exceptions were small bequests to her son, some friends, and longtime employees. Her grandson was left only one dollar.

"She was very smart, you know," the woman confided to me, "I heard some reporters talking. Besides her lawyers, she had her pastor, a judge who is a friend, and a psychiatrist as witnesses that she was of sound mind and knew exactly what she was doing."

I'm sure that my gossipy informant did not realize that my Website probably triggered both the will change and the heart attack. It was a hollow victory for me. I remembered that gracious, stately woman offering condolences for Andrea's death the day of the funeral.

I was glad to escape into the elevator before a reporter recognized me and connected me with the breaking story.

• • •

Mrs. Stroebel was already in the corridor waiting for me. Together we went into Paulie's room. His bandages were now much smaller. His eyes were clearer, and his smile was warm and sweet. "My friend, Ellie," he said. "I can count on you."

"You bet you can."

"I want to go home. I'm tired of being here."

"That's a good sign, Paulie."

"I want to get back to work. Were there many people in for lunch when you left, Mama?"

"Pretty good crowd," she said soothingly, with a contented smile.

"You shouldn't be here so much, Mama."

"I won't have to be, Paulie. You'll be home soon." She looked at me. "We have a little room off the kitchen at the store. Greta has put a couch and television in there. Paulie can be with us, do whatever he feels up to in the kitchen, and rest in between."

"Sounds good to me," I told them.

"Now, Paulie, explain what it is that worries you about the locket you found in Rob Westerfield's car," his mother encouraged.

I simply didn't know what to expect.

"I found the locket and gave it to Rob," Paulie said slowly. "I told you that, Ellie."

"Yes, you did."

"The chain was broken."

"You told me that, too, Paulie."

"Rob gave me a ten-dollar tip, and I put it with the money I'd saved for your fiftieth birthday present, Mama."

"That's right, Paulie. That was in May, six months before Andrea died."

"Yes. And the locket was shaped like a heart, and it was gold and it had pretty blue stones in the center."

"Yes," I said, hoping to encourage him.

"I saw Andrea wearing it, and I followed her to the garage and saw Rob go in after her. Later I told her that her father would be angry, and then I asked her to go to the dance with me."

"That's exactly what you said earlier, Paulie. That's the way it happened, isn't it?"

"Yes, but something is wrong. *You* said something, Ellie, that was wrong."

"Let me think." I tried to reconstruct the conversation as best I could. "The only thing I remember that you didn't just mention is that I said Rob didn't even buy Andrea a new locket. He had the initials of their first names, Rob and Andrea, engraved on a locket some other girl had probably dropped in his car."

Paulie smiled. "That's it, Ellie. That's what I needed to remember. Rob didn't have the initials engraved on the locket. They were already there when I found the locket."

"Paulie, that's impossible. I know Andrea did not meet Rob Westerfield until October. You found the locket in May."

His expression became stubborn. "Ellie, I remember. I am sure. I saw them. The initials were already on the locket. It wasn't 'R' and 'A.' It was 'A' and 'R.' 'A.R.,' in very pretty writing."

43

I LEFT THE HOSPITAL with the sense that events were spinning out of control. Alfie's story and the diagram I had put on my Website obviously had the desired effect: Rob Westerfield had been cut out of his grandmother's will. By doing that, Mrs. Westerfield might just as well have erected a sign saying, "I believe my only grandchild planned the attempt on my life."

That heartbreaking realization and painful decision had undoubtedly caused her to have the massive heart attack. At ninety-two, it seemed unlikely to me that she could possibly survive.

Again I remembered the quiet dignity with which she had walked out of our house after my father ordered her to leave. He was the first to humiliate her because of her grandson. Or was he? Arbinger had been the school that her husband, the senator, had attended. It seemed doubtful that she would have been unaware of the reason Rob was asked to leave there.

The fact that she changed the will and took every precaution to see that it could not be legally challenged meant to me that she not only believed he had planned the attempt on her life, but also at last might even be convinced that Rob was responsible for Andrea's death.

Which of course brought me to the locket.

The locket already had the initials "A" and "R" engraved on it before Rob met Andrea.

That fact was so stunning, so utterly out of context with everything I had been thinking, that for the first few minutes after I left Paulie, I had to let it sit in my mind until I could get used to it.

The gray morning had evolved into an equally gray afternoon. The car was at the far end of the hospital's visitors' parking lot, and I walked briskly to it, my coat collar turned up as protection against the damp, cold wind.

I drove out of the hospital grounds and realized that the beginnings of a headache were being caused by the fact that it was one-thirty, and the last time I'd eaten was seven-fifteen this morning.

As I drove, I began looking for a coffee shop or restaurant and passed several that looked pretty good. The reason I kept passing them became evident when I rejected still another popular luncheon spot. It was because being out in public in Oldham made me feel vulnerable now.

I went back to the inn, glad to be there and equally eager to be on my way to the anonymity of downtown Manhattan. Mrs. Willis was at the desk and handed me an envelope. I knew it was the obituary notice that Joan had left for me.

I took it upstairs, phoned room service, ordered a club sandwich and tea, and then sat down in the chair that overlooks the Hudson. It was the kind of view Mother would have loved, with the palisades rising in the mist, the water gray and restless.

The envelope was sealed. I slit it open.

Joan had clipped the obituary from the *Westchester News*. It read:

Cavanaugh: Genine (née Reid) in Los Angeles, Ca., age 51. Beloved former wife of Edward and loving mother of Gabrielle (Ellie) and the late Andrea. She was active in her church and community, and created a happy and beautiful home for her family. She will always be missed, always loved, always remembered.

So Mother wasn't the only one who remembered the good years, I thought. I had written my father a churlish note to inform him of Mother's death and to ask if her ashes could be interred in Andrea's grave.

I'd been so wrapped up in my own pain that it never crossed my mind that the news of her death might affect him deeply.

I decided the lunch with my father that I'd promised Teddy would take place sooner rather than later. I put the clipping in my suitcase. I wanted to pack right away and leave as quickly as possible. Then the phone rang.

It was Mrs. Hilmer. "Ellie, I don't know if this is helpful at all, but I remembered where it was that I read a reference to someone named Phil."

"Where, Mrs. Hilmer? Where did you see it?"

"It was in one of the newspapers you gave me."

"Are you sure?"

"I'm positive. I remember because I was reading it when I was at my granddaughter's house. The baby was asleep, and I was going through those papers for names of people who still lived around here whom you might want to interview. And Ellie, as I told you when we had dinner, reading about the trial brought everything back, and I was crying. Then I read something about Phil, and that was very sad, too."

"But you're not sure what it said about him?"

"You see, Ellie, that's why I think that even if I can find the item, I've probably got the wrong person in mind."

"Why do you think that?"

"Because you're looking for a man named Phil. I read something about a young *girl* who died whose family called her 'Phil.' "

I beat *Phil* to death, and it felt good.

Dear God, I thought, *was he talking about a girl?*

A young girl who was a homicide victim.

"Mrs. Hilmer, I'm going to read every one of those papers line by line."

"That's what I'm doing, Ellie. I'll call you if I come across it."

"And I'll call you if I find it."

I pushed the "end" button to terminate the call, laid the phone on the night table, and grabbed the duffel bag. I unzipped it, turned it upside down, and dumped the yellowing, crumbling newspapers on the bed.

I took the first one that came to my hand, sat down in the chair that faced the river, and began to read.

The hours passed. Every so often I would get up and stretch. At four o'clock I sent for tea. Tea peps you up. Hadn't that been the advertising slogan of one of the tea companies?

It does pep you up. And it helped me to keep focused.

I concentrated intensely, reading line by line the newspapers, reading again in horrifying detail the story of Andrea's death and Rob Westerfield's trial.

"A.R." Was the locket totally unimportant after all? No. Absolutely not. If it was unimportant, Rob would never have taken the chance of going back for it.

Was "A.R.," the girl who owned the pretty gold locket, yet another victim of one of his murderous rages?

At six o'clock I took another break and turned on the news. Mrs. Dorothy Westerfield had expired at 3:30. Neither her son nor her grandson had been at her bedside.

I went back to reading the papers. At seven o'clock I found it. It was in the memorial section of the obituary page the day of Andrea's funeral. It read:

Rayburn, Amy P.
Remembering you today and every day. Happy 18th birthday in heaven, our darling Phil.
    Mom and Dad

"*A.R.*" Did the initials on the locket stand for Amy Rayburn? Her middle initial had been P. Could it have been Phyllis or Philomena, shortened to Phil?

Paulie had found the locket in early May. Andrea was dead twenty-three years. If Amy Rayburn had owned the locket, had she died twenty-three and a half years ago?

I called Marcus Longo, but there was no answer at his home. I was frantic to have him check Amy Rayburn's name against homicide reports from that year.

I knew there was a complete Westchester phone book in the drawer of the night table. I pulled it out, opened it, and turned to the "R" section.

There were only two Rayburns listed. One lived in Larchmont, the other in Rye Brook.

I dialed the one in Larchmont. The modulated voice of an older man answered. There was no way to be indirect. "My name is Ellie Cavanaugh," I said. "It is necessary for me to speak to the family of Amy Rayburn, the young woman who died twenty-three years ago."

"For what reason?" The voice had suddenly become frosty, and I knew that I had made contact with someone who was at least a relative of the dead girl.

"Please answer one question of mine," I said, "and then I will answer all of yours. Was Amy the victim of a homicide?"

"If you do not know that already, you have no business calling our family."

The phone was slammed down.

I called back, and this time the answering machine picked up. "My name is Ellie Cavanaugh," I said. "Nearly twenty-three years ago my fifteen-year-old sister was bludgeoned to death. I believe I have proof that the man who killed her is also responsible for Phil's death. Please call me back."

I began to leave my cell phone number, but the phone was picked up on the other end. "I'm Amy Rayburn's uncle," he said. "The man who murdered her served eighteen years in prison. What do you think you're talking about?"

44

THE MAN I HAD CALLED, David Rayburn, was the uncle of seventeen-year-old Amy Phyllis Rayburn, who was murdered six months before Andrea. I told him about Andrea, about Rob Westerfield's confession to a fellow inmate in prison, about Paulie finding the locket in Rob's car, and about its being taken from Andrea's body.

He listened, asked questions, then said, "My brother was Phil's father. That was Amy's nickname in the family and among her close friends. Let me call him now and give him your number. He'll want to talk to you."

Then he added, "Phil was about to graduate from high school. She'd been accepted at Brown. Her boyfriend, Dan Mayotte, always swore he was innocent. Instead of going to Yale, he spent eighteen years in prison."

Fifteen minutes later my phone rang. It was Michael Rayburn, Phil's father. "My brother told me about your call," he said. "I won't try to describe my emotions or those of my wife at this moment. Dan Mayotte had been in and out of our home since he was in kindergarten; we trusted him like a son. We have had to make our peace with the death of our only child, but to think that Dan may have been wrongly convicted of her death is almost more than we can bear. I'm a lawyer, Ms. Cavanaugh. What kind of proof do you have? My brother talked about a locket."

"Mr. Rayburn, did your daughter have a heart-shaped gold locket with blue stones or gems on the front and her initials on the back?"

"Let me put my wife on."

From the moment she spoke I admired the composure of Phil's mother. "Ellie, I remember when your sister died. It was only six months after we lost Phil."

I described the locket to her.

"That has to be Phil's locket. It was one of those inexpensive trinkets you pick up at a shopping mall. She loved that kind of jewelry and had several chains with any number of pendants she'd slip on them. She would wear two or three at the same time. I don't know if she was wearing the locket the night she was murdered. I never missed it."

"Do you think you might have a picture of Phil wearing it?"

"She was our only child, so we were always taking pictures of her," Mrs. Rayburn said, and now I could hear tears in her voice. "She was fond of the locket. That's why she had it engraved. I'm sure I can find a picture of her wearing it."

Her husband took the phone from her. "Ellie, from what you told my brother, I understand that the convict who says he heard Westerfield confess to my daughter's murder is missing."

"Yes, he is."

"I have never in my heart believed that Dan could attack Phil so violently. He wasn't a violent person, and I know he loved her. But as I understand it, there is no hard-and-fast proof to actually tie Westerfield to Phil's death."

"No, there isn't, at least not yet. Maybe it's too soon to go to the district attorney with what I know, but if you tell me the circumstances of your daughter's murder and why Dan Mayotte was charged and convicted, I can put it out there on the Website and see if it brings in more information. Can you do that?"

"Ellie, we've been living that nightmare for twenty-three years. I can tell you everything about it."

"Believe me, I understand. The nightmare that my family endured broke up my parents' marriage, eventually killed my mother, and has tortured me for more than twenty years. So, yes, I understand that you're always living it."

"I'm sure you do. Dan and Phil had quarreled and hadn't seen each other in a week. He did tend to be jealous, and Phil had told us that the week before, when they were buying sodas and candy in the lobby before a movie, some guy started talking to her, and Dan got angry. She never described the guy or mentioned his name.

"She and Dan didn't speak for a week after that. Then one day she went to the local pizza parlor with some of her girlfriends. Dan came in with some of his friends and went over to Phil. They talked and I guess began to make up. Those kids were crazy about each other.

"Then Dan spotted the guy who'd been flirting with Phil in the movies. He was standing at the counter."

"Did Dan describe him?"

"Yes. Good-looking, about twenty years old, dark blond hair. Dan said that at the refreshment stand of the movie house, he'd overheard him tell Phil that his name was Jim."

Jim! I thought. That had to be one of the times Rob Westerfield was wearing his dark blond wig and was calling himself Jim.

"Seeing the guy there at the pizza parlor made Dan jealous all over again. He said that he accused Phil of planning to meet Jim there. She denied it and said she hadn't even noticed he was in the place. After that, she got up and stalked out. Everyone could see that she and Dan were angry with each other.

"Phil was wearing a new jacket that night. When she was found there were traces of dog hairs on it that came from Dan's Irish terrier. Of course she'd been in his car many times, but because that jacket was brand-new, the hairs were proof that she'd been in his car after she left the pizza parlor."

"Did Dan deny that Phil got in his car?"

"Never. He said he persuaded her to get in and talk things over.

But when he told her it was too much of a coincidence for him to believe that Jim just happened to be in the pizza parlor, she got sore at him again and got out of the car. She told him that she was going back to her friends and for him to get lost. According to him, she slammed the car door and started to walk from the parking lot, heading back to the restaurant. Dan admitted he was furious and said that he gunned the engine and took off.

"Phil never made it to the restaurant. When it started to get late and she hadn't come home, we called the friends she'd gone out with."

Mother and Daddy called Andrea's friends. . . .

"They told us she was with Dan. At first we were relieved, of course. We thought the world of him and were glad they'd made up. But hours passed, and when he finally did get home, Dan claimed that he'd left Phil in the parking lot and she was going back to the restaurant. The next day her body was found."

Michael Rayburn's voice broke. "She died of multiple fractures of the skull. Her face wasn't recognizable."

I beat Phil to death, and it felt good.

"Dan admitted that he'd been angry and upset after she got out of his car. He said he drove around for an hour or so, then parked near the lake and just sat there for a long time. But he had no one to back up his story. No one had seen him, and Phil's body was found in a wooded area about a mile from the lake."

"Didn't anyone else see Jim at the pizza parlor?"

"People said they remembered a guy there with dark blond hair. But he apparently didn't talk to anybody, and nobody noticed when he left. Dan was convicted and sent to prison. It broke his mother's heart. She'd raised him alone, and, sadly, she died much too young and never lived to see him paroled."

My mother died much too young as well, I thought.

"Where is Dan now?" I asked.

"He got his college degree in prison instead of at Yale. I've heard he works as a counselor to former inmates. I never in my heart really believed he could do that to Phil. If it turns out that your theory is right, then I owe him a profound apology."

Rob Westerfield owes him a lot more than an apology, I thought. He owes him eighteen years—and the life he should have lived.

"When are you going to put this on your Website, Ellie? Michael Rayburn asked.

"As soon as I can write it. That should take about an hour."

"Then I won't keep you. We'll be looking for it. Let me know if any new information comes in."

I KNEW that I was already in jeopardy from the Westerfields and that by mounting this new assault I was being downright reckless. I didn't care.

When I thought of all the victims Rob Westerfield had claimed, I became enraged.

Phil, an only child.

Dan, his life destroyed.

The Rayburns.

Dan's mother.

Rob's grandmother.

Our family.

I started Phil's story with the headline: "WESTCHESTER DISTRICT ATTORNEY, TAKE NOTE!"

My fingers flew over the keyboard. At nine o'clock it was finished. I read it over once and, with grim satisfaction, sent it to the Website.

I knew I had to clear out of the inn. I closed the computer, packed in five minutes, and went downstairs.

I was at the desk, paying my bill, when my cell phone rang.

I thought it might be Marcus Longo, but it was a woman with a Hispanic accent who responded to my quick greeting.

"Ms. Cavanaugh?"

"Yes.

"I have been watching your Website. My name is Rosita Juarez. I was housekeeper for Rob Westerfield's parents from the time he was ten years old until he went to prison. He is a very bad person."

I gripped the phone and pressed it closer to my ear. This woman had been the housekeeper at the time Rob committed both murders! What did she know? She sounded frightened. Don't let her hang up, I prayed.

I tried to make my voice sound calm. "Yes, Rob *is* a very bad person, Rosita."

"He looked down on me. He made fun of the way I talk. He was always nasty and rude to me. That's why I want to help you."

"How can you help me, Rosita?"

"You are right. Rob used to wear a blond wig. When he put it on, he would say to me, "My name is Jim, Rosita. That shouldn't be too hard even for you to remember.""

"You saw him put on the wig?"

"I have the wig." There was sly triumph in the woman's voice. "His mother used to get very upset when he wore the wig and called himself Jim, and one day she threw it in the garbage. I don't know why I did it, but I took it out and brought it home. I knew it was expensive, and I thought maybe I could sell it. But I put it in a box in the closet and forgot all about it until you wrote about it on your Website."

"I'd like to have that wig, Rosita. I'll be glad to buy it from you."

"No, you don't have to buy it. Will it help to make people believe that he killed that girl, Phil?"

"I believe it would. Where do you live, Rosita?"

"In Phillipstown."

Phillipstown was actually part of Cold Spring, not more than ten miles away.

"Rosita, may I come and get the wig from you now?"

"I'm not sure."

She was starting to sound worried.

"Why not, Rosita?"

"Because my apartment is in a two-story house, and my land-lady sees everything. I don't want anyone to see you here. I am afraid of Rob Westerfield."

For the moment all I cared about was getting my hands on the wig. Later, if Rob was put on trial for Phil's death, I would try to persuade Rosita to be a witness.

Before I could try to convince her, she volunteered, "I live only a few minutes from the Phillipstown Hotel. If you want, I could drive there and meet you at the back entrance."

"I can be there in twenty minutes," I said. "No, make it half an hour."

"I will be there. Will the wig help to put Rob in jail?"

"I'm sure it will."

"Good!"

I could hear the satisfaction in Rosita's voice. She had found a way to get back at the nasty teenager whose insults she had endured for nearly a decade.

I rushed to finish paying my bill and quickly put my bags in the car.

Six minutes later I was on my way to acquire the tangible proof that Rob Westerfield had owned and worn a dark blond wig.

I was hoping that samples of Rob's DNA would still be linger-ing within it. That would be definitive proof that the wig had be-longed to him.

45

SOME TIME AFTER DARK the light mist had turned into a cold, battering rain. The windshield wipers of the car I had rented needed to be replaced, and before I had driven a mile, I found myself straining to see the road.

The traffic became lighter the farther north I drove on Route 9. I could tell by the readout on the dashboard that the temperature outside was dropping, and within minutes I saw that the rain was turning into sleet. As ice began to collect on the windshield, it became harder and harder to see more than a few yards ahead, and I was forced to stay in the right lane and drive slowly.

As the minutes passed, I became frantic that I would miss Rosita. She had sounded so nervous that I was sure she would not wait around if I didn't show up on time.

I was concentrating all my energy on watching the road in front of me and only gradually became aware that I was starting to go up a hill. It dawned on me that it had been a while since I'd seen any headlights coming from the opposite direction.

I glanced at the odometer. The Phillipstown Hotel was not more than ten miles from the Hudson Valley Inn, yet I had already driven twelve miles and still wasn't there. Obviously, somewhere I had veered off Route 9. The road I was on now was clearly not the main highway and was getting narrower.

I looked in my rearview mirror to check for headlights. There were none. Frustrated and furious at myself, I jammed on the brakes—a stupid thing to do, because I started to skid. I managed to straighten out the car and carefully began to make a U-turn. In that instant a red dome light went on behind me and blinding headlights flashed in my eyes. I stopped the car, and what appeared to be a police van pulled up beside me.

Thank God! I thought. I rolled down the window to ask the cop to please give me directions to the Phillipstown Hotel.

The window of the van rolled down as well, and the man in the passenger seat turned to face me.

Though there was no light directly on his face, I saw immediately that it was Rob Westerfield, and he was wearing a dark blond wig. With an unmistakable Hispanic accent, and with his voice pitched to sound like a woman, he mockingly called, "He was nasty to me. He made fun of the way I talk. He told me to call him Jim."

My heart almost stopped. Horrified, I realized that Rob, pretending to be Rosita, had made the phone call to lure me out. Past him I could just make out the face of the driver—it was the man who had threatened me in the parking lot of the railroad station near Sing Sing prison.

Frantically, I looked around for a way out. I could not get around them. My only hope was to straighten out the car, floor the gas pedal, and keep driving blindly ahead. I had no idea where the road might lead. As I accelerated, I saw that there were woods on both sides of me and that the road was steadily narrowing. The tires were slipping, causing the back of the car to fishtail.

I knew I could not outrun them. I could only pray that I would not end up in a cul-de-sac, that this road might take me toward some kind of highway.

They had turned off the dome light, but their bright headlights were still shining straight into my rearview mirror. Then they began to toy with me.

They pulled up on my left, and the van slammed into the side of the car. The door behind the driver's seat took the impact, and I heard grinding steel as the car lurched and my head banged into the steering wheel.

They dropped back as I skidded from side to side, trying now to stay in the middle of the road. I knew I was bleeding from a cut on my forehead, but I managed to hang on to the wheel and keep the car on the road.

Then suddenly they shot by me, angling in front of me and tearing the fender off my car as they hit me again. I could hear the fender scraping and dragging as I struggled to stay on the road, praying that soon I'd come upon an intersection or at least see another car coming toward me.

But there were no other cars, and I sensed that a third attack was coming. Clearly they would aim to make it the final one. As the road curved sharply, they slowed and moved fully into the left lane. I hesitated briefly, then accelerated, hoping to break ahead of them again. However, they quickly pulled up even with me again.

For a split second I glanced at them. The interior light was on in the van, and I could see that Rob was waving something at me.

It was a tire jack.

With a final burst of speed, the van cut sharply to the right, directly into my path, forcing my car off the road. Helplessly, I tried to turn the wheel, but I felt the tires losing traction. The car went into a spin and then tumbled down the sloping embankment, heading toward a wall of trees thirty feet away.

I managed to hang on to the steering wheel as the car turned over several times. I covered my face with my hands as the car, right side up again, slammed into a tree and the windshield shattered.

The sound of crashing metal and glass had been deafening, and the sudden silence that followed was ghostly.

My shoulder hurt. My hands were bleeding. My head was throbbing. But I could tell that by some miracle I had not been seriously injured.

The final impact had caused the driver's door to spring open, and sleet was pelting at me from every side. The cold sting against my face may have kept me from losing consciousness, and suddenly my brain felt clear. It was totally dark, and for a moment, I felt extraordinary relief. I thought that when they saw my car tumbling down the side of the road, they decided that I was finished and had driven away.

But then I became aware that I was not alone. Nearby I heard harsh, labored breathing, followed by the high choking sound that as a child I had described as a giggle.

Rob Westerfield was out there in the dark, waiting for me, just as he had waited for Andrea nearly twenty-three years ago in the darkness of the garage-hideout.

The first blow of the tire jack missed me and hit the headrest behind me. I clawed at the clasp of the seat belt and managed to release it.

As I scrambled over to the passenger side, the second blow came so close that I felt it graze my hair.

Andrea, Andrea, this is the way it was for you. Oh, God, please . . . please help me. . . .

I think we both heard it at the same time, a car roaring around that last bend in the road. Its headlights must have caught the wreckage of my car, because it turned and came rushing down the slope to where I was trapped.

Rob Westerfield, the tire jack in his hand, was illuminated in the glare. But so was I, and now he could see exactly where I was.

Snarling, he twisted around and turned back toward me. He leaned inside the car until his face was only inches from mine. I tried to push him away as he raised the tire jack, about to smash it over my head.

I heard the scream of sirens filling the air as I shielded my head with my arms and waited for the blow to land. I wanted to close my eyes, but I could not.

I heard the thud before I saw the look of shock and pain on Westerfield's face. The tire jack fell from his hand onto the seat be-

side me as he was suddenly thrust forward and disappeared. Unbe-
lieving, I stared out.

The car that had driven down the slope was filling the space
where he had stood. The driver had seen what was happening and
had done the only thing possible to save my life: He had crashed his
car into Rob Westerfield.

As the blazing lights of the police cars turned the area into vir-
tual daytime, I looked into the faces of my rescuers.

My father was driving the car that had hit Rob Westerfield. My
brother was beside him. On Daddy's face I saw again the agonized
expression that I remembered from when he knew he had lost his
other little girl.

One Year Later

I OFTEN LOOK BACK and realize how close I came that terrible night to sharing my sister's fate. From the time I left the inn, Dad and Teddy had been following me from a distance. They had seen what they believed to be a police van behind my car and assumed that I had finally requested protection.

However, they lost me when I veered off the highway, and Dad called the Phillipstown police to be sure the van had stayed with me.

That was when he learned that I had no official escort. The police told Dad where I probably had taken the wrong turn and promised immediate response.

Dad told me that when he came around the turn, the driver of Westerfield's van had started to pull away. He'd been about to follow him, but Teddy spotted the wreckage of my car. Teddy—the brother who never would have been born if Andrea had lived—saved my life. I often reflect on that irony.

Both of Rob Westerfield's legs were broken when he was hit by Dad's car, but they mended in time for him to walk into court for his two trials.

The District Attorney for Westchester County immediately reopened the investigation into Phil's death. He obtained a search warrant for Rob's new apartment and found a cache of his trophies, mementos of his hideous crimes. God knows where he had them stashed while he was in prison.

Rob had kept an album containing clippings of newspaper stories about both Andrea and Phil, starting from the time their bodies were found. The clippings were in sequence, and next to them were pictures of Andrea and Phil, photographs of the crime scenes, the funerals, and the other people caught up in the tragedies, including Paulie Stroebel and Dan Mayotte.

On each page Rob had written comments, cruel and sarcastic commentary on his actions and the people he hurt. There was one picture of Dan Mayotte on the witness stand swearing that a guy named Jim with dark blond hair had been flirting with Phil in the lobby of the movie theater. Next to it Rob had written, "I could tell she was crazy about me. Jim gets all the girls."

Rob had been wearing the dark blond wig when he pursued me. But the most telling proof of his guilt in Phil's death was that he had kept her locket; it was pasted on the last page of the album. The caption under it read: "Thanks, Phil. Andrea loved it."

The district attorney requested the criminal court judge to vacate Dan Mayotte's conviction and to schedule a different trial: *The People vs. Robson Westerfield.* The charge was murder.

I saw the locket exhibited at the trial, and my mind flew back to that last evening in Andrea's bedroom when, close to tears, she had slipped it around her neck.

Dad was sitting next to me in court and closed his hand over mine. "You were always right about the locket, Ellie," he whispered.

Yes, I was, and at last I have made my peace with the fact that, because I saw her wearing it and believed she had gone to the hideout to meet Rob, I did not immediately tell my parents when she was missing. It may already have been too late to save her, but it is time to relinquish the possibility that it may *not* have been too late, and to stop letting it haunt me.

Robson Westerfield was convicted of the murder of Amy Phyllis Rayburn.

In a second trial Rob and his driver were convicted of attempted murder for their attack on me.

Rob Westerfield's sentences are consecutive. If he lives another 113 years, he will be eligible for parole. As he was being escorted out of the courtroom, after the second sentencing, he stopped for a moment to check his watch against the courtroom clock. Then he adjusted it.

"Don't bother," I said to myself. "Time has no meaning for you anymore."

Will Nebels, when confronted with the evidence of Westerfield's guilt, admitted that he had been approached by Hamilton and offered a bribe to lie about seeing Paulie go into the garage that night. William Hamilton, disbarred attorney, is now serving his own prison term.

My book was rushed out for publication in the spring and did very well. The other book—the sanitized version of Rob Westerfield's sorry life—was withdrawn. Pete introduced me to the Packard Cable executives, and they offered me a job as an investigative reporter. It seemed like a good opportunity. Some things never change. I report to Pete.

But that's fine. We were married three months ago in the St. Christopher Chapel at Graymoor. Dad gave the bride away.

Pete and I bought a house in Cold Spring overlooking the Hudson. We use it on weekends. I never tire of the view—that majestic river framed by the palisades. My heart has finally found its home, the home I have been seeking all these years.

I see Dad regularly. We both feel the need to make up for lost time. Teddy's mother and I have become good friends. Sometimes we all go up to see Teddy at college. He's on the freshman basketball team at Dartmouth. I am so proud of him.

The circle has taken a long time to close. But it *has* closed, and for that I am deeply grateful.